"I'm thinking

Recognize

Anna Segee stood stock-still as Ethan Knight walked through the gate.

As of one hour ago, he'd become her boss. He'd been waiting for this moment for weeks, and he grinned to himself.

Anna's hard hat was tucked under her arm, and her hair hung down in a braid as thick as a man's wrist. It was light brown, with highlights that Ethan knew hadn't come from a bottle. Several strands had worked free, framing her face. She'd washed her jacket, and her boots had been polished.

Ethan's grin broadened. She'd obviously put her best foot forward for the new owners of Loon Cove Lumber. Would she have been so eager, if she had known who that was?

And did she realize whom she had agreed to rent her cabin to?

Lord, this was going to be fun.

THE STRANGER IN HER BED
is also available as an eBook

The
Stranger
in Her Bed

JANET
CHAPMAN

POCKET STAR BOOKS
New York   London   Toronto   Sydney

An *Original* Publication of POCKET BOOKS

 A Pocket Star Book published by
POCKET BOOKS, a division of Simon & Schuster, Inc.
1230 Avenue of the Americas, New York, NY 10020

This book is a work of fiction. Names, characters, places and incidents are products of the author's imagination or are used fictitiously. Any resemblance to actual events or locales or persons, living or dead, is entirely coincidental.

ISBN-13: 978-1-4165-0528-0
ISBN-10:   1-4165-0528-8

This Pocket Star Books paperback edition February 2007

10 9 8 7 6 5 4 3 2 1

POCKET STAR BOOKS and colophon are registered trademarks of Simon & Schuster, Inc.

Cover design by Min Choi
Cover art by Alan Ayers

Manufactured in the United States of America

For information regarding special discounts for bulk purchases, please contact Simon & Schuster Special Sales at 1-800-456-6798 or business@simonandschuster.com.

To Paul Michael Byram,
We know you're enjoying heaven, dear brother,
because we hear the angels laughing at your jokes.

The Stranger in Her Bed

Chapter One

The man appeared out of nowhere, walking directly into the path of the loader Anna Segee was driving. She jerked the wheel to the right and hit the lever that lowered the forks, to drop her center of gravity, but she couldn't stop the heavy load of logs from shifting. Tires screeched for purchase on the frozen ground as the loader skidded into the ditch, causing her cargo to scatter like giant toothpicks.

Anna barely had time to cover her head as she was tossed against the side of the cab, then down to the floor as the massive machine rolled onto its side with a jarring thud. A log crashed through the windshield, raining crystals of glass over her like hail as several more logs slammed into the cab with deafening bangs, drowning Anna's scream in the chaos.

Then everything went suddenly still but for the rapping knock of the huge diesel engine. Anna cautiously lowered her arms. She was alive, apparently, and except for the throbbing pain in her right shoulder, she didn't seem to be hurt. She reached over and turned the key in the ignition to put the beast out of its misery, hearing it cough once before it fell eerily silent. Anna closed her eyes, but couldn't block out the image of the man's horror when he had realized he was about to be crushed by several tons of logs and machinery.

Lord, that had been close.

Trembling with delayed shock and no small amount of anger, Anna twisted around the heavy log wedged in her seat and pushed at the door of the cab. It wouldn't budge. Feeling the cold February air on her face, and realizing the side window had blown out as well, she banged her hard hat against the metal casing as she popped her head out and looked toward the loading ramp. The man she'd barely avoided was just picking himself off the ground, brushing a mixture of dirt, snow, and bark off his pants.

Anna grabbed the tire iron wedged behind the seat. A lumber mill was no place for idiots, and the stupid fool had nearly killed them both with his inattention. Using the tire iron to knock away what was left of the glass, Anna scrambled out the window and climbed to the ground. She waved away several men running toward her and stalked toward the idiot gaping at her, still hefting the tire iron. He took a step back as she advanced, held up his hands in supplication, and sheepishly grinned.

A log suddenly fell behind her. Anna turned just in time to see it roll off the loader, taking the headlights with it and forcing two men to jump out of the way to avoid being crushed. What a mess. The expensive loader was sitting on its side in the ditch, its cargo strewn around it like scattered bowling pins. And to her experienced eye, there were several thousand dollars' worth of damage to the big rig.

She repositioned her grip on the tire iron with a growl of disgust, turned back to the man, and stepped straight into his oncoming fist. Anna's brain rattled inside her hard hat again as her head exploded in pain, lights flashing in the back of her eyes as she crumpled to the ground amid angry shouts.

"Aw, shit! Dammit. I didn't know she was a woman!" she heard above her, the voice backing away. "She was coming after me with that tire iron. Dammit, I didn't know!"

Anna wanted to stay right where she was, motionless and curled up in a ball; the less she moved, the less it would hurt. But as much as she'd like to see the idiot taught a lesson, that lesson might turn into murder if she didn't get up. So she rolled to her side and pushed herself up on her hands and knees, then stood, finally opening her eyes to see four men from her crew backing her attacker against the saw shed. Two other men rushed to her side to hold her up, but she shrugged them off. "Leave him alone," she said through the pain in her jaw. She stepped up to the four men just as one of them drove his fist into the idiot's belly. "Dammit. Back off!" she snapped as she shoved them away.

Anna pointed at the hunched, gasping man. "This is a sawmill, not Disneyland. You can't walk around here with your head in the clouds. Do you know what happens to a body when twelve tons of timber and steel run over it?"

"Yes, ma'am," he acknowledged with a gasped cough.

And there it was again. That grin. Was it a nervous reaction, or was he really an idiot?

"Look," he said, stepping toward her. "I wouldn't have hit you if I'd known you were a woman."

Anna took a step back and pointed at the mangled loader. "That piece of equipment costs more than you can earn in two years, but I had to ditch it so your heirs couldn't sue us right out of business. Now who the hell are you, and what are you doing walking around my mill yard?"

"I'm Ethan. I work here."

"Not anymore, you don't. You're fired."

"What!"

Anna reached down for her tire iron before she looked back at him. "We don't pay people to be stupid. You're a walking accident, and next time someone could be killed."

"I hired Ethan this morning," Tom Bishop said as he hustled over. Her aging boss wrapped one arm around her, moved her hand so he could examine her jaw, then gave her shoulder a fatherly squeeze. Anna stifled a wince as pain shot across her back and down her arm.

Tom Bishop owned Loon Cove Lumber, and he had the right to hire and fire anyone he wanted. But as his foreman, Anna was annoyed that Tom hadn't told her he was adding to her crew.

"I'm sorry, Tom. I didn't know she was a woman," Ethan said. "And she was coming at me with that tire iron," he added in his own defense, pointing at her right hand.

Tom took the heavy tool from her and gave it to one of the men. "Haven't I told you that piece of hardware would get you in trouble?" he said, sounding more like her father than her boss.

Anna gaped at him. "The man just wrecked your loader and struck one of your crew, and you're scolding *me?*" She stepped out of his grip. "I'm firing him, Tom," she said with all the grit she could muster. She turned to Ethan. "I want you off this property in sixty seconds."

It was the idiot's turn to gape. He looked at Tom. "She can't fire me," he said.

"Now, Anna," Tom said, looking as shocked as Ethan. "Don't be rash. Maybe you can give him another chance. It was an accident."

"You know my rules. There's no second chances when it comes to safety. I run a tight yard."

"But, Anna," Tom entreated, darting a worried glance at the man in question.

Anna cupped her swelling jaw. She had to get some snow on it soon or she wouldn't be able to open her mouth tomorrow. "It's either him or me, Tom. Your call."

"But Ethan's worked in the woods all of his life," Tom told her. "The Knights own a logging operation on the other side of the lake. He knows his way around machinery."

Anna shot her gaze to Ethan on an indrawn breath. Good God, this hard-punching, devil-handsome, grinning idiot was Ethan Knight? _Her_ Ethan Knight? It took all of her willpower to merely raise a brow at the man who stood as tall as a mountain and looked to be made of steel.

He also looked like he couldn't believe his fate rested in the hands of Tom Bishop's female foreman. "He's probably here because he stepped in front of a skidder at home," she told Tom. "It's him or me," she repeated.

Tom looked around at the gathered men waiting to hear which worker he chose, but Anna spoke first. "Davis," she said. "Escort Mr. Knight to the gate, and make sure he doesn't destroy anything else on his way out." She turned toward the wreckage. "Come on, people. We have a mess to clean up."

There was a heartbeat of silence before a dozen or more men suddenly scrambled to follow her orders.

"Jeeze Louise," Keith said as he fell into step beside her. "You've got balls, lady."

Anna kept walking, not looking at Keith. "Tom

needs me more than he needs to worry about some accident-prone idiot. I know it, and he knows it."

She suddenly stopped and bent at the waist, propping her hands on her knees and taking deep breaths. The throbbing in her head was only slightly worse than the throbbing in her shoulder, and she felt like she was going to pass out.

"Jeeze, boss lady. We can take care of the loader. Go home," Keith told her, putting an arm around her waist, obviously afraid she was going to fall flat on her face—which was fast becoming a possibility.

Anna closed her eyes and tried taking shallow breaths to see if that wouldn't work better. "Is Knight headed for the gate?" she asked, not looking up, not daring to move her head.

"Yeah. He's leaving. And if looks could kill, you'd be one dead foreman right now."

"I'm just going to sit here a minute," she whispered, sidling over to a low stack of lumber and letting Keith help her sit down. "And I think I will go home. See what you can do about righting that loader."

"Are you okay to drive?"

Anna looked up and attempted to smile. "I'll be fine, thanks. I just need a minute."

Keith examined her with a critical eye. "That was a mean punch he threw. Your jaw's already turning purple."

Anna touched her jaw as she looked over to see Ethan Knight spinning out of the parking lot. She also saw Tom Bishop, his face a mask of concern, headed her way. Damn. She didn't want his coddling. Ethan may have caused the accident, but she'd been as much of an idiot to go after him with a tire iron.

"Just look at you, girl," Tom said, the worry evident in his voice. "Come on. I'm taking you to see a doctor."

"No, I'm going home." She motioned for Keith to get to work on the loader. "I'm fine, Tom. Really. I just need an ice pack and some of Grampy's tea."

Tom frowned. "Samuel's tea could skin the hide off a beaver. Don't tell me there's still some of that old rotgut hanging around."

She nodded. "I seem to have inherited a whole case of it along with Fox Run Mill."

Tom rolled his eyes. "Sam must have figured you'd need it, if you intended to keep that ghost camp."

Anna lifted her swollen chin. "I'm keeping it."

"But it's no place for a woman alone, Anna. And don't think I didn't try to talk him out of leaving it to you."

"It's my heritage."

"It's falling down around your feet."

"The main house is sound."

"Which is why the animals have taken it over," he shot back. He took hold of her shoulders to help her stand and held her facing him. "Sell the place, Anna. Save out a couple of acres on the lake if you're determined to stay here, but sell the rest."

Anna stepped back and tucked her balled fists

in her jacket pockets. "We've had this conversation before, Tom. My grandfather left Fox Run to me, and I'm keeping it."

Tom put his hands in his pockets with a tired sigh. "It was Samuel's dream you'd come back here someday and restore Fox Run Mill," he admitted. "But you were eleven when he made out his will, and no one was planning to build a resort next door back then. Samuel talked to me just a few months before he died, and said he was reconsidering putting you in the middle of this mess. They're going to keep up the pressure, you know. You can't fight big business."

"Sure I can. By refusing to sign on the dotted line."

"You think that will stop them from putting up their condos? Anna, they'll just build around you."

"Then let them. I have enough land that I won't even see the resort."

"But they need your mile of lake frontage, too. How about the historical society? Couldn't you work out a deal with them, to protect yourself from the developers?"

She shook her head, then immediately regretted it, wincing in pain.

"Then at least get a dog to scare away your ghost."

Anna walked over and picked up her hard hat. "I have a dog," she reminded Tom.

He snorted. "The most Bear could scare off is himself, if he looked in a mirror."

She started walking toward the gate. "I'm not bringing in a replacement while Bear's still breathing.

Keith can handle things here tomorrow, Tom. I'm going home, taking some aspirin, and going to bed. I'll be back to work on Monday."

"You need a keeper, Anna Segee."

"I can take care of myself," she said automatically, not taking offense. Tom was, after all, a man. She opened the door of her truck, got in, put the key in the ignition, then looked back at Tom. "Why did you hire Ethan Knight without talking to me first? And didn't his house burn down yesterday? It was the talk of the mill yard this morning. Someone said the Knights were moving into those old sporting camps farther up the lake."

Tom nodded.

"Then why wasn't Ethan helping his family get settled?"

"I asked him that same question," Tom said. "He told me his dad and brothers insisted he show up his first day of work here, since there wasn't anything for him to do that they couldn't do themselves." He suddenly grinned. "The older Knight boy, Alex, got himself a new wife."

"You still haven't explained why you hired Ethan without telling me."

"I was doing his father a favor." Tom looked down at the ground, then back at her with serious eyes. "Ethan didn't recognize you. Is that the real reason you got mad and fired him?"

Anna would have scowled if it wouldn't have hurt. "I'm relieved he didn't recognize me."

"Somebody's bound to put two and two together one of these days," Tom warned. "Then what are you going to do?"

"I'm not eleven anymore."

"Samuel sent you to live with your father in Quebec because he knew it was impossible for you to live here." Tom shook his head. "And nothing's changed in eighteen years, Anna. Hell, half the men in this town have a history with your mother."

Anna glared at Tom. "You've spent the last three months convincing me Samuel sent me away because he loved me, so maybe you should consider that he brought me back for the same reason."

"He never stopped loving you, Anna," Tom whispered, his eyes clouding with emotion. "You were all he talked about."

"Yeah, well," she growled, looking out the windshield of her truck. "He didn't love me enough to stay in contact. He sent a confused, heartbroken little girl to live with complete strangers, and he never once came to see me. He didn't even write or call."

"That was your father's doing," Tom countered. "André Segee insisted that if he took you, the break must be clean." He lifted a brow. "I don't recall you trying to contact Samuel, once you came of age."

Anna twisted the key in the ignition and started her truck. "I wasn't about to chase after someone who didn't want me."

Tom touched her sleeve. "Samuel loved you more than life itself, Anna. He spent eighteen lonely years living with his decision to send you away. And he didn't dare call or go see you once you grew up because he preferred to live with the hope that you could forgive him, to risk the reality that you never would."

Anna closed her eyes. "I forgave him," she whispered. She looked back at Tom, her eyes wet with tears. "I was simply too stubborn to make the first move."

"Not stubborn," Tom said, squeezing her arm. "Scared. You were just as scared as Samuel." He pulled his hand away and rocked back on his heels. "Ethan Knight was what . . . twelve, thirteen when you left?" He shook his head. "That boy spent the entire summer with his arm in a cast because of you. And even though you've changed a great deal, he'll recognize you eventually. Then what are you going to say to him? 'I just thanked you for rescuing me eighteen years ago by firing you'?"

"Then why did you put me in such a terrible position?" Anna snapped. "Of all the people you could have hired to work here, why Ethan Knight?"

"Because Grady Knight asked me to."

"You can't run a business hiring men for favors, Tom."

"I hired *you* as a favor to your dead granddaddy," he said, puffing up his chest.

"No, you hired me because I'm the best damn foreman you could ever hope to have."

Tom let his chest sink back into his belly with a

sigh of defeat. "Dammit, Anna. What am I going to tell Grady Knight?"

"You tell him to keep his son away from large machinery."

"Ethan's more competent than most men. All the Knights are. Half our sawlogs come from North-Woods Timber."

"Then what's he doing at your mill? Why isn't he seeing to his own business if he's grown into such a hotshot logger?"

Tom's gaze dropped to the ground. "Grady said Ethan wanted a change of scenery," he muttered, his voice so low Anna had to strain to hear him.

She gave Tom a hard look. "And what would you be telling Grady now, if I'd run over his precious son?"

All the color drained from Tom's face. "Hell, Anna. You saved Ethan's life."

"For all the thanks I got," she muttered, touching her jaw.

Tom's eyes grew misty again. "Thank you for being the best damn foreman I could ever hope to have," he said thickly.

Good Lord, she had to get out of here before she started bawling. She ached from head to toe, and this conversation stirred uncomfortable memories for her. "Go back to your office and shuffle some papers," she gently told him. "And call Grady Knight if it will make you feel better, and tell him to be thankful his son is alive. And tell him that I fired Ethan, not you—that it was out of your hands."

She closed the door, then rolled down the window. "Oh. And while you're at it, tell him he might want to keep his son away from their wood chipper. Ethan's liable to get eaten up."

She put the truck in gear and headed for home.

It was eight miles from Loon Cove Lumber to Fox Run Mill, and Anna spent the drive trying to figure out how this day had gone so terribly bad. Probably because it had started so badly, just ten minutes after midnight, when her ghost had returned.

Bear, who was deaf in one ear and could barely hear with the other, had slept through the visitation, but Anna had been awakened by a noise coming from the old stables. She'd gotten out of bed and looked out her upstairs window, but hadn't been able to see a thing. She also hadn't been brave enough to venture out into the moonless night to investigate.

Instead she'd crept downstairs, made sure the house was locked up tight, and then taken Samuel's old shotgun back to bed with her. This morning she'd found nothing in the stables to account for the noise, but she could sense that someone had been in there. Things just weren't right, though it was more of a feeling than something she could put a finger on.

Then, when she'd gotten to work, the head sawyer at Loon Cove Lumber had met her with the news that the parts for the carriage that rode the logs into the saw blade were on back order, and their number two saw was going to be down for several days while they fabricated the new parts themselves. And then an idiot—who turned out to be Ethan Knight, of all people!—had stepped in front of her loader. If old Samuel Fox were alive, he'd say tree-squeaks were causing her troubles, or maybe those pesky side-hill gougers.

All through her childhood, Samuel had filled Anna's head with tales of the gremlins who lived in the forest and wreaked havoc on the loggers intruding on their domain. As a child she'd sat on his knee and listened to his tall tales—and had believed the miniature monsters existed. Which was why she still refused to venture outside at night. To this day, Anna was petrified of the dark—almost as much as she'd been afraid of seeing Ethan Knight again.

Her twelve-year-old knight in shining armor certainly had grown into a handsome man. His eyes were even more arrestingly blue than Anna remembered. And even through his bulky clothes, Ethan's masculine strength had been evident.

Anna had grown used to rugged men over the last eighteen years, hanging out and eventually working in her father's logging and mill yards in Quebec since age eleven. She had four burly half brothers, a brawny and somewhat autocratic father, and three uncles on her daddy's side. Except for a stepmother and an absentee mama who was mostly a memory, Anna had been brought up in an all-male world and had learned to look beyond gender. Usually, she didn't even notice the brawn.

But she had today.

Ethan Knight could make a woman drool in her sleep. And Anna knew her anger had been as much at herself for noticing his looks as it had been at his stupid stunt. Her first reaction, upon seeing him step in front of her rig, was that she'd gladly ditch the loader before she'd harm one hair on his beautiful body. Why had *that* popped into her head?

Anna feared it was genetic, that her mother's legacy was instilled in her so deeply, her true nature had inadvertently spilled out. But she had successfully fought her hormones since puberty, so why had they surfaced today? And why with Ethan Knight of all people?

Anna refused to dwell on the reasons.

She finally stopped her truck in front of the main house of Fox Run Mill, shut off the engine, and with a sigh, rested her forehead on the steering wheel. Lord, she ached. Her jaw was throbbing so painfully, she feared several teeth might be loose. Ethan Knight sure did pack a powerful wallop.

The scratch of tiny claws on the windshield and flutter of tiny wings on the glass made Anna look up to find Charlie perched on the wiper. The tiny chickadee tapped on the windshield with his beak, and Anna smiled, only to grab her jaw with a moan. She opened the door and slid out of the truck, and Charlie landed on her head.

"I don't have any seed, little one," she told her tiny friend, who was now working his way down her hair to sit on her shoulder. "You'll have to wait until we get inside."

Several more chickadees appeared, dive-bombing her with frantic urgency. By the time Anna made it onto the porch of the old house, she was covered with birds hitching a ride to dinner. Her spirits immediately lifted.

These little sprites were the one true constant in her life lately, and appeared from the cover of the forest that surrounded Fox Run Mill whenever she stepped outside, ever present, ever playful, and always hungry.

Samuel must have tamed them. From birth to age eleven, Anna's life at Fox Run had been filled with wonder and discovery, exploring the old mill site of a long-dead empire that had been passed down for generations. She couldn't even fathom how many generations of chickadees Samuel had fed over the years.

This generation, however, had spawned a little daredevil she'd named Charlie. He was the boldest of the birds, and sometimes got into more trouble than his rapidly beating heart could handle. He was constantly wiggling into any pocket he saw, searching for seed. More than once Anna had pulled his panicked little body out of entangling clothes, then had to spend the next ten minutes calming him down.

Still, he never learned. Just last week an unsuspecting visitor—a developer from Boston hoping to talk her into selling—had found his shirt pocket frantically squirming, and had beat at his chest in horror. Charlie had spent the following two days healing in a box beside the woodstove.

"Shoo, guys," she said as she walked through the door of the house, sending a flutter of tiny black, gray, and white bodies to the curtain rods. Bear scrambled out of his bed beside the woodstove, his eyes blinking with sleep as he lumbered arthritically toward her.

"Hello, Bear. Anything exciting happen today?" she asked as she sat down in an overstuffed chair and pulled Bear's head onto her lap. He looked up at her with nearly opaque eyes and gave a wheezy woof.

"I know how you feel, pup." She scratched behind his ears. "No ghostly visits today? No resort people knocking on my door?" She tickled his chin. "No historical fanatics snooping through the outbuildings?"

Anna bent forward and kissed his nose. "You wouldn't know if the roof caved in on top of you, would you, old boy? Come on. I'll give you something for your aches, and then I'm taking some of your medicine myself." She slowly rubbed her jaw on his broad head. "You might not have noticed, but I kinda got beat up today."

When all she got for sympathy was another soft whine, Anna stood and walked to the kitchen. Bear's toenails sounded on the floor behind her, letting her know he was following. But before she could dole out the pain relief, Anna had to set out some sunflower seed on the shelf beside the window. The frenzy that had followed her and Bear into the kitchen finally settled into a polite meal as half a dozen chickadees descended on the shelf.

Anna noticed all the acorns had disappeared, and her gaze followed the trail of dusty squirrel tracks leading to the tiny hole cut in the outside wall, covered with a flap of leather. Samuel must have decided that if he didn't want the squirrels ruining everything in sight, he'd better feed them as well.

Anna put some water to boil on the stove, then opened the cupboard. She took down a brown bottle of pills and ran her finger over the name typed on the prescription label. Samuel Fox. Gramps, she used to call him. Anna held the bottle to her chest as she groped behind her for one of the kitchen chairs, sat down, and burst into tears.

"Oh, Gramps," she whispered. "Such a waste of eighteen years, just because we were both too stubborn to make the first move."

Bear lumbered over and settled his head on her knee with a whine. Anna blindly reached out and petted him. "I know. I know. You miss him, too," she said, soothing her old friend's broken canine heart. The kettle on the stove began to whistle into a rolling boil, and Anna gave Bear one last pat and stood up. "Maybe it's Gramps roaming the mill at night," she told him as she wiped away her tears. "Maybe he's our ghost."

Anna poured the boiling water into the teapot and left it on the stove to steep. She returned to the cupboard, put back the bottle of pills and took down the buffered aspirin, went to the fridge and got a slice of cheese, then folded one of the buffered aspirin inside it.

"Here you go, pup. This will make you feel better," she said as she fed Bear the medicinal treat. Then she popped four aspirin in her mouth and washed them down with a glass of water. If she had survived Ethan's punch, a couple extra aspirin weren't going to kill her.

She grabbed an old towel from the rack and opened the back door, scooped some snow off the porch railing into the towel, then tied it in a knot and gingerly touched it to her cheek. A little late with the ice pack maybe, but it still felt good. Back in the kitchen, she poured herself a cup of tea, then made her way into the living room, pushed several magazines off the couch, and lay down with a sigh. Her tea forgotten on the coffee table, Anna fell asleep in less time than it took to get comfortable—and dreamed of Ethan Knight charging to her rescue that long-ago summer.

Chapter Two

It was a long drive back around the lake as Ethan headed for home. He slapped the steering wheel with a curse, still unable to believe he'd been fired. And on his first day on the job! He hadn't even gotten a proper look at Loon Cove Lumber.

That's what he'd been doing when he'd stepped in front of the loader being driven by Anna, the tyrant foreman. He'd almost gotten them both killed. And if he hadn't killed her in the wreck, he'd nearly killed her with his fist. Dammit! He hadn't known she was a woman. All he'd seen was an angry body coming at him with a tire iron, and instinct had taken over.

Just as Anna had instinctively saved his life by driving the loader into the ditch.

Ethan hit the steering wheel again as he drove

past the lane to his old home, which was nothing but ash now. He should have stayed and helped his family settle into the sporting camps three miles up the shoreline, but oh, no. Everyone had insisted he start his new job at Loon Cove Lumber today.

By suppertime, Ethan realized he should have just kept driving deeper into the woods instead of coming home.

"I was fired," he told his eleven-year-old niece, Delaney.

"Fired!" his father and younger brother, Paul, repeated in unison.

Ethan scowled at them. "The crazy woman fired me!"

"Woman?" Delaney asked, tugging on his sleeve to gain his attention again.

"Fired?" Paul repeated.

"Well, I did knock her flat on her ass—er—her fanny," Ethan added sheepishly.

"You *hit* her?" Delaney gasped.

"What!" Grady shouted.

Ethan saw his father head for the back door, probably to get a pail, since Grady was in the habit of dousing his sons with cold buckets of water whenever he was mad at them.

Delaney punched him in his side. "Shame on you," she chastised.

"I didn't know she was a woman at the time," he repeated, acutely aware he'd told his story all wrong.

His sister-in-law, Sarah, shook her head, but then a little smile broke on one corner of her mouth.

"There's a woman working at Loon Cove Lumber, and she's in a position to fire you?" She laughed then. "I wish I could have seen that."

Ethan held up his hand to forestall his father, who had just finished filling his bucket at the sink. "I didn't know she was a woman!" he shouted. "She was wearing a hard hat and coming toward me with a tire iron, obviously mad enough to use it." He ran a hand through his hair. "I just reacted and swung. It wasn't until she fell down and her hard hat came off that her hair came tumbling out." He looked at Sarah and Delaney beseechingly. "I just thought she was a short, wiry Frenchman."

"Why was she coming at you with a tire iron?" Paul asked.

"I—uh—stepped in front of the loader she was driving. It was carrying a full fork of logs at the time, and she had to ditch the machine. It rolled over, dumping the logs and landing on its side." Ethan closed his eyes. "She came climbing out of the rig, cursing and waving that tire iron."

"But who is she?" Alex asked. "How come we've never heard of her before?"

Ethan shook his head. "It's the damnedest thing. But from what I can tell, all the men respect her. Ron Davis escorted me to my truck at her order, and told me she can handle anything with an engine better than any man on the payroll. He said her name is Anna Segee, and that Bishop hired her three months ago when she moved into town."

"Segee?" Alex repeated, his brow raised. "As in Segee Logging and Lumber of Quebec?"

"How in hell would I know?" Ethan shook his head. "She can't possibly be related to the Quebec Segees, although she did have a bit of a French accent. But why would she be down here working for Tom when her family owns a timber operation half the size of the state of Maine?"

"I've met André Segee," Grady said, his gaze speculative. "And he didn't strike me as a man who'd want a woman anyplace near his business. How old is this Anna Segee?"

"She can't be a day over twenty-two," Ethan said.

"Maybe she's André's daughter, and she's down here because they had a falling-out," Grady surmised.

"Why doesn't André Segee want women in his business?" Sarah asked. "All the hard physical work is done by machinery."

"It's still a male-dominated industry for the most part," Grady told her. "And André has at least two, maybe three sons who'll inherit the business."

Ethan poured himself a cup of coffee. "We don't know if Anna is even related to the Quebec Segees," he said, sitting down at the table. "But I do know I'm not going to like being a millwright. Bishop's yard is busier than downtown Greenville in the summer."

"So let me get this straight," Grady said, looking at Ethan through narrowed eyes. "You stepped in front of a loader?"

Ethan didn't quite meet his father's gaze. "Yeah."

"And you're planning on thanking Bishop's foreman for saving your life by firing her just as soon as we own that mill, aren't you?" Grady asked in a whisper-soft voice.

Ethan looked him square in the eye. "A mill is no place for a woman."

"Tom Bishop seems to think it is."

"Bishop's getting old," Ethan returned. "He's obviously grown soft in the head. Will I be the one running Loon Cove Lumber or not? With the power to hire and fire?"

"Tom Bishop is leaving for Florida the day after we sign the papers," Grady said. "I couldn't talk him into staying even a month to help with the transition. And you don't know a damn thing about running a mill. That leaves Anna Segee."

"There's got to be competent men working there," Ethan said. "Bishop's got a crew of thirty."

"And he hired Anna as their foreman."

Ethan glared at him. "Do I have autonomy or not?"

"That depends. You going to cut off your nose to spite your face? Loon Cove is running in the black right now, but if you try to fix something that's not broke, it won't stay that way. We have a lot riding on this venture."

"Okay then, I won't fire her." Ethan lifted his cup to his mouth and grinned behind it. "Not unless she makes me."

Chapter Three

*N*o *wonder* you can't make friends around here, if that's how you greet people," Tom said as he climbed out of his truck, his face a grin from ear to ear. He pointed at the shotgun in her hand. "Is it loaded?"

Anna broke open the ancient weapon and looked at the sky through the empty barrel. "I don't trust the old shells Samuel had. And I haven't had time to buy new ones."

"Then I suggest you buy a new shotgun while you're at it. That one's liable to blow up in your face."

Anna leaned the useless weapon against the wall inside the house and turned back to watch her friend mount the porch stairs.

"You look like hell," Tom said as he inspected her face.

"Thank you." She leaned to the side to look behind him. "What have you got back there?"

"Something to cure your ills. Mildred baked you a blueberry pie," he told her as he pulled a deep, heavy-looking dish from behind his back. "And this," he added, reaching into his pocket and pulling out a pint bottle, "is from me."

Anna immediately opened the chocolate milk and took a long swallow, carefully wiped her sore mouth on her sleeve, and smiled at Tom. "Thanks. I needed that."

"Now tell me who you're gunning for," he said, waving her inside ahead of him.

"You must have met them on your way in," she said, leading the way to the kitchen, knowing Tom expected her to share Mildred's gift.

"I met a car full of suits, so I'm guessing they were the developers and not the historians," he said, taking a seat at the table as he tossed his jacket onto another chair.

"Bingo. They brought in the big guns this time," she said, putting the water on to boil. "From Boston."

"So you decided to show them *your* big gun?" Tom sighed and shook his head. "You have to stop confronting men with tire irons and empty shotguns. One of these days someone's going to call your bluff."

She rubbed her swollen jaw. "Someone already did."

"And you didn't learn a damn thing, did you?"

"I learned to stay out of reach," she said, sitting

down across from him and leaning her arms on the table. "So, what brought you here today?"

"I'm being a concerned friend. Isn't that enough?"

"No." She nodded at the pie. "That's nice, but it's not the reason you're here. So, what's up?"

Tom stood and started opening drawers until he found a knife, and Anna patiently waited. He came back to the table and sat down, then began to methodically cut into the pie as if he were doing surgery. "I've sold Loon Cove Lumber," he said, his voice whisper soft.

Anna leaned back in her chair and stared at him.

Tom finally looked up, his face nearly as red as hers. "We sign the papers next month."

Still she didn't speak.

Tom set down the knife. "I'm tired, Anna. And I'm cold. I want to live where I don't have to wade through four feet of snow to go get the mail, I want to walk on the beach in Florida in January in my shorts, and I want to see my grandchildren more than once a year."

She opened her mouth to respond, but nothing came out.

Tom leaned across the table and took her hands in his. "Nothing will change. You'll still have your job. You'll just have a new boss."

"Who?"

He pulled away and stood up again, then started opening cupboard doors until he found the plates. He returned to the table and began dishing out the pie.

He wouldn't look at her. "I can't say just yet, because I promised not to. But they're good people. And they're locals. They'll run the mill with the workers in mind."

"Locals," she repeated. "Which means they won't like having a woman foreman."

He finally looked at her, frowning. "Why wouldn't they? You're a damn good foreman."

Anna threw up her hands with a laugh. "This is Maine, Tom, where men are men, and women belong at home cooking and cleaning and making babies." She laughed again at his glower. "How hard was it for you to hire me? You had so many reservations about your men taking orders from me that you stood over my shoulder for an entire month and scowled at the crew, just daring them to give me a hard time."

"You've proven yourself. And I've made provisions in the sale. They can't fire any of my crew for the first twelve months."

Anna sat back in her chair. "How long have you been thinking about selling?"

"A long time," he admitted. "Mildred's been after me for years to retire."

Anna went to the stove when the kettle started to boil, put tea bags in the pot and set it on the table, took down two cups and set them out, then went to the fridge and got Tom some milk.

"I'm seventy-two, Anna. It's past time I began reaping the rewards of my labor," he continued. "And both of my sons have established themselves out of state. Nothing's holding me here."

"There's the woods," she said. "And elbow room." She reached out and grabbed his hand reaching for the milk. "All you're going to find in Florida are people. They don't even have real trees down there, Tom."

He reversed their grip and squeezed her hand. "It's done, Anna. And I'm glad. Now be glad for me."

She covered his hand and squeezed back. "I am, Tom. I'm just a little surprised, is all." She smiled. "I still can't picture you in shorts."

The red returned to his face and he pulled his hand free and dug into his pie. "Ah, there's another thing," he said just before he filled his mouth.

Anna had forked up a piece of her own pie, but she stopped with it halfway to her mouth. "And what would that be?"

"I've offered one of your cabins to the new owner who'll be running the mill," he said, quickly following that bit of information with a gulp of tea. He sputtered and choked into his napkin. "Damn. That's hot."

Anna just glared at him

He smiled back. "He'll pay rent," he offered as enticement. "Six hundred dollars a month."

"What!"

"With a six-month lease," he added, ignoring her shock. "You can put the money toward your taxes."

"The man's going to be livid when he sees what

he's renting. The only cabin I've got that's habitable doesn't even have running water."

"And having a tenant means you'll have some muscle around when your ghost returns," he continued, ignoring her protests. He smiled broadly at her. "That's the best part."

"For you," she snapped.

He nodded. "I'll feel better knowing you're not living way out here alone." He looked at Bear curled up by Anna's feet. "You wouldn't get a new watchdog, so I got one for you."

"And did you tell this man that ghost-busting was part of the lease?" she asked. She stood up and leaned her hands on the table. "I can take care of myself."

"Six hundred dollars, times six, is thirty-six hundred dollars, Anna. That'll put a nice dent in your tax debt."

Anna blew out her breath, sat back down, and rubbed her aching jaw, realizing she'd been gritting her teeth. Tom was right, it would put a very nice dent in her tax debt. And it shouldn't be too hard to get the water running to the old cabin. "Who is he?" she asked, picking up her fork again.

"You'll meet him next month."

"Who?"

"I can't say, Anna. I promised. The buyers are local, and they don't want anyone knowing about the sale until it's final." He smiled. "Which is happening faster than I expected. We weren't supposed to close until April first, but my lawyer called yesterday and told me we can sign the fifteenth of March."

"You're sure about this, Tom? You know what you're doing?"

"I'm sure, Anna girl."

"Then I truly am glad for you. Samuel would be glad, too, don't you think?"

"He'd also be glad you're getting a tenant," he said. "He didn't stop to think about you living out here all alone when he left you this place."

"I doubt he was thinking I'd be here this soon, since he wasn't planning on crashing into that ravine."

Before filling his mouth with pie again, Tom muttered something about being glad the old goat hadn't died in his bed. Anna looked down at her own dessert.

Yes, the Samuel Fox she remembered wouldn't have wanted to spend the last days of his life in a nursing home, and he hadn't. Still, she wished he'd waited until they'd reconciled before getting himself killed.

"I'm not sure I want a male tenant," she said, more for conversation than anything else. She gave Tom a wistful look. "It's been kind of peaceful around here, with no men sticking their noses in my business."

"The new owner will be too busy learning to run a sawmill to bother you," he told her, a twinkle suddenly lighting his eyes. "And he's probably more afraid of ghosts than you are."

Anna rolled her eyes. "Oh God. He's going to try

bossing me around at work, sticking his nose in every aspect of the mill."

Tom finished off the last of his pie, followed it with the last of his tea, then stood up and put on his coat. "Don't create trouble before it happens, Anna girl. If the man knows what's good for him, he'll leave the bossing to you." He walked to the kitchen door and looked back at her. "Just don't go after him with a tire iron for the first few days."

Just as soon as Tom left, Anna headed for the only cabin that wasn't leaning badly enough to scare off her new tenant. In its heyday, Fox Run had been a bustling lumber mill that had run two ten-hour shifts a day. The main camp, made up of two dozen buildings scattered over nearly ten acres, sat on two thousand acres of dense forest situated between the main road and Frost Lake. Most of the buildings were in sad shape, with some completely caved in. The stable, which had housed some thirty horses, was the soundest structure. The building that covered the main saw, stretching long and low for nearly a hundred and fifty feet, was also in pretty good shape. So were the cookhouse and bachelor bunkhouse. But several sheds and many of the family cabins had given up their battle with nature, and were slowly melting into the encroaching forest.

Lumbering had been labor intensive a hundred years ago, and Fox Run had been the winter home for nearly ninety lumberjacks and sawyers as well as several families. Now it was a ghost camp. And as of three months ago, it was all hers—including the ghosts.

Strange things had been happening around the mill since Anna had moved in. Odd noises came from the various outbuildings some nights, waking her from a sound sleep. In the morning she always investigated and found tools and old equipment rearranged, as if her ghost had been looking for something. One morning she'd found that even her truck had been searched.

But if the truth be told, ghosts were the least of her problems at the moment, as the tax collector was far more threatening. Samuel had left a sizable sum of back taxes due on the mill when he'd died, and Anna was up to her armpits in debt. As much as she hated to admit it, Tom Bishop was right: thirty-six hundred dollars would go a long way toward securing her heritage.

And what was one more man in her life, anyway? She hadn't met one yet she couldn't handle with a bit of calculated charm. She grinned. And if that failed, there was usually a tire iron or shotgun nearby.

Anna stopped in front of the straightest cabin and inspected it with a critical eye. It was leaning to the left and the roof sagged, but it looked sound enough to shelter the new owner of Loon Cove Lumber. And best of all, it was a goodly distance from her house.

Charlie suddenly landed on her head. "Aw, pest. I don't have time to play right now," she told the bird, perching him on her finger so she could hold him up to her face. "And you've got to stop sneaking up on people," she admonished. "We've got a new tenant moving here in a month, and I don't need you and your gang driving him off."

Charlie blinked at her and canted his head, giving a little chirp. Anna threw him into the air, watched him flutter to a nearby branch, and walked up the stairs of the cabin.

The door was frozen shut. She shoved against it, but her shoulder was still sore from her loader accident yesterday, so she didn't even try to bang it open. She walked to the window instead and wiped the glass to peer inside. The place looked dry and downright filthy, so she trudged to the old machine shed and returned pulling a sleigh of tools. It took her ten minutes using a pry bar, but she finally gained entrance to the cabin, took two steps inside, and immediately started sneezing. There was enough dust in there to bury a body.

For three hours she cleaned and straightened and tossed out broken furniture until she had a pile outside the door that would fill a dump truck. Finally, it was time to fire up the old woodstove, but first she had to climb up on the roof and check the chimney.

Not wanting to bother with a ladder, and thankful for the snowdrift that was in all likelihood propping up the back side of the cabin, she carefully worked her way onto the roof, then bounced a couple of times to make sure it would support her weight. She was just pulling the cap off the tin chimney when a car drove up to her house across the yard. Anna watched a man get out, climb the steps, and knock on the door.

"I'm over here," she shouted.

The man turned and scanned the camp, looking for the direction of her voice.

"Up here!" she yelled, waving at him.

He finally spotted her and headed toward the cabin. Charlie and his gang intercepted him. Startled, the man began waving his arms at the marauders, ducking his head inside his coat collar. Anna sat down on the snow-covered roof with a chuckle and watched the poor guy start running toward her. Just then Bear, having finally noticed they had company, stood up from the porch below and started barking, sounding quite pitiful as he rushed at the man. The guy stopped dead in his tracks and went stone still.

"He won't hurt you," Anna hollered down over the chirping birds and barking dog. "Neither will the chickadees. They're just hungry."

"Is the dog hungry?"

"No. He's just glad to see you."

"I'm Frank Coots, your absentee neighbor."

"Oh. That name sounds familiar," she said, sliding closer to the eave of the roof. "Doesn't your daddy own Kent Mountain?"

"I own it now," he said with a nod. "They told me in town that an Anna Segee was living here. You her?"

Anna nodded.

"Any relation to Segee Logging and Lumber in Quebec?"

She nodded again.

"You have something against white snow?" he asked, motioning at the roof she was sitting on.

Anna looked down and burst into laughter. The snow was more black than white. She looked at herself and found that she was even dirtier. She wiped the hair out of her face and grinned at the man standing below her. "I'm cleaning the chimney."

He gazed around the camp with a frown. "Alone?" he asked, looking back up at her.

"Just me and the chickadees. I'm trying to figure out how to get one of them to fly down the pipe with a rag in its beak."

He didn't smile; in fact, his frown deepened. "You shouldn't be up on the roof when no one's around."

Anna ignored his concern. "Are you going to sell your mountain to the developers?" she asked, standing to brush off her pants.

He seemed caught off guard by her question. Instead of answering her, Frank took another swipe at Charlie dive-bombing his pocket. Anna returned to cleaning the chimney by running the brush down the pipe, scrubbing it up and down the inside several times before replacing the cap. Then she walked to the back of the cabin and jumped into a snowdrift, landing in the soft powder up to her waist.

She smiled when Frank came running around the

building. "Well? Are you selling?" she asked as she wiggled back and forth to get unstuck.

"Lady, you're crazy. There could have been something solid under that snow."

" 'Cause if you are, you can just take your butt back out of here. We don't need another resort around here." She grabbed his offered hand and pulled herself free. "Personally, I like the mountain just as it is."

He stepped away, rubbing his dirty hands in the snow, and Anna studied him. Frank Coots was handsome; not too tall, with blond hair cut in a modern style, eyes the color of pine needles in winter, and the face of a cherub. He could stand to lose about thirty pounds.

"You want to buy it instead?" he asked when he straightened.

Anna snorted. "I can't afford the taxes on *this* place. I'd hate to guess what they are for the mountain, much less what your asking price would be."

"There's three thousand acres," he told her. "All old growth. You could sell timber to pay the taxes."

She started walking toward her house. "That's true. But the grade's steep, and most of it probably isn't cuttable. There would be erosion control and reseeding costs, not to mention the roads that would have to be built."

"I guess you do know the timber business."

"I know something about it. Where you living now, Frank?"

"Boston. I'm in advertising."

THE STRANGER IN HER BED   39

She walked up on the porch, opened the door, and entered the house ahead of him. "So what are you doing here?"

"You get right to the point, don't you?" He started to close the door behind them, but several chickadees flew through the doorway. "Hey! What are they doing?"

"I feed them in the house. They sleep in here, too, when it's stormy."

Coots looked blank, and Anna decided he didn't have much of a sense of humor. "Well? Are you moving back to Maine, or just up here long enough to sell your mountain?"

"Just visiting. The pace in Boston is killing me."

She laughed. "The pace around here is just as liable to kill you with boredom."

"Will you have dinner with me tonight?"

It was Anna's turn to be caught off guard. "Dinner?"

Frank's cherub face lit with humor. "Assuming you clean up okay," he added, motioning at her sooty clothes and face.

Anna looked down at herself. Maybe he did have a sense of humor, considering she looked like the inside of a vacuum cleaner bag. Only now the snow was melting, turning the dust to mud. She wiped her cheeks with her gloves.

"What happened to your face? Did you fall?" he asked, reaching out to touch her cheek.

Anna backed up and spun around. "I rolled a loader at work yesterday." She turned on the faucet at the kitchen sink and started splashing her face, watching the water run black down the drain. She grabbed a towel and wiped herself dry as she turned to face her guest. "I thank you for your offer of dinner, but I've got too many chores." She motioned toward her bruised jaw. "And I'm not presentable for public dining."

He waved her excuses away. "Makeup will cover that, and I'll help you finish your chores," he offered.

The only problem was, she didn't own any makeup. "That's sweet of you, but I'll take a rain check and give you a piece of pie instead."

Frank looked sincerely surprised by her refusal—as well as a bit angry. She picked up the kettle and started to fill it with water.

"I'll have to take a rain check as well," he said, putting on his gloves. "I'll call back again when you're less busy."

She set the kettle on the cold burner. "Okay."

"Who are you renting the cabin to?"

"One of the workers at Loon Cove Lumber," she told him. "He needs a temporary place to stay."

"When's he moving in?"

Frank Coots was a rather nosy neighbor. "In a couple of weeks."

"Well, that'll be nice. You shouldn't be staying way out here all by yourself."

Great, another man who didn't think she was capable of taking care of herself. Anna headed to the living room. "I'm glad you stopped by and introduced yourself. And I hope you enjoy your vacation. How long are you staying?"

He shrugged one shoulder. "I haven't decided."

"Just long enough to sell Kent Mountain?"

He stepped onto the porch and turned to face her. "How about your father? Would Segee Logging and Lumber be interested in buying Kent Mountain?"

Anna shook her head with a laugh. "Not unless you can move it over the border to Canada."

He lifted a brow. "What happened to the old guy who used to own this place?"

"He died three months ago."

"Oh. Did you buy it from his daughter? He had a daughter named Madeline, didn't he?" Frank's eyes suddenly widened. "You didn't buy the mill to restore, did you?" he asked, scanning the decaying buildings before leveling his gaze back on her.

"I haven't decided what I'm going to do with it," she said, giving him back his earlier words. "Right now my only focus is paying the taxes."

His gaze sharpened. "You got stuck with back taxes?"

The man was getting far too interested in her plans and problems. Anna stepped back into the house. "Nothing a phone call to Quebec won't fix. It was nice meeting you, Frank."

He clearly didn't like being dismissed. Anna closed the door on his disgruntled face, leaned against the doorjamb, and asked for forgiveness for her little fib.

If only it *were* that easy. Her father had told her, in the plainest words he could find, that she was on her own if she insisted on moving back to Fox Run Mill.

She hadn't lied when she'd told Frank that her father wanted nothing to do with Maine.

Anna waited until she heard him leave before she ventured back to the old cabin, newspaper and kindling in hand, to finish the job she'd started. Why had he come here, and what had he hoped to learn? He hadn't answered her question as to whether or not he intended to sell to the developers. In fact, he'd sidestepped it quite nicely by asking her to dinner.

But something about him had made her say no. She didn't trust him. Maybe it was his slick city looks, or the fact that he smiled too easily, or maybe it was that little flash of anger that had crossed his face when she'd also eluded his questions. Then again, maybe it was because he didn't like her chickadees.

Whatever, she intended to treat Frank the same way she was treating all her problem visitors—by ignoring every damn last one of them until they gave up and left her alone. So she spent the rest of Friday, Saturday, and all of Sunday making the cabin rentable with furniture from the main house.

Three weeks to her first rent check, and she'd finally be able to put enough money down on Fox Run's taxes to keep it from being foreclosed on by the town. If she wasn't so determined to prove that she didn't need her family's backing, she wouldn't have to put up with a tenant, developers, historians, or pesky ghosts. Though stubbornness could sometimes be a handicap, it could also be as powerful a motivator as guilt.

Chapter Four

Is it true, boss? Is Tom really selling the mill?"

Anna sat on the stack of rough-cut boards waiting to be taken to the planer shed and opened her thermos. "As we speak," she told the obviously worried men taking their morning break. "He's in Greenville signing the papers right now."

Several more men joined the somber crew. Word had traveled fast. The rumor had broken this morning, likely by Tom Bishop himself, who had known the men would be looking to Anna for answers.

Loon Cove Lumber was Tom's creation, and he'd run it for nearly forty-five years. Now, though, he couldn't bring himself to tell his men he was selling, so he'd started a rumor instead. Anna looked down

at her shoulders, wondering if they were wide enough
for thirty grown men to cry on.

"It could be worse," she told them. "Most of the
mills around here have shut down for one reason or
another, but Tom was able to sell Loon Cove because
it's still making money. Your jobs are safe—and that's
what really matters."

"Who's buying it?"

"I don't know. But Tom said they're locals. That's
in our favor."

"Locals?" Keith repeated. "Maybe it's Clay Porter.
I heard talk in town he was trying to drum up capital
for something."

Several men groaned. "Hell. Not Porter," one of
them said. "He's a logger, and doesn't know anything
about running a mill. He'll come charging in here
and change everything."

"He'll fire some of us," another said.

Anna shook her head as she swallowed her tea.
"He can't. Tom made provisions that no one gets fired
for one year."

"He can do that?"

"Yup," she assured them. "That's common practice
when small, family-run businesses change hands. The
seller can stipulate that no one loses his or her job as
a result of the purchase."

Keith suddenly smiled at her. "Does that mean you
can't fire anyone for a year, boss lady?"

"No. Just like the guy who stepped in front of the
loader last month, you screw up and you're out of here."

The men quietly ate their snacks and drank their coffee while they mulled over the news. Anna scanned their worried faces. They were good men, every one of them, hard workers, family men, decent folks. Though she'd only been here four months, they were her friends.

Her first few weeks here had been almost comical. Several of the men had needed to adjust their mind-set about taking orders from a woman who, in some cases, was younger than their own daughters. But Anna had proven herself by calmly and patiently showing them that she knew timber and sawing and that she wasn't a threat to either their livelihood or manhood. She'd built a good working relationship, as well as friendships, with most of them.

"Oh, come on, guys," she admonished, poking Keith with her elbow. "This could be an excellent move for Loon Cove Lumber: new blood, new capital, new ideas. We're likely to grow in the next few years and become a force to be reckoned with in this industry."

Keith rubbed his ribs and frowned. "I'm just trying to figure out who has that kind of money around here." He shook his head. "Nobody local that I can think of."

"Well, we're about to find out," she said, nodding toward the front gate. "Here they come."

All eyes turned to the outer parking lot and watched as Tom drove his truck into his usual space. A blue SUV parked beside him, and all four doors opened. It was quickly followed by a red pickup with two men inside.

Anna groaned. "Oh God. Kids." She looked at her crew. "No one starts any equipment until they're gone. Got that?"

Every man present nodded. Most of them had kids of their own, and they knew that young people and machinery were a dangerous combination. Two children jumped out of the SUV and immediately headed for the gates. They were chased by a woman who, even from this distance, Anna could see was beautiful, and every man in her crew suddenly perked up.

An older gentleman got out behind the children and made his way over to Tom. Another man, tall and dark haired, waited for the two men to get out of the red pickup.

"Well, hell," Keith said, jumping up as he gaped at the group walking through the gate with Tom Bishop. He turned and looked down at Anna with a crooked smile. "I'm thinking you're in trouble, boss lady. Recognize that guy in the middle?"

Anna sat stock-still as Ethan Knight walked through the gate beside her used-to-be boss and friend. She suddenly felt every eye of her crew on her. Anna snapped the cover down on her thermos and stuffed her half-eaten donut back in its bag. "Come on, people. We don't want them to think we're slackers. Let's get back to work."

"What about the kids?" Keith asked.

Anna stopped. "Okay. Put everyone to work on anything that doesn't have an engine." She waved at the yard. "Shovel the snow off the storage shed roof. Grease the machines and catch up on the maintenance. The saws are shut down as of now, until I tell you to start them again."

Grinning like a fool, Keith crossed his arms over his chest and looked at her. "And what will you be doing?"

She walked up and shoved her thermos and lunch bag at his stomach. "I'm going to greet our new owners," she told him sweetly through gritted teeth. She pivoted around, squared her shoulders, and headed for the group of people standing outside the office.

It had been all he could do to contain himself these last few weeks waiting for exactly this moment. Ethan stood beside his father and brothers and watched Anna Segee walk up to Tom Bishop, her stride determined, her smile forced.

Ethan grinned to himself. As of one hour ago, he'd become her boss.

Ethan had known the minute she had recognized him; he'd seen her entire body stiffen just as she was about to take a drink from her thermos. All the men had turned to her, to see her reaction.

He had to give her credit, she'd kept a cool head. But he'd bet their newly purchased mill that the lady was cursing a blue streak under her smile as Tom Bishop introduced her to Grady.

She came up to his father's nose, which made her tall for a woman. Her hard hat was tucked under her arm, and her hair hung down her back in a braid as thick as a man's wrist. It was light brown, with highlights in it that Ethan knew hadn't come from a bottle. Several strands had worked free and were framing her decidedly young face.

Ethan quickly changed his earlier estimate that she couldn't be a day over twenty-two. Hell, she looked young enough to still be in high school, though he knew that was impossible. It was strange enough that Bishop's crew took orders from a woman, and even stranger still that they seemed to respect her.

She'd washed her jacket, and her boots had been polished. Ethan's grin broadened. She'd obviously put her best foot forward for the new owners of Loon Cove Lumber. Which meant that Bishop had kept his word and hadn't told a soul who was purchasing his mill, not even his foreman.

Would Anna Segee have been so eager if she had known?

And did she realize who she had agreed to rent her cabin to?

Lord, this was going to be fun.

"Why are the saws stopped?" Tom asked, apparently just now realizing how silent the mill was.

A tinge of color appeared in Anna's cheeks as she glanced at Delaney and Tucker and then back at Tom. "I thought this would make a good maintenance day."

Tom gave her a quizzical look, and Ethan knew she was lying. She darted another glance at the children, and Ethan realized Delaney and Tucker were the reason the mill had been shut down. Anna Segee had already proven herself a safety tyrant, and she wasn't about to take any chances with the children of the new owners. Nor did she want to blame them for bringing thirty men to a standstill.

"I've been waiting all month to meet you," Sarah Knight said, grabbing Anna's hand and shaking it. "I was surprised to learn there's a woman working here as foreman. Or should I say forewoman?"

Anna Segee smiled and politely returned the handshake. "Foreman's fine. You're in the majority, Mrs. Knight," she returned. "But Tom's an open-minded businessman."

"You can drive all this machinery?" Sarah asked, her voice excited and her look expectant.

"Yes. I grew up driving large equipment."

Alex grabbed his wife and hugged her to him. "No, Sarah, she hasn't got time to teach you," he said with a laugh. He looked at Anna. "How about a tour of the mill?" Alex turned and motioned to his kids. "But first, you should meet the rest of the family. This is Delaney, and this is Tucker."

"I'm seven," Tucker told her. "You fired Uncle Ethan."

Anna Segee didn't miss a beat. She smiled at the young man and said, "Yes, I did, because your uncle did a very foolish thing. I hope you're smarter than he is. As we tour the mill, you'll need to keep on your toes. There's lots of dangerous equipment here, and I wouldn't want you to get hurt."

She followed her little lecture with a pat on Tucker's head, and Ethan addressed his nephew. "That's right, Tuck. Behave yourself or she's liable to make you wait in the truck."

Sarah took hold of Tucker's hand. "Don't worry. They know the dangers of a working yard," she assured Anna.

"Even if my son doesn't," Grady said, turning a frown on Ethan. He looked at their new foreman. "And if he didn't properly thank you for saving his life, I certainly will. Thank you, Miss Segee."

"You're welcome," she whispered, her face coloring again.

"I'm Paul," Paul said, stepping past Alex to take her hand. "Are you free for dinner tonight?"

Anna Segee's face turned even redder. She quickly pulled her hand away and stuffed it in her pocket. "You'll probably want to get settled at Fox Run tonight, Mr. Knight," she told him. "And I never mix business with pleasure."

"Oh, Paul won't be running Loon Cove," Grady said, his face wrinkled into a grin. "Ethan will. And thanks for renting us one of your cabins. That will save him from having to drive clear around the lake each night."

Anna looked like she'd just swallowed a pine-cone, though Ethan would bet it was more likely curses she was choking on.

She finally looked at him, forcing another smile. "I hope you don't mind roughing it. I haven't been able to get water running to the cabin yet."

And she wasn't going to put herself out getting it there now, he guessed. The smile he gave her was wholly sincere. "I'm sure I'll manage just fine."

"Yes. Well." She turned to Grady. "What would you like to see first?"

"The saws," Grady said. "And I'd like to meet the crew."

Anna spun on her heels and started walking toward the office. "I'll get you some hard hats," she called over her shoulder as she disappeared into the building.

"She's a tad disconcerted," Tom said. He looked at Ethan. "She didn't know you were going to be her tenant when I talked her into renting one of her cabins."

"And why is that?" Ethan asked.

Tom Bishop's face wrinkled in a frown. "Because I don't want her living alone out there, and I knew she would have refused if she had known who her tenant would be."

That was an understatement. Ethan would bet the lady was racking her brain right now, trying to figure out how to get out of the lease. But he had signed a six-month lease this morning, along with the purchase papers. Anna was stuck with him.

"What's wrong with her living alone?" Sarah asked. "She seems capable of taking care of herself."

"Oh, she is," Tom quickly agreed. "It's just that Anna's been having some trouble lately, and I'll sleep better knowing there's a man around."

"What kind of trouble?" Ethan asked, wondering if his role as tenant had just become that of babysitter. "Has she got an old boyfriend bothering her?"

Tom shook his head. "It's nothing that simple." He glanced at the office before looking back at Ethan. "Some developers are trying to get her to sell Fox Run to them. And there's a group of historians after her to sell it to them for a museum."

"And she doesn't want to?" Sarah asked.

"No. She's told them that several times, but neither group is willing to accept it. And then there's her ghost."

"Ghost?" Paul repeated.

Tom nodded. "Someone's been visiting Fox Run at night. So far they've just been going through the old buildings, but I'm worried. I don't know if it's the developers, the historians, or someone else."

Ethan snorted. "She just has to show them her tire iron."

Both Tom and Grady glared at him. Ethan spun around and headed for the saw shed, leaving his family behind. He did, however, look both ways before crossing the yard.

During the ride home that evening it was snowing hard enough to make driving seem like a carnival ride, with four inches of snow on the main road and at least seven inches covering the mile-long lane leading down into Fox Run. And if that wasn't bad enough, Anna had the headlights of another pickup behind her, constantly reminding her that she was being followed home by a man who made her stomach do flip-flops.

Her insides had been in a state of chaos all day. She'd tried to blame it on the fact she was escorting her new bosses around the mill, as well as on not getting enough sleep lately because she'd been trying to get water running to the cabin for her tenant. She'd even blamed her bout of nerves on the arriving storm.

But she knew better. She'd greedily signed the lease agreement before a name had been put on the contract, and now she would not only have to deal with Ethan Knight all day at work, he'd be following her home and sleeping just several hundred feet away every damn night for the next six months.

Which meant it wouldn't be ghosts keeping her awake anymore.

Damn, he'd grown into a ruggedly handsome man.

And he still hadn't recognized her. On the one hand it was a relief, but on the other it hurt like the devil. How could he not remember her? He'd been beaten black and blue protecting her eighteen years ago, and had spent the whole summer with his arm in a cast—though she hadn't been able to console him because she'd been whisked away to Canada right after the "incident."

Her firing Ethan a month ago had been Anna's first contact with her childhood hero in eighteen years.

He'd hugged his family good-bye at Loon Cove, then bowed like the knight he was, waving Anna toward her truck to lead the way home. And he'd grinned the whole time, like the proverbial cat who was about to discover where the canary lived.

Anna rounded a steep curve and automatically sent up a prayer to Gramps as she approached the spot where he'd gone off the road four months ago. Suddenly her truck lost traction and started to fish-tail, and Anna quickly cut the wheel and let her foot off the gas, trying to keep from skidding off the road. The front right tire slid off the lane, the momentum pulling her toward the ravine. She quickly straightened the wheel and pushed the gas to the floor, maneuvering out of danger.

A sudden cloud of blinding snow cut her visibility and Anna felt the truck's front tire slip again, this time past the point of no return. Tiny trees snapped, her truck scraped against rocks and stumps, and the steering wheel jerked out of her hands as the pickup suddenly rolled, slamming her against the door and then into the ceiling as it slid on its roof down the steep bank with a deafening roar.

Hanging from her seat belt, Anna covered her face with her arms as branches smashed through the windshield and side window, battering her body. Snow poured into the cab, covering her head and shoulders and sliding under her jacket like icy needles.

The churning suddenly stopped with a violent thud of finality, knocking the breath out of her. The truck shuddered and then died, silence engulfing her in a cocoon of twisted metal and snow laced with bark and branches, the smell of pine filling the air as she hung upside down from her seat belt.

Anna opened her eyes to an eerie white darkness. The stillness was suffocating; the faint smell of gasoline made her heart pound at the thought of it spilling onto the hot engine. She twisted, rocking back and forth, trying to open a cavity around her. Her arms worked, she could wiggle her toes, and nothing seemed to be broken, but she was definitely trapped.

She squirmed to reach the buckle on her seat belt and more snow fell up the back of her jacket, sending a shiver along Anna's spine that chilled her to her soul. Oh God. Had Gramps gone through this? Had he lived several hours, trapped like she was?

Something banged into the side of her truck with a muted thud, followed by a very welcome curse.

"Anna!" came Ethan's muffled voice through the whiteness surrounding her. The truck rocked, jostling her against her belt. "Anna!"

She punched at the snow in the direction of the door. "I'm stuck," she shouted back. "I can't release my seat belt."

"I can't get the door open," he told her. "I'm going around to the other side. Hang tight."

She snorted. She *was* hanging. And the snow that had gone up her coat was beginning to melt and run up her back in an icy rivulet. Silence descended again, but for an occasional curse from the man outside. Anna continued to squirm, widening her cocoon enough to allow her to claw the snow toward the passenger's side. The truck shuddered again and began slipping farther down the ravine.

"Dammit! Quit moving!" Ethan shouted.

"Get me out of here!" she shouted back. "I smell gasoline!"

"I've got to brace the truck first," he said, his voice fading away.

Carefully, in small increments, Anna dug at the snow to make a tunnel. She needed air. She knew she wasn't in danger of suffocating, but it damn well felt as if she were. Her rescuer was suddenly beside the driver's door again.

"Anna, can you hear me?"

"Yes."

"I've braced it, but I don't know how long it will hold. I can't get either door open. I don't dare pull you out the windshield because you'll get caught on the steering wheel, but your side window is blown out. I'm going to dig toward you and then pull you out this way."

"I can't get my seat belt off. I can't reach the release."

"I've got a knife."

His hand suddenly appeared through the snow beside her, and Anna grabbed it.

"Hey, easy now," he said, his voice closer. He pulled his hand away. "Let me get rid of this snow."

The truck shifted again, settling against whatever he'd used to brace it.

"Hurry up!" she cried.

She thought she heard a chuckle come through the tunnel he'd dug. The packed snow slowly disappeared around her until Anna saw Ethan, though he was upside down.

He smiled at her through the tunnel he'd made. "You and my sister-in-law have a thing for accidents, it seems," he said, brushing the snow from her face and hair. "Are your legs stuck, or any bones broken that you can feel? Because I'm going to cut the belt and pull you out all in one motion."

"My legs are free, and nothing's broken."

He straightened and removed a knife from a sheath on his belt, squinting against the swirling snow as he looked toward the back of the truck. "When I cut the belt, you'll drop like a stone, and that just might send this baby to the bottom." He looked back at her. "Hold on to me as tightly as you can when I pull you out."

Or go down with her, she realized as she nodded agreement. Anna suddenly felt eleven again as she remembered the determined look in his twelve-year-old eyes that long-ago summer.

He stepped closer and held out his hand. "Grab my arm and be ready to scramble."

She grabbed him with shaking hands and felt his muscles bunch beneath her grip.

"Easy," he soothed her. "I won't let you go down with the truck."

"I know."

He grinned. "Do you, now? Then why are you shaking like a pine in a gale?"

"I'm cold," she snapped. "Half the snow on this hill is up my jacket. Do it, Knight. Cut the belt."

He turned serious. "Are you sure nothing's broken? Your neck and back feel okay?"

"I'm fine, if I can just get out of this damn truck!"

"Okay. Hang on tight," he said, reaching in and grabbing the front of her jacket in his fist.

Anna dug her fingers into his sleeve and closed her eyes. The belt holding her suddenly let go and she fell to the ceiling, The truck shuddered with the impact, and began sliding down the ravine. Her scream was lost in the shriek of metal scraping against rock as Ethan pulled her out. She banged her head on the door, her hip smashed into the outside mirror, which caught her jacket pocket . . . and Anna felt herself going down with the truck.

Ethan's grip never wavered. He held on to the front of her jacket and used his knife to slash at her pocket. She was the prize of a deadly tug of war that lasted mere seconds, then she was free and the bed of the truck went rushing past her in a blur of black twisted metal.

As Anna frantically scrambled up Ethan's body, he wrapped both arms firmly around her and hugged her to him. Trees below them snapped as her pickup gained momentum, rolling over and over until it landed in the bottom of the ravine and burst into flames. A plume of fire exploded toward them, and Ethan rolled them over, pinning her deep in the snow as branches and debris rained down.

The man weighed a ton. She couldn't breathe, but she didn't care. He'd saved her life. The deadly rain of fiery missiles eventually stopped, and Ethan slowly lifted his head and looked down at her. Smiling again.

"You seem to have a thing for ditches, Segee."

"Bite me," she said through gritted teeth, squirming to get free.

He didn't give an inch, but grabbed her hand pushing against his chest. "Are you shaking from the cold, or do I make you nervous?"

"I'm going to throw up."

That worked. He rolled away and sat up, pulling her with him, then grabbed her by the neck and shoved her head down between her knees. "Deep breaths," he said as he peeled off her coat.

She grabbed for her jacket. "I'm freezing to death!"

"You're soaked, and you've got a snowdrift up your back," he said, running his hand under her sweater.

His fingers burned like glowing embers, and a shudder racked Anna's body. Oh God. She *was* going to throw up. She scrambled to her feet and promptly fell flat on her face.

"Easy there," Ethan said, standing and wrapping his arm around her waist to hold her steady. "Your head's still spinning. You can't jump to your feet like that."

He started climbing the hill, not once loosening his hold on her, and Anna was grateful for his help. Her knees were knocking with the realization that she'd nearly been killed.

"Unless it's my charm that's making you light-headed," he said just as he lifted her onto a boulder halfway up the slope.

She blinked at him. His face was shadowed, wreathed in a halo of flames from her still-burning truck. "Charm?"

He cocked his head. "Yeah. I got the charm in my family."

She snorted and moved out of the way when he jumped onto the boulder and sat down beside her. Personally, she thought he'd gotten the looks in his family, not that she ever intended to say so. "What you've got is more muscle than brain," she said.

He sat beside her, and the snowstorm continued around them, the wind plastering the large wet flakes to her hair and face.

"That muscle just saved your life."

"And my brain saved yours last month."

A grin slashed his face. "We're even, then. Take

off your sweater." He slipped out of his jacket. "It'll take us ten minutes to climb up to my truck. You'll freeze to death before that."

She hesitated, but knew he was right. "Turn around."

He laughed, but turned. Anna pulled her sweat-shirt off over her head, but when she got her face free, she saw that he'd turned back to her. And he was no longer laughing.

She shoved him with all her might, sending him off the rock, swiping his jacket out of his hands as he fell. "You no good dirty jackass!" she said to his shocked face.

"Hey, I was checking for injuries."

"Yeah, right."

She slipped into his coat and buttoned it up to her chin, engulfing herself in heavenly warmth. "To hell with my tire iron, I'm buying a gun. One that holds nine bullets and has laser sights."

He held out both hands to her. "You planning on hatching that rock, or do you want to get home before morning?"

She looked down the ravine. "I totaled my truck," she said, more to herself than to him. "Now what am I going to do?"

"Was it insured?"

"Only liability."

"Just call your daddy. I'm sure he'll buy you a new one."

She snapped her gaze to his. "How do you know my father?"

Ethan shrugged. "I don't. But I'm guessing there aren't many women named Segee who know about sawmills. And your accent is definitely French Canadian. You have to be related to Segee Logging and Lumber of Quebec."

Anna stared at her burning truck again, not disputing his guess. It didn't matter if he knew who her daddy was; nobody would link Samuel Fox to André Segee. "He'll just add this accident to his list of reasons why I should come home."

Anna suddenly felt two hands at her waist and was pulled backward off the boulder until she was plastered up against a rock-hard chest. "I know someone who can give you rides to and from work until you buy a new truck."

She wiggled free, stepped away, and turned to face him. "I'll drive my snowmobile."

He grabbed her hand and started pulling her up the hill. "You've got to be the most hardheaded woman I know."

"Thank you."

He stopped and glared at her.

Anna continued climbing past him.

But it didn't take them ten minutes to reach the top, it took them twenty. Her legs just wouldn't cooperate. Ethan had to help her most of the way, and when they finally made it to the road, Anna threw herself down in a snowbank, exhausted.

"We can't stop. You're getting hypothermic."

"Just a minute," she said, panting with each spasm

that racked her muscles. She knew that she wouldn't be able to wiggle one finger come morning, every inch of her ached, from her hair to her toes.

Ethan sat down beside her, not even winded from their climb. "You need to get home and soak in a tub of warm water."

She looked around the darkened woods. The flames from her truck had faded, and the forest was eerily foreboding. Lord, she hated the dark. "Where's your truck?"

"Down the road. I saw you spinning out of control, but I couldn't stop." He looked behind them. "The road must be pure ice under this snow."

Anna rubbed her forehead. "This is where Samuel Fox was killed. The exact same thing happened to him." She looked at the man sitting beside her. "Only he didn't have someone to pull him out. I was told it was two days before anyone found him."

"How did you end up with Fox Run? You related to Samuel?"

When she only rubbed her forehead with a tired sigh, Ethan turned his attention to the skid marks zigzagging from one side of the lane to the other. He reached down and brushed the snow beside him. "There must be a spring running over the road. There's glaze ice under this snow."

"There's never been a spring here before. There's one about a quarter mile from here, but it's off in the woods."

He snapped his gaze back to hers, and Anna could

see his eyes had narrowed. "I've lived here all winter, and I've never seen this spot get icy," she quickly said. "And there's a map at Fox Run that shows a spring someplace over there," she added, waving toward the main road.

After several heartbeats of silence, Ethan finally stood up. "Springs can be worse than old girlfriends, suddenly popping up in the damnedest places."

"A recurring problem of yours?" she asked, taking his offered hand to stand.

He didn't answer. They slipped and slid to his truck, which was nearly off the road, the left front tire buried in the snowbank. She followed the line of skid marks to it.

"Very impressive," she said as she opened the door.

"Hey, my truck is still on the road."

"But stuck."

"The engine still works, so you can get warm. I've got a come-along in the back that'll get us out."

"I'll help."

He lifted her onto the seat. "No, you won't. You'll sit here with the heater running. You've stopped shivering and your words are slurring together. You're fading, Segee."

"Fine. Be the macho man. I'll just lie here and die."

"You can't go to sleep. Start the truck, unzip my jacket, and take off your shoes."

She blinked at him. He *was* looking a bit blurry.

And she did know the dangers of falling asleep and never waking up. But it irked her to be at Ethan's mercy.

"There's a thermos of coffee in the seat," he told her. "It should still be lukewarm."

"I hate coffee."

The glare Ethan gave her could have turned back a bear. But just to show him she wasn't dead yet, Anna pushed him away with her foot and pulled the door shut, then turned the key in the ignition.

Ethan reached into the truck bed and pulled out the block-and-tackle device he could hook to a tree to rachet the truck out of the snowbank. Anna unzipped his jacket and started working at the frozen laces of her shoes. She managed to get one boot off but couldn't keep her eyelids open any longer. She lay her head on the seat with a sigh and gave in to sleep.

Chapter Five

Guessing that the wheezing barks coming from inside meant he'd found the right building, Ethan kicked in the door, carried his listless patient inside, and laid her down on the couch. The large black dog immediately began washing Anna's face.

She didn't even stir.

Not good. He would have preferred to take her to the hospital, but the fifty-mile drive would have taken too long in the storm. Ethan headed to the back of the house and found the kitchen, but none of the light switches worked. He stumbled around until he found a battery-powered lantern on the table and continued exploring until he found the bathroom just off the kitchen. He put the plug in the bathtub drain and started running it full of lukewarm water, hoping the well tank had enough pressure to fill the tub. Walking back through the kitchen, he stopped long enough to put the kettle on to boil, then returned to the living room and stopped dead in his tracks.

There were half a dozen chickadees perched on Anna's chest and head, chirping at her. The old black dog was sitting beside the couch, his head resting on her arm. Ethan walked over and propped the damaged front door shut, then gently pushed the dog away with his knee, shooed the birds into flight, and touched Anna's forehead to find it cold and dry. He started undressing her and couldn't help but smile. She was going to be damned pissed off when she woke up and discovered he'd stripped her naked.

Ethan found one beautiful woman under her masculine work clothes: her chilled skin was alabaster, her toned muscles gently sculpted, her long legs perfectly suiting her athletic body. Her breasts were full—and damn if they weren't encased in a delicate yellow satin bra.

What a delightful surprise. Anna Segee was all woman beneath her masculine uniform, with matching bra and panties that had to be the sexiest thing Ethan had seen in months. He started to sweat, though he was already soaked to the skin himself. It had been a while since he'd had the pleasure of handling a beautiful woman—even though this one happened to be unconscious.

Ignoring his instinct—or was it his libido?—telling him to complete his chore, Ethan left her cute little underwear on, quickly covered her with a quilt from the back of the couch, then went to work unbraiding her wet hair. He brought the lantern into the bathroom and shut off the faucet, then came back and carried Anna to the tub. She finally stirred when he lowered her into the water, then opened her eyes and gasped.

"Easy, now. It'll only sting for a minute."

"I'm naked."

"Not quite," he pointed out, grabbing her flailing hands and holding them in front of her. "Just sit quietly and let the water do its job."

She pulled her hands free to cover her chest, sinking into the water up to her chin, but immediately gave a cry of pain, and she tried to bolt from the bathtub.

"I know it hurts, but we need to raise your temperature."

"But it stings!" She went still, then huge tears ran down her cheeks.

Ethan closed his eyes. Lord, he hated to see a woman cry. The kettle, which had been screaming the fact it was boiling, finally entered his consciousness. "Can you keep yourself from drowning while I get you something hot to drink?"

She quietly nodded, her head bowed, her tears landing in the water in front of her. He hesitated, then left the lantern with her, allowing the light to spill into the kitchen.

Ethan put a tea bag in a mug, along with several spoonfuls of sugar from one of the canisters on the counter, and poured in the boiling water. When he returned to the bathroom, Anna was adjusting a large wet towel over her body.

"There's a flock of chickadees in your kitchen, Segee. They keep buzzing around me like flies."

"They're hungry," she said, not looking up.

Her cheeks were bright red, and though he hoped it was heat returning to her body, more likely the woman was blushing all the way to her toes. Either way, she seemed to be warming up.

He walked to the tub, hunched down, and handed her the tea. "What do I feed them?"

"There's seed in the tall canister on the counter," she whispered, holding up the cup to blow on the steaming drink.

She still wouldn't lift her eyes to his, and Ethan looked down. Yup. Even her feet were pink. "I need to know if you're hurt anyplace. That was quite a ride you took."

"I'm sore, but everything works."

He didn't know whether to believe her or not. "I'll take you to the hospital in Greenville once you're warm. You might have internal injuries."

"I'd know if I did. I'm just lame. All the snow that came in the cab actually protected me."

"Okay. Where's your generator? I'll start it up, then build a fire in the hearth."

"Out the back door, in the shed at the end of the porch. You have to choke it," she instructed, still not looking at him.

Ethan found the generator, got it going, threw the switch, and light suddenly flooded the shed and glowed through the kitchen windows. He went back inside and built a roaring fire in the hearth, then returned to the bathroom to find Anna's mug sitting on the floor, empty.

"Where's your bedroom? I'll get you some dry clothes."

"Upstairs. The first one on the right."

"Good. I can't wait to go through your underwear drawer."

She gasped, snapping her gaze to his.

Ethan gave her a lecherous grin. "I'm on to you, lady, now that I know what's under all those layers of men's clothes."

"One word to the men at work, and I promise to use all nine bullets on you."

He laughed as he headed upstairs.

Anna dressed, then dried her hair, cursing the man making himself at home in her house. The arrogant jerk. He'd brought her a cream cashmere sweater and black leggings, her pink panties and bra nestled on top, and shot her a wink just before he'd closed the bathroom door. Getting dressed proved to be a trying task, as she felt like someone had taken a stick to her. Anna looked in the mirror and saw several small bruises on her face, interlaced with tiny scratches. Dammit, she was not normally prone to accidents— they'd only started since Ethan Knight had appeared back in her life. Anna's stomach churned just thinking about walking into the living room.

He saved your life tonight, she told herself.

And he undressed you, her reflection returned.

How was she going to survive work, now that Ethan knew about her sexy underwear? Would he give her knowing looks or make snide remarks that only she would understand? Anna sighed and tucked her riotous curls behind her ears. She would just have to brazen it out. She needed her job at Loon Cove, and she wasn't about to let Ethan drive her away. She opened the door to the bathroom, but took only two steps before she grabbed her back with a groan. She ached so badly she ended up hobbling into the living room.

The first thing she noticed was that the couch had been moved in front of the fireplace and made up as a bed. Then she noticed the suitcase sitting on the floor at the foot of the stairs. Ethan was sitting in a chair beside the roaring fire, drinking tea, his clothes changed and his hair combed.

"You are not sleeping on my couch," she said as she walked into the living room, ruining her edict with another groan.

The grin he was wearing disappeared. His eyes widened as his gaze moved up and down her body, finally stopping at her rioting curls. His smile just as suddenly returned. "No, I'm not. You are."

"Excuse me?"

He nodded at her hand bracing her back. "I doubt

you can make it upstairs, so I'll sleep in your bed and you can sleep down here."

Over her dead body was he taking her bed. She'd never be able to sleep in her bed again, knowing he'd been there—probably naked. She shook her head. "Your cabin is across camp. The generator's going, so its porch light will be on. And the fire in the woodstove is probably dead, but there should be enough embers to get it going again.

"But it doesn't have running water, and you do." He took a sip of his tea and settled deeper into his chair. "I think I'll bunk with you until we get that fixed."

She hobbled over to stand in front of him. "I live alone. And unfortunately, you live next door."

He stood up. Anna backed up a step, not liking that she had to look up to glare at him.

"Sit down before you fall down. You're so beat up, you can't stand without swaying."

She turned on her heel to head to the kitchen, lost her balance, and started to fall. Ethan caught her before she hit the floor, scooped her up, and gently set her on the couch.

"And you called *me* an idiot last month," he muttered, grabbing the blanket and tossing it over her. "You're too stubborn for your own good, Segee."

"Anna. My name is Anna."

"And I prefer Ethan. I'll try to remember if you do."

He left the living room, returned with another cup of tea, and handed it to her. Anna wrinkled her nose. She didn't even have to take a sip to know it was laced with sugar again. "I drink my tea black," she said, holding out the cup.

He simply sat down in his chair. "I guessed as much when I had to hunt for the sugar. But you need the boost right now. Your body's had a shock."

Since he'd doubtless pour the foul concoction down her throat, Anna sipped the tea while watching the flames dance over the logs in the fireplace.

"That was close tonight," he said into the silence. "The accident was bad enough, but then you scared the hell out of me by passing out." He paused, staring at her, and then said, "Tell me about your ghost. Tom told me you have one haunting your mill."

She snorted. "I'll just bet he did. Tom Bishop has more imagination than discretion. Just finish your tea and head to your cabin. I'll loan you my shotgun if you're afraid."

He set his cup on the hearth and leaned his elbows on his knees, his gaze piercing. "I'm sleeping here tonight, Anna. You may have injuries you don't know about."

"Who died and left you king?"

That infuriating, devastating smile returned, and Anna felt her stomach flip. Ethan leaned back in his chair and laced his fingers together over his belly. "I seem to have stumbled onto the title all by myself."

"I don't need a babysitter."

"There's safety in numbers, you know," he said. "And if your ghost shows up, I can help you call the ghost-busters."

"It's probably just the historians who want to buy Fox Run," she told him. "They're a bit obsessed with this place. They're the ones snooping through the old buildings."

"But why at night? Why not during the day, when you're at work?"

She frowned. She hadn't really thought of that.

"Just how badly do the resort people want your land?"

"Bad enough that several three-piece suits came up from Boston to have a go at changing my mind."

"Maybe they're trying to scare you into selling."

"I've thought of that."

"How about an old boyfriend?" he asked, his eyes taking on a definite sparkle. "Got a disgruntled old beau back in Quebec who wants to see you return home?"

She choked on her tea. "No. Just four brothers, one father, and several uncles even more obnoxious than you."

Ethan suddenly stood up and stretched his arms over his head with a loud yawn. Anna tried to close her eyes, she really did, but they simply refused to work. God, he was beautiful. His shirt lifted, exposing a very flat, very male stomach, and his muscles rippled over his rib cage, stretching his shirt. Anna's belly knotted again.

"Are you hungry?" he asked.

Come to think of it, she was hungry. Maybe *that* was causing her stomachache. "No. I couldn't eat a thing. But I left some staples in your cabin; you can fix yourself something when you get there."

He headed for the kitchen and Anna was left staring at the fire again. She'd had this problem all of her life: men ignoring her wishes, brushing off her ideas and suggestions like cobwebs, always "knowing" what was good for her. Anna sighed and took another sip of the terrible tea. Too bad. It would be nice to meet a man who wasn't so full of himself. She knew they were out there; she just hadn't been able to find any in her neck of the woods.

And maybe that was the problem—the woods. Logging was physical, dangerous, demanding work. It took a keen intelligence to succeed in this industry, as well as the ability to make difficult decisions and live with them. And since bad decisions could result in failure or even death, the men who worked the woods were a cocky, confident bunch. They had to be, in order to survive.

And that little trait spilled over to the rest of their lives. Even in this day and age, women were still the partner who stayed at home, kept the fires burning, and raised the babies. It was okay for wives to have jobs to supplement the family income, but those jobs were always secondary. Women could waitress and keep books and even occasionally drive the trucks that brought the logs to the mills; they could not, however, be in positions of power.

Which was why her job at Loon Cove Lumber was

so precarious. Which was also why she was going to have a tough time with her new boss. The man in her kitchen would be watching every move, just waiting for her to give him a reason to fire her.

Oh, yes. Her new tenant was just as autocratic, just as infuriatingly male minded as the rest of them. He was staying the night to oversee her recovery, he'd just appointed himself watchdog of her ghost per Tom Bishop's suggestion, and he was going to butt in where he wasn't wanted—all because he "knew" what she needed for her own good.

"Hey! Get out of here, you furry weasel!" came Ethan's shout from the kitchen.

Anna smiled. Her flying squirrel wanted supper. They were nocturnal creatures and Casper usually came looking for his share of treats after the lights went out, but the storm must have made him impatient, and he was trying to filch whatever meal Ethan was making.

"Segee! There's more wildlife in your home than in a nature preserve. It's a wonder you don't have rabies." He walked into the living room, a tray in his hands and a scowl on his face.

"You don't have little critters on your side of the lake?" she asked, taking a sandwich from the tray he held to her.

"In the woods, not our house."

She separated a piece of her sandwich and shared it with Bear, then took a giant bite for herself. "Casper probably smelled the peanut butter," she said, her mouth full of sandwich. She washed it down with the terrible tea and took another bite.

"Casper would be the little varmint who hasn't grown into his skin yet?"

"He's a flying squirrel," she explained around another mouthful, licking her fingers as she eyed the tray sitting on the table beside him. "You going to share that soup?"

He stopped with his sandwich halfway to his mouth. "You said you weren't hungry."

"I lied."

He shook his head. "That's a bad habit to get into, Segee."

"Whatever works, *Knight*."

He nodded at her reminder and handed her a bowl of soup. "Did you know Samuel Fox very well?" he asked, tossing another log on the fire before making himself comfortable again. "You said your truck went off the road in the same place his did."

Anna blew on her bowl of soup and decided not to answer his question. "Yes, it was the exact same spot, according to what I was told. They didn't find him for two days. They said there was barely any snow then, so the crash must have been even more violent than mine. I hope he didn't suffer."

"He probably died instantly. He was eighty, wasn't he?"

"Eighty-three . . . I was told."

He nodded. "Then he would have been too frail to survive the wreck. Did you buy Fox Run from his daughter? Madeline's her name, I think." He suddenly chuckled. "There's no telling what her last name is by now."

"What do you mean by that?"

Ethan's grin widened. "Madeline Fox was on her sixth or seventh husband, last I heard." He looked past Anna's shoulder, his thoughts obviously turned inward. "She had a daughter named Abby. Abby Fox would be about seven or eight years older than you." He leaned forward, resting his elbows on his knees. "Did you meet her when you signed the papers to purchase Fox Run? She wasn't at Samuel's funeral," He looked off, his eyes distant again. "I was hoping to see her."

How the hell old did he think *she* was? Anna decided the conversation was straying into dangerous territory. "Everything was done through a lawyer in Quebec. I don't understand it," she quickly added, wanting to change the subject. "Since I've been here, I've been watching that spot where Samuel went off the road, but I've never seen ice there until tonight. If it's a spring, it's not always running."

He shrugged as he chewed, then swallowed his food. "Springs can be fickle."

"Why did your family buy Loon Cove Lumber? My crew told me you Knights own several hundred thousand acres of timberland. Why get into sawing?"

"My dad thought we should diversify." He ate another bite, then picked up his soup. "We could see the outlets for our timber drying up, so rather than send our logs to Canada to be milled, we decided to buy our own mill."

"You'll still have to compete with Canadian lumber."

"With your family?" he asked with a grin.

She didn't smile back. "Yes."

"You could give us an edge with inside information."

"I'm mad at my family, not vindictive."

He nodded concession. "I find it hard to believe they'd let you move here all by yourself."

"They couldn't exactly lock me in my room."

"I would have, if you were my sister. Hell, you must have just barely graduated from high school."

Anna choked on her soup.

"Are you even through school?"

Anna set down her bowl on the hearth, fighting the blush creeping into her cheeks. "I'm old enough to know what I'm doing, Mr. Knight, and I have worked in mill and logging yards since I was fifteen. There isn't a piece of machinery I can't run or a problem I can't solve when it comes to sawing. For the last five years I've worked in one of my family's mills in Quebec and earned the respect of every man there the hard way—by being reliable in a crisis."

"Then what are you doing here?"

"Marching to the beat of my own drum," she said. "My father's so set in his ways, there's no future for me at Segee Logging and Lumber. My brothers will inherit the business."

Ethan snorted and leaned back in his chair. "I'm sure you won't be left sitting on a sidewalk with a tin cup in your hand."

"Oh, I'll be taken care of for the rest of my life. My family will buy me vehicles, a house, even a husband if I decide I want one. But they won't let me make decisions, run my own mill, or help move our operation into the twenty-first century."

His eyes widened. "You don't expect to put *this* place back into operation, do you?"

"Why not?"

"It's a rotting pile of buildings."

"With enough land to give me plenty of leverage."

His eyebrows drew together. "Leverage for what?"

"There's nearly a mile of shore frontage on Frost Lake. I could build a campground or sporting camps, or use it as collateral to buy more timberland."

"That's ridiculous."

"And then there's my family's leverage," she continued, ignoring his remark. "They love me, they just don't know what to do with me. I could use Fox Run to buy myself a place in Segee Logging and Lumber."

He shook his head. "You can't buy family acceptance, Anna. It doesn't work that way."

"Says the man whose own family banished him to Loon Cove Lumber."

He stood up with a scowl. "I volunteered," he muttered, gathering up the dishes. "Grady's too old, Paul's too busy chasing women, and Alex couldn't very well uproot his family."

Anna handed him her bowl. "But you don't want to be a millwright, do you?"

"I'd rather be working in the woods. I have no desire to shuffle papers and fight loggers over the price of timber."

"There's a lot more to it than that."

He stopped in the kitchen doorway and looked back. "Yeah. There's dealing with a female foreman who dresses like Paul Bunyan and looks like she should be worrying about what to wear to her senior prom."

Well, he'd won their little battle this evening and was comfortably snuggled in Anna's frilly bed. Too bad she wasn't in it with him. But twenty, or even twenty-two, was a world away from thirty years old, which made the lady off limits in his book—even if she did have more self-confidence than was healthy for a woman. Actually, Ethan admired Anna's determination to make her own way in the world instead of letting her family make it for her. She had plenty of grit all right, nicely packaged in an utterly feminine body.

Ethan stared up at the ceiling of the old house. He would likely have a riot on his hands at work if he let Anna go. Besides, he was sort of curious as to how she did it; how she could get thirty grown men to respect her enough to let her boss them around. She claimed she knew her job, but Ethan would bet there was more to it than that. It was a rare woman who understood the male mind enough to tame it, work with it, and get it to listen to reason.

It was probably her upbringing. Her entire life must have been a study of male thinking, how to manipulate and ultimately emulate men. Anna Segee intrigued him; she challenged his mind, stirred his blood, and made him feel alive. And he couldn't remember the last time a woman had made his heart race the way his had been racing all day.

It had been way too long since he'd been attracted to a woman, since he'd even gotten close enough to flirt. Ethan knew the love his brother Alex and sister-in-law, Sarah, shared was rare. That Alex had returned from the dead to find himself married to a beautiful, guileless woman was a fluke. The odds that another such woman would suddenly show up in this neck of the woods had to be one in a billion.

He would love to get Anna Segee in his bed and capture some of that passion she kept hidden under all those layers of men's clothes. Seeing her sexy-as-hell underwear had been quite an insight—and more than Anna had been comfortable with, judging by the snit she'd thrown when she had realized she'd lost the battle over their sleeping arrangements.

When he'd started up the stairs with suitcase in hand, she'd thrown a book at him with amazing accuracy. Then she had tried to get that poor pathetic dog to take a bite out of his hide. Bear had whined and tried to follow, but he couldn't even make it up the first step. So Ethan had left Anna fuming downstairs with her woodland creatures and wheezing dog, his "good night" answered by a very unladylike curse.

He couldn't wait for the fun to *really* begin.

Anna lay on the couch, her hand resting on Bear's head on the floor beside her, and looked up at the curtain rod full of sleeping chickadees. The low fire in the hearth cast dancing shadows over the entire room and made her feel as if the old house was laughing at her.

She wasn't even queen of her own castle. Ethan Knight was sleeping in her bed upstairs, surrounded by all her frilly, feminine things. He probably wasn't even able to sleep, he was laughing so hard.

She'd let him get too close tonight. She never should have talked about her family problems, and she sure as hell shouldn't have passed out and let him undress her. Now he would be seeing her as a woman, not his foreman, and it would take a miracle to gain back the ground her underwear had lost her.

She needed a plan. Something simple, something that wouldn't be obvious to the arrogant jackass. Anna racked her brain for nearly an hour, but nothing came to mind other than pretending everything was business as usual.

Anna guessed she'd be laid up for at least two days, and not going to work tomorrow was a definite risk. The crew was crackerjack; they could practically manage themselves. Would Ethan think he didn't need her, since he was more than capable of running a crew himself?

Keith knew the mill as well as she did. Would the two men form a team? Would she still have her job in three days? Anna reached behind her on the table, picked up her cell phone, and dialed Keith's number.

"Keith, this is Anna. I'm calling to tell you that I won't be in for a few days. Can you handle things at the mill?"

"Sure, boss lady. What's wrong? Did you get into an argument with our new owner already?"

"No. I had an accident with my truck coming home, so I'm laid up for a few days."

"Are you all right?"

"Yeah, just shaken up a bit. Nothing's broken."

"What happened?"

"I skidded off the road and crashed my truck."

There was a long silence. "Jesus, Anna. You sure you're okay?"

"I'm fine, Keith. Ethan Knight was right behind me, and he pulled me out."

"Thank God."

"Ah, about Mr. Knight. I won't be there to orient him."

A chuckle came over the line. "And you're worried he'll decide he doesn't need you if he survives this week without you, is that it?"

Anna frowned at the fire. "Something like that."

"Don't worry, boss. I'll take care of it. Ethan will be praying for your return by the end of the week."

"No foolishness. I don't want you getting in trouble," she warned.

"Ah, hell, Anna. What would work be without a little fun now and then? I'll just misplace a few lumber orders and have Jeremy lose the keys to the loader. Things like that."

The fact that Keith was willing to help her warmed Anna's heart. She smiled into the phone. "Thanks, friend. I owe you one."

"Remember that if I ever step in front of your loader."

"I will."

"Well, good night then," he said. "And don't worry. You just take it easy and get better."

"Oh, one more thing, Keith. Can you put out the word that I'm looking for another truck? Something within my budget."

"Totaled it, huh?"

"Down to the floorboards."

"Hell, if not for Ethan, you could have been killed. You're lucky you've got a new tenant."

Anna looked in the direction of the stairs. "That remains to be seen. Good night, Keith."

She hung up the phone and snuggled herself into the blankets with a sigh. There. That little problem was taken care of. She'd have to give Keith a couple of personal days off as thanks.

Satisfied with her efforts, knowing she might have

lost tonight's battle but not the war, Anna drifted off to sleep—and dreamed of a knight in shining armor finding her shivering in Frost Lake as three boys taunted her, the ensuing fight so violent that she'd been able to slip away without being seen.

Chapter Six

It took Anna two days to get off the couch and get Ethan Knight out of her bed. The man was adamant—he wasn't leaving until he got running water, and he wasn't giving up her comfortable bed because the couch was shorter than he was.

He had come home from work the last two nights, eaten supper with her, then gone out to battle the frozen water lines leading to his cabin. But nothing he tried worked. Around nine last night, he'd finally rigged a large tank in the loft of his cabin, pumped it full of water using a long hose from her house, and let gravity feed the water into his sink and bathroom. If he conserved, he'd only have to fill the tank every few days.

That was fine with Anna; anything to get him

out of her house. The man complained about the weather, about the primitive living conditions, and about her woodland friends. He did not, however, complain about work at Loon Cove.

And it was precisely that work, Anna guessed, that was making him grumpy. She knew from personal experience that loggers were used to plenty of space and didn't like operating equipment within the confines of a busy mill yard.

Keith might be overdoing it in the problem department. Ethan had mentioned over supper on the second night that their number one saw was down. He'd paused as if waiting for her to comment, but Anna had merely shrugged her shoulders and continued eating. She wasn't about to ruin Keith's efforts by revealing that their number one saw was fickle sometimes and probably only needed a good rap with a tire iron in just the right place.

Now it was Thursday, day three of her recuperation. Ethan had moved his suitcase to his cabin, and Anna was finally, blessedly, alone. She was getting around without groaning anymore, and enjoying her minivacation by ice fishing. It wasn't difficult. She had a power auger to drill the holes, and she and Bear spent most of their time soaking up the healing rays of the weak winter sun. Bear had a thick blanket to nap on, and Anna sat in a lawn chair. Her box kite was tied to a stick she'd wedged into an ice hole.

The lake was active. Snowmobilers zoomed past

out on the cove, some occasionally coming close enough to wave to her. Several more fishermen were set up a quarter mile away, nestled against one of the islands dotting this part of the lake. Anna had her cell phone sitting on her lap, and was studying the truck section of a statewide classified ad magazine.

She hated shopping for a truck, especially a used one. Hers had been ten years old, but it had been reliable. Buying a used one was a gamble that could quickly turn into a disaster. Then there was the problem of finding a way to go see it, register it, not to mention paying the sales and excise taxes. It wasn't something she was looking forward to, considering the size of her bank account.

A snowmobile approached from the lake and pulled up beside hers, parked just a few yards away. A man got off and removed his helmet, and Anna smiled when she saw who it was.

"Hi, Daniel," she said, closing her magazine. "Out looking for bad guys?"

The game warden shot her a boyish grin. "Hello, Anna. And no, I'm just pretending to work today." His eyes suddenly widened. "What happened to you?" he asked, only to turn red in the face. "I'm sorry. It's just that . . . well, did you have an accident?"

"I totaled my truck four days ago." She held up the magazine. "And now I'm looking for another one."

He sat down on the cooler beside her lawn chair. "Too bad." He nodded in her direction. "That's quite a bump on your forehead. You okay?"

"Yeah. I'm just sore."

Bear lumbered over and shoved his nose under Daniel's hand. Daniel dutifully began to scratch Bear's chin. "Hello, old boy. You helping Anna catch fish?"

For answer, Bear closed his eyes and basked in the massage Daniel was giving his ears.

"We got three," Anna said. "All legal. Want to see them?"

"Salmon or trout?" he asked, looking around the snow for her catch.

"Two salmon, one lake trout," she told him, pointing at the cooler he was sitting on.

He stood up and opened it and looked at her catch. "Mmmm. They should be good eating."

"You're welcome to stay for supper. I've got canned fiddleheads to go with them."

His expression was wistful. "Sounds tempting."

"I make a mean wild rice pilaf," she added.

He shook his head, though he licked his lips.

"Oh, come on," she urged. "I know you don't get to fish often, since you're too busy protecting them. When was the last time you had salmon and fiddleheads?"

"Too long."

"Then it's settled. You help me pull in my traps, and I'll cook you supper."

He hesitated only a moment before he stood up. "I shouldn't be doing this. I don't even have a fishing license," he said, going over to the nearest trap and pulling it up.

"Doesn't the state give you a free one?"

He grinned at her. "Nope. They make us buy one, like everyone else. I just haven't gotten around to it yet this year."

Anna pushed herself out of her lawn chair and shook her head. "Daniel Reed, you need to get a life."

He pointed at the kite flying above them. "Like you? You're fishing out here all alone, flying a kite."

Anna lifted her chin. "I'm recovering from my accident."

He was about to respond but suddenly straightened as he looked toward shore. "You've got company."

Anna followed his line of sight, groaned, and headed for another one of her traps. "It's nobody. Just my new tenant."

"Hey, that's Ethan Knight."

She stopped and looked at Daniel. "You know him?"

"Of course. I know his whole family." He looked from Ethan to her. "I heard the Knights bought Loon Cove Lumber. You say he's your new tenant?"

"He rents one of my cabins." Anna reached down and pulled up her trap, tossed the bait on the ice for the birds, then began winding in the line.

"You got a license to fish these waters, Reed?" Ethan asked as he walked over.

"Hello, Ethan." Daniel glanced at the sun, then back at Ethan. "You sneak out of work early, or did you get fired again?"

Anna looked up just in time to see Ethan's glare,

which he turned on her before looking back at their mutual friend. "I sent everyone home. Half that blasted mill is either broken or lost," he said with a growl in his voice.

Daniel looked surprised. "But I thought Bishop ran a tight operation."

"He did," Ethan said, walking past Daniel, not stopping until he was standing over Anna's fishing hole. "But it seems to have gone down the tubes suddenly. Any idea why, Segee?"

She looked up at his scowling face and gave him a bright smile. "Not a clue, Knight," she said, moving to step past him.

He grabbed her jacket sleeve and slowly turned her back to face him. Yup, he definitely was angry.

"You're going to work tomorrow, lady, and you're going to get my mill running smoothly again. Understand?"

She looked down at his hand on her sleeve and then back at him. "What makes you think I can fix it?"

"You can fix it because *you're* the problem."

"Me? I haven't been near Loon Cove Lumber for three days."

"Which is why all the men are working so hard to make sure you come back. They're sabotaging my mill, and you're going to make them stop."

"I'm still too sore to work."

"I'll fire every damn last one of them," he threatened. "And you can explain to their families why Easter dinner will be canned beans this year."

"You can't legally do that. Besides, you'd be bankrupt within the month. It takes years to assemble a crew that good."

"Hey, are you two going to argue all day? I'm hungry," Daniel said, picking up another trap.

Ethan's glare moved to his friend. "What's your belly got to do with it? If you're hungry, then go home."

Anna would swear Daniel Reed suddenly stood a little taller and that his chest puffed out a few inches. "Anna invited me to dinner. She's cooking salmon and fiddleheads."

"Is she, now?" Ethan said softly.

Anna looked him right in the eye. "I thought it would be nice to have a meal with pleasant conversation for once. Growls, grunts, and complaints are not good for my digestion."

"Just how many fish did you catch, while *recuperating?*"

"Enough for two," she answered. "Now that your cabin is fit to live in, you're on your own. Meals were not included in your lease."

Just then a gust of wind sent Anna's kite spiraling into a violent downward arc. All three of them ducked to avoid being struck, and Bear started barking. Ethan reached up and grabbed the string, and Anna watched, amazed, as he skillfully subdued the huge box kite. He slowly worked his way down the string until he came to the stick she'd wedged in the ice, kicked it free, and began unwinding more string.

"You didn't have enough string let out," he told her, his eyes trained on the suddenly obedient kite. "A beauty like this needs to fly high, to catch the steadier winds."

He was acting like a kid with a new toy. He played with the kite, sending it into a graceful dance, making it dip and soar and then arch skyward before slowly working it back to earth.

Anna heard Daniel chuckle and realized her mouth was hanging open. She closed it with a snap and headed for her snowmobile, put the cooler on the tow sled, packed up her chair and Bear's bed, motioned for Bear to come over, then helped the dog climb up in front of her.

"When you guys are done playing, you can finish pulling my traps. I'm going home to start supper," she told them, not at all sure they even heard her.

Daniel was still chuckling and Ethan was actually talking to her kite now, his voice soft and coaxing. Anna's belly tightened again. She started up her snowmobile and gave it some gas, then headed for shore.

Ethan turned at the sound of a snowmobile leaving and saw Daniel Reed packing up her fishing traps.

Reed had gotten himself invited to Anna's table tonight, for what he surely intended to be the first of many such dinners. Ethan dismantled the kite and put it in the fishing pack.

"I'll tell Anna you got a call and can't make dinner tonight," he said, once Daniel had straightened with the pack basket. Ethan took it from him and hefted it over his shoulder. "I'll give her your regrets."

Daniel's eyes narrowed to slits. "Oh, no you don't. You're not running me off. I found her first."

Ethan grinned. "Not exactly. I'm already living with her, and possession is nine-tenths of the law."

Daniel took a step closer. "Dammit, you Knights can't claim every pretty woman around here. I'm not backing off, Ethan. Anna Segee is fair game."

Ethan settled his weight back on his hips and contemplated his friend. "You don't have time to date. You work around the clock and you live a good thirty miles from here. Besides, you're old enough to be her father."

"I'm only three years older than you are."

Ethan started walking toward Daniel's snowmobile. "So if *I'm* too old for her, that makes you way out of the ballpark," he said, holding out Daniel's helmet to him.

"What in hell are you talking about? Anna's twenty-nine."

Ethan stilled. "She's what?" He shook his head. "She can't be a day over twenty-two, Reed. She looks like she just got out of school last year."

"She's twenty-nine," he told Ethan. "Her birth date's on her fishing license. That was the first thing I checked when I came across her fishing out here in January." Daniel thumped his chest. "Which means *I* saw her first."

Anna was twenty-*nine*? That meant she was around the same age as Samuel Fox's granddaughter, Abigail. He looked back at Daniel. "Don't make me get nasty," Ethan warned. "Be the gentleman and bow out. We've been friends too long not to be civilized about this."

Daniel snorted. "There isn't a civilized bone in your body when it comes to women, and there's not a damn thing you can do or say that will make me back off."

Ethan lifted a brow. "I could always ask your boss why the state had to repair both your and my sister-in-law's trucks, when the accident was obviously Sarah's fault."

Daniel's scowled. "You wouldn't do that. You'd be causing trouble for Sarah."

"But more for you, for taking the blame for the accident."

"A *gentleman* would let Anna decide whom she wants to have dinner with," Daniel said.

"Yes. A gentleman probably would."

"Dammit! It's salmon and fiddleheads! Do you know how often I get asked to a home-cooked dinner by a beautiful woman?"

Ethan repositioned Anna's pack on his shoulder. "This beautiful woman is going to be more trouble than you have time to deal with, my friend. I'll give her your regrets, and you can have the next pretty woman that comes along."

Daniel climbed onto his snowmobile and drove his

helmet down on his head. "The way my luck is running, your brother Paul will beat me to her." He shot Ethan one last disgruntled look before speeding out of the cove in a cloud of snow. Ethan watched until the sled disappeared behind an island, then started walking to shore, whistling the whole way.

Anna heard the stamping of heavy boots on the porch, and shoved the salmon under the broiler, then went to the living room to greet her guest. The door opened and Ethan walked in carrying her basket of fishing equipment, closing the door behind him.

Anna opened it back up. She looked around the porch, then out at the lake, but didn't see Daniel. She went back inside, where Ethan's jacket was now hanging on the peg by the door.

"Where'd you find the fiddleheads?" he asked as he peered down into the steaming pot on the stove. He opened the oven door and looked inside. "You only cooked one of the fish," he said, turning to face her.

"Where's Daniel?"

"He got called away. Trouble down the lake or something."

"What kind of trouble?"

Ethan shrugged. "I don't know. But he sends his regrets." He turned back to the stove and looked under the cover of another pot. "Are those black specks wild rice?" He looked over at her and frowned. "If you know how to cook, how come I got stuck doing it all week?"

Anna walked up to the stove, took the cover out of his hand, and slammed it back on the pot. "Because I was recuperating. And what *you're* having for supper depends on what you bought for groceries." She went to the table and removed one place setting.

"Hey, you've got enough for two. I'll eat Daniel's share."

She turned to face him. "I am not feeding you anymore, Mr. Knight. You're eating me out of house and home."

"You were going to feed Reed."

"That's different."

"How?"

Anna took a calming breath. "Daniel Reed is one of the nice guys, and I've been wanting to invite him to dinner for the last couple of months."

"What do you mean, 'one of the nice guys'?" he asked, his eyes narrowing.

"Nice," she repeated. "Safe, steady as a rock—not full of himself."

"Daniel Reed is a confirmed bachelor."

"Only because he hasn't met the right woman yet."

"And you think you're the right woman?"

Anna lifted her chin. "I didn't say that. All I said was that I think he's a nice guy."

He snorted. "Well, good luck trying to date him. Reed doesn't even have the time to fix up that shanty he calls home, much less go on dates." Ethan leaned back against the counter and crossed his arms over his chest. "So that's what you're looking for? A safe, shy, steady-as-a-rock man?"

Anna crossed her arms under her breasts. "Yes. I only date nice, sensitive men."

Ethan snorted again. "Don't let Reed's shy facade fool you. Beneath his lazy smile beats the heart of a predator. Why do you think he's a game warden? He loves a good hunt better than most."

"You chased him off, didn't you?"

Ethan was suddenly all innocence. "He got called away."

"Yeah, right."

"Tell me more about your 'dream guy.' What other qualifications must this paragon of manhood possess?"

"Well, for one thing," she said, getting out a dinner plate again when she realized she wasn't going to get rid of Ethan short of shooting him, "he won't be a woodsman."

"What's wrong with loggers?"

"In a word? Neanderthals." She grabbed a fork and knife from a drawer. "I haven't met one yet who's man enough to accept a woman as his equal. Most loggers, when they're not busy beating their chests, are giving me orders as if I were a witless child."

"Probably because you look—and *act*—like a child," he muttered, straightening to his full height.

Anna turned and opened the oven and pulled out the salmon, hiding her smile. Lord, she hadn't had this much fun in ages. It was so easy to push Ethan's buttons. He was getting so riled up, she could see the cords in his neck bunching.

"I'm going to date a man whose job tells me he's open to my opinions, ideas, and dreams."

He followed her to the table. "Your opinions?" he echoed. "There is no such man."

She finally let her smile escape. "Maybe there's a doctor or veterinarian I can cook for." She headed back to the stove, drained the fiddleheads, and put them in a bowl. "A veterinarian would have to be a sensitive man to work with animals." She looked over at the chickadees on the shelf, happily munching their seed. "And he wouldn't mind my pets." She turned back to Ethan and widened her grin. "Isn't there an unattached veterinarian in Greenville? Dr. Knox?"

The cords in Ethan's neck bunched again, and a small twitch appeared in his right cheek. "Knox wouldn't know what to do with a woman if one shoved her chest in his face," he growled, following her back to the counter.

Anna hid her smile again. "I'll have to see if that's true. It's about time Bear went in for a checkup."

She was suddenly spun around by hands of steel, and brought face to face with eyes of snapping ice. "You're not asking Knox out. Or any other man, for that matter."

She'd done it now. She'd uncovered the beast, and he was looking at her as if he intended to have her for lunch.

The hands on her shoulders moved to her back, wrapping her in a strong, unbreakable band of muscle. Ethan kissed her full on the mouth, taking possession as if it were his God-given right.

Anna's belly started to cartwheel. Her heart stopped beating and started again with such force, it took her breath away.

He was relentless in his assault, determined to soothe the ego she'd soundly battered. She'd asked for this, although for the life of her, she didn't know why.

She was *not*, however, going to kiss him back.

Chapter Seven

Anna crawled out of bed with a curse and a groan. She didn't want to go to work, and not because of her physical condition; she simply didn't want to deal with Ethan today.

And that made her mad. She usually loved facing whatever surprises the mill might throw at her, having the satisfaction of knowing she could meet every demand and probably win. So why couldn't she consider her new boss just another challenge? It shouldn't matter that when the light touched his eyes just right they reminded her of liquid steel, or that the man had taken kissing lessons from Cupid himself.

He was not going to stay in his office where he belonged; he'd be out in her yard, bugging her and her crew, sticking his nose in everything. Especially after last night's kiss, which had been one of those *I'm losing this battle so I'll just kiss her* kisses that men gave women when they didn't know what else to do. Now Ethan probably would be sticking his nose in her private life as well, because he *knew* he had curled her toes. She never should have kissed him back. For that matter, she never should have pushed him that far to begin with.

What *had* she been thinking?

He'd broken off the kiss just as soon as he'd felt her respond, and stared down at her with dark, unreadable eyes. And then he had suddenly turned on his heel and walked out of the house, not looking back, not saying a word.

Anna started dressing in several layers of warm clothes. If the temperature in the house this morning was any indication of the temperature outside, she needed plenty of wool. She could actually see her breath as she put on her long johns, two pairs of socks, a turtleneck, wool pants and a sweatshirt. She hurried downstairs and stirred the fire in the stove just as Bear headed for the door with a whine. Anna opened it to let him out, and nearly got knocked on the nose by Ethan's fist.

"So, did you catch him?" she asked instead of noticing how particularly handsome he looked this morning.

"Catch who?"

"The ghost. There was enough noise coming from the saw shed at two this morning to wake the dead."

When he merely lifted a brow, Anna rolled her eyes, spun on her heel, and headed to the kitchen. "Great. Tom found me a watchdog who's as deaf as the one I already have."

Ethan followed her into the kitchen, carrying the old shotgun he'd picked up in the living room. "If you heard the ghost, why didn't you send a shot his way? I would have heard that."

Anna took the gun away from him and leaned it against the wall in the corner, then filled the teakettle with water to put on the stove. "I don't have shells for the gun," she muttered. "I need to pick some up."

"Then you should have pounded on my cabin door, and we could have gone after your ghost together."

She wasn't about to admit that a herd of horses couldn't have dragged her outside. "You're getting cheap rent to go after my ghost."

There was a moment's silence, then Ethan said, sounding a bit surprised, "You're afraid of the dark."

"I am not."

"That's why you haven't bought shotgun shells. That's your excuse for not confronting whoever's snooping around your mill."

"If I bought shells, then I'd have to shoot them," she growled. "And then I'd have to hire a lawyer to help me explain to a judge that I was defending myself, and I can't afford a lawyer on the salary you pay me."

"Speaking of which, we're going to be late for work."

"The only reason I'm going in this morning is to save my crew's jobs," she said over her shoulder as she opened one of the cupboards.

"And your own," he added, shutting off the burner. He picked up the kettle and poured the boiling water into the two traveling mugs she placed on the counter. "Hey, what are you adding to my tea?" he asked when she put a dropper full of liquid in each of the mugs.

"It's milk thistle. It's good for your liver."

He scowled down at his tea. "There's nothing wrong with my liver."

She opened another bottle, shook out two pills, and handed one to Ethan. "And this is a multivitamin. You should take one every day," she said, opening another bottle and shaking out two more pills. "And this is vitamin E," she explained, handing him one.

He looked at the two pills in his hand. "I haven't taken vitamins since I was ten."

Anna popped her own pills in her mouth. "My grand-père and grand-mère on my father's side had the physiques of sixty-year-olds," she said. "If they hadn't died in an auto accident at ninety-four and ninety-three, they probably would have lived to be a hundred. They took herbs and vitamins every day."

"You really believe this stuff works?" he asked, popping the pills in his mouth. "Maybe your grandparents simply had good genes."

"Maybe," she acknowledged, taking her tea into the bathroom. She closed the door, set her cup on the shelf, and stared at the woman in the mirror. Damn, she needed to get it together if she hoped to survive working with Ethan.

She splashed water on her face. When he wasn't haunting her during the day, Ethan was haunting her dreams. Last night she'd dreamt they'd had a candlelit dinner of salmon and fiddleheads in front of a roaring fire. She had been dressed in a prom gown, and he had worn a tux.

He'd been damn handsome in that tux.

Anna blinked at herself in the mirror. It had been a guilt dream. She'd kissed Ethan as if he were the only man on earth, and then sat down—alone—to a meal of salmon and fiddleheads that had tasted like sawdust. Then Ethan had walked into her house this morning, all confident and cocky, and already the butterflies were back.

It was going to be a long day.

"If Loon Cove Lumber is such a dangerous place, why is it okay for Bear to come to work with us?" Ethan asked, frowning at the huge dog sitting on the seat between him and Anna, drooling all over the dash of his truck.

"Bear's used to being around machinery," she said, turning to give him a satisfied smile.

Well, she should be feeling smug with her eighty-pound chaperone between them. "What's he going to do all day?" he asked, pushing Bear's head away, then wiping his drool-covered sleeve on the dog.

"He'll probably sleep in the office with you."

"Then he's going to be lonely. I'm not staying in the office," Ethan said

"Somebody's got to line up the shipments of logs," she said. "Here. Stop here," she suddenly said, reaching for her door handle.

Ethan stopped the truck just as she opened the door. "Where are you going?"

She got out, fished around in her pocket, and produced a key. "I'm locking the gate," she told him, leaving the door open while she walked to the rear of the truck.

Ethan shoved Bear's head out of the way and watched in his mirror. Specifically, he watched Anna's sexy little butt sashay down the road to the gate, and decided the woman was put together quite nicely.

Her lips were nothing to complain about, either.

Ethan chuckled to himself. She'd goaded him into kissing her last night, and he hadn't let up until she'd responded. But then he'd felt all the blood in his body rush to his groin, and had run from the house as if burned. Not because he hadn't wanted her, but because he had; because she'd felt too good in his arms, smelling of wool and sunshine and tasting like butter.

It was her damn underwear! Ethan had known he was in trouble the moment he'd spotted that lace the day he'd undressed her, and his libido had been in a downward spiral ever since. Sleeping in her frilly bed for three nights, surrounded by all her feminine stuff, had driven him crazy. How in hell was he supposed to work with her when he knew exactly what was under all those layers of clothes?

She hadn't said a word when he'd broken off their kiss; she'd simply stood there in the middle of her kitchen, her lips swollen and wet, and stared at him as if he'd just sailed in from another planet. So he'd left before she could slap his face.

"There. That will keep the honest people out," she said, sliding back in the truck and closing the door.

Ethan pushed Bear's head aside again to shift out of four-wheel drive, and pulled onto the main road. "Tell me about the resort people trying to buy your land."

"There's not much to tell, really. A group of Boston investors has been buying up all the land they can around this area to build a resort."

He looked out his side window, at the mountain they were passing. "And Fox Run Mill is one of the parcels they want?"

"Yes."

"Have they made you an offer?"

"Yup. Two hundred and fifty thousand dollars."

Ethan snorted. "Not much for prime shoreline."

"The historians matched their offer."

"Not bettered it?"

"No. They think I should want to preserve the mill's heritage or some such nonsense," she said. She smiled over Bear's head. "I'm betting old Samuel Fox would turn over in his grave if either group got that mill."

"Samuel couldn't have cared about Fox Run too much if he left it to his daughter. He should have left it to his granddaughter, Abby."

Anna shrugged and remained silent.

"Where is Madeline Fox?" he asked.

"She could be on any one of the seven continents, with husband number twelve by now." She looked over and smiled again. "Madeline's a good person, I hear. She just can't seem to sit still long enough to grow roots."

"She didn't go to Samuel's funeral. My whole family went, and we didn't see either Madeline or Abby."

Anna merely shrugged again.

"Why not ask your father for the tax money you owe?"

She snapped her gaze to his. "Who told you I owe back taxes?" She held up her hand. "Never mind. Tom Bishop, right?"

"Tom's just worried about you."

"Not too worried, if he saddled me with you for a tenant."

"So why not ask Daddy for the money?"

"Because he didn't want me getting Fox Run in

the first place," she said. "He thinks I should just find a good man, get married and have babies, and live happily ever after."

"He's just being a father, Segee. He can't help it if he wants to see you settled."

"Is that how you'd treat a daughter? Would you insist that she not have a life of her own, but do what *you* thought was right for her?"

He looked back at the road and frowned.

"What about your niece? Do you expect her to marry a logger, have babies, and never go farther than Greenville all her life?"

"No."

"What if she wants to be a businesswoman? Or an astronaut? Would you encourage her to follow her dream?"

"I'm not a chauvinist. Delaney can be anything she wants."

She snorted. "Yeah, right. Tell me that when she's nineteen and wants to move to Boston or New York."

Ethan gripped the steering wheel until his knuckles whitened. "It's not the same," he told her. "You're not wanting to go out and explore the world; you're trying to make this world fit into *your* mold. And you're trying to fend off some very determined men who have a lot of money at stake."

"I'm not in any real danger."

"No? You think your resort people are going to let one stubborn woman get in the way of their plans? What about your ghost?"

"I don't believe in ghosts."

"Okay, what about your midnight intruder, then?"

She dismissed his question with another shrug, then suddenly straightened in her seat. "Why are all the trucks backed up at the gate?" she asked.

Ethan frowned at the four twenty-two wheelers loaded with logs idling outside the gates of Loon Cove Lumber. "I told them to come back this morning," he said, glaring out the windshield. "Everything around here is jammed tighter than an ice dam. I didn't have anyplace for them to unload."

The smile she gave him was rather snarky. "Looks like I recovered just in the nick of time."

Ethan pulled his truck past the waiting loggers, who were scowling at him for keeping them waiting, and parked in Tom Bishop's old space. Anna was out the door and already stepping into the middle of the gathered truckers before he got the engine shut off. Ethan followed at a more leisurely pace, Bear trailing behind him, and stopped beside his rear bumper, amazed when the expression on each driver's face turned from sullen to thankful. To a man, each glare turned into a grin as Anna Segee agreed with every one of their complaints.

Ethan unlocked and rolled back the large gate. He could see his crew going about their business inside, but not one of them had ventured out to let the loggers in. Anna followed him through the gate, riding on the running board of the lead truck, laughing at something the driver was saying.

Within minutes Loon Cove Lumber was bustling with chaos. Machinery started up, trucks were unloaded, and both the number one and number two saws began sending sawdust out their chutes like confetti. Ethan walked into his office and threw himself in his chair, lay his head on the desk, and closed his eyes with a frustrated groan.

Chapter Eight

$\mathcal{W}$*ork was going well*—likely because her crew was happy to have her back on the job—and Anna was even happier to be working again. When she was at the center of a busy mill yard, all her problems seemed to magically disappear. All except for one; Ethan was still a pain in the neck, alternating between sulking and glaring because everything was running as smoothly as a well-oiled clock.

"Keith, can I borrow your truck to run into Oak Grove?" Anna asked.

"Sure, boss lady. The keys are in it. Take it for as long as you need." Keith stopped inspecting the pile of lumber in front of them, wrote something down on his clipboard, and smiled at her. "You can take it home tonight. I'll bum a ride with Davis."

"Thanks, but I only need it over lunch."

"I was just headed into town myself," came Ethan's voice from behind her. "I'll ride with you."

Anna spun around. "I'm taking a two-hour lunch."

He lifted a brow. "On the clock?"

"No. On my own time."

He lifted his other brow. "Your check's going to be small this week."

Anna patted her leg to call Bear and headed for the gate. "It better not be. I have sick days coming."

Ethan fell into step beside her. "Did you find a truck for sale? I'll tag along to make sure you don't buy a lemon."

"I going to the gun shop."

He spun her around to face him. "You're not really serious about buying a handgun. They're dangerous."

"Only for the person on the wrong end," she shot back, heading for Keith's truck again.

Ethan climbed in the passenger's side and fastened his seat belt. "It doesn't take two hours to buy a gun," he said over Bear's head.

Anna hid her smile by watching for traffic as she pulled out of the parking lot toward Oak Grove. "I'm also taking Bear in for a checkup. I hear Dr. Knox has a gentle way with his four-legged patients, and I can't wait to meet him."

Silence settled inside the cab of the truck. She knew better than to push Ethan's buttons, but it was so sinfully easy. Besides, she owed him for that mind-blowing kiss that had made her toss and turn in bed until dawn.

"Knox is a good three inches shorter than you, he's missing most of his hair, and he always smells of antiseptic," Ethan said, pulling Bear down onto his lap to see her. "And he's at least ten years older than you."

"So he's thirty, then?"

"I know you're twenty-nine. I have your employment records, remember? Knox is a pudgy gnome."

Anna finally smiled directly at Ethan. "What do looks have to do with personality? And besides, I hear gnomes are cuddly."

The look Ethan gave her should have turned Anna to toast, but she merely broadened her smile and pulled into a parking spot in front of the Drooling Moose Café. "I'll meet you back here in two hours," she said, getting out and motioning for Bear to stay put. "I'll bring you back a burger, pup," she said, locking the door and heading to the café.

Ethan fell into step beside her and ushered her into the bustling restaurant ahead of him. Anna walked to the counter and took the only empty stool available, between an elderly gentleman she didn't know and a woman with two toddlers that she did know.

"You've got your hands full, I see," she said with a laugh, snatching a fork away from the two-year-old girl in Jane Trott's lap before she could poke Jane in the eye—who was busy catching the four-year-old boy trying to slide off his stool. "You're still babysitting for your sister, I see. How's her husband doing?"

Jane looked over, smiled apologetically, and plopped the screaming two-year-old in Anna's lap. "Pete's doing real well. Could you watch Megan for me? Travis needs to go potty."

Anna gave Megan a spoon to replace the fork she'd stolen, and the girl immediately shoved it in her mouth and went blessedly silent. "Sure."

"Oh . . . ah, hi, Ethan," Jane said, her face turning crimson as she scrambled around him and headed toward the front of the café with Travis in tow.

"A table just freed up in the corner," Ethan said, plucking Megan out of Anna's arms before she could protest, then turning and striding away with the suddenly laughing little girl who was now trying to shove the spoon in his mouth.

Dammit, why couldn't she stay one step ahead of the man? Just when she thought she'd ditched him, he'd found a way to get right back in her face. Anna grabbed the large diaper bag Jane had left under the counter and ran after him.

"This will be better for the kids," he said as Anna sat down and began moving silverware and coffee mugs out of Megan's reach. "I can't believe Jane dared to venture out in public with these bandits," he continued, capturing Megan's swinging fist.

"She's been watching them since Pete's accident, so her sister can stay in Bangor with him. She's probably going stir-crazy at home and thought it would be fun to take them out to lunch. Have you heard any news about how Pete's doing?" Anna asked, rummaging around in the bag until she found a green crayon, which she handed to Megan. The little girl dropped the spoon, grabbed the crayon, and immediately began scribbling on the paper place mat.

"He's in slightly better shape than his logging truck, which was totaled. He'll need physical therapy, but he should be back hauling logs in two or three months."

"He works for you, doesn't he?"

Ethan guided Megan's hand to draw a stick person. "He contracts to haul for us," he confirmed, looking up. "They're having a benefit dance for Pete next Saturday, to raise money to help pay his bills until he can get back to work. You going?"

"Of course. I always go to benefits."

Ethan suddenly stilled, got the strangest look on his face, and lifted Megan off his lap. "Aw, hell," he muttered.

Anna covered her mouth to stifle her laughter as Ethan stood up and looked down at the wet patches on his thighs. "She peed on me," he growled, scanning the café for Jane. "Stop laughing," he said under his breath, tucking the child under his arm like a football, grabbing up the diaper bag, and striding toward the restrooms.

He returned two minutes later with Travis in his arms. Anna stood up and slipped back into her jacket.

"I've decided I'm not really that hungry. I'll see you back at the truck in about an hour and a half," she said, not waiting around for his response but heading to find Jane.

She ran into her just coming out of the restroom. "Where are you going?" Jane asked a bit desperately. "Where's Travis?"

"With Ethan."

"Oh, please don't leave me alone with Ethan," Jane pleaded. "Go get Travis, then walk me out to my car. Please?"

"You're not afraid of Ethan, are you?" Anna asked in surprise. "Weren't you dating his brother Paul before I met you?"

Jane shifted Megan on her hip and nodded. "That's why it would be awkward to sit with Ethan. Please go get Travis. I'll fix you lunch at home, and we ... maybe we could talk?" She stepped closer. "Please, Anna? I really need to talk to someone, and my family has enough to deal with right now."

There was such desperation in Jane's eyes, Anna couldn't refuse. Jane had been the first friend she'd made in Oak Grove, when the woman had offered to share her table in this very café four months ago. Since then they'd visited often, even traveling the ninety miles to Bangor to shop at the mall and take in a movie.

"Of course I'll have lunch with you," Anna quickly returned, spinning on her heel to go fetch Travis. "Change of plans," she told Ethan, picking up the boy. "I'm helping Jane take the kids home and having lunch with her."

"What about the gun shop and Bear's checkup?"

"They'll have to wait until tomorrow," she said, handing him the keys to Keith's truck. "Buy Bear a burger and take him back to the mill for me, will you? I'll catch a ride from Jane's sister's house."

"How?"

"It's on the main road. I'll hop in with a logger hauling to the mill later this afternoon."

"You are not hitchhiking."

Anna rolled her eyes. "I know all the drivers."

"What about work? You can't just take off whenever you feel like it. We have a mill to run."

"It's running itself now. I'll be back no later than three," she said, turning away before he could say anything else, carrying Travis through the crowded room. "My, aren't you a big boy," she told him, repositioning the toddler on her hip.

"Megan pee-peed on him," Travis said.

"Yes, she did," Anna said. "I owe her big-time for that."

Anna swallowed her suddenly dry bite of sandwich. "But I thought you broke up with Paul Knight months ago?"

"I did," Jane said, looking down at her plate. "He's seeing Cynthia Pringle now."

"And you're how far along?" Anna asked gently.

"Just over four months. I've been driving to

Bangor to see a doctor so no one would find out."

"So Paul doesn't know?"

Jane shook her head.

"Nobody knows?" Anna asked. "Not your parents or sister?"

She shook her head again.

"Jane. You have to tell someone."

"I'm telling you."

Anna leaned back in her chair. "*Paul*. You have to tell Paul Knight that you're having his baby," she said. "You can't keep something like this bottled up inside you. And besides, *everyone* will know soon," she said, waving toward Jane's belly. "And I'm pretty sure Paul can count well enough to realize he's the father." Anna sat forward, sliding her plate out of the way to rest her arms on the table. "He deserves to hear this from you, not from some town busybody, and the sooner the better. You both need to decide what you're going to do."

"But I don't know how to tell him," Jane whispered.

Anna took hold of her friend's cold fingers. "Ignoring the facts won't make them go away, Jane, and you can't continue to deal with this all by yourself. Not telling him is not fair to Paul, to you, or to your baby." She patted Jane's hands, then leaned back in her chair again. "Believe me, I know what I'm talking about. My mother never told my father about me, and I spent my entire childhood wondering who he was. Who *I* was."

Jane looked up in surprise. "You never knew your father?"

Anna smiled softly. "I was eleven when I finally met him. But he made up for lost time, and is a doting, overprotective dad to this day."

"How did your mother keep you a secret from him?"

"They didn't live in the same town. My dad and mom met at a logging show, had a fling, and walked out of each other's lives at the end of the week." She rested her arms on the table again. "But you and Paul will be seeing each other all the time. The Knights are good people, aren't they? Paul will do what's right."

"But what *is* right?"

Anna shrugged. "I don't know. You've made a baby together, and you and Paul are the ones to decide what's best for the three of you. Do you love him?" she asked softly.

Jane blinked at her. "Yes. But I'm scared."

"Of Paul?"

"Yes—no, of his whole family." Jane shifted nervously. "The Knights don't have a very good track record when it comes to women—especially women who get pregnant. Alex Knight's first marriage ended in disaster, and it was common knowledge that Charlotte had gotten pregnant so he'd have to marry her. And Ethan . . ." Jane visibly shivered. "There was a terrible scandal several years back involving Ethan and a woman named Pamela Sant. Rumor has it they had a huge fight, there was a chase down a remote tote road, and Pamela died when her car missed a turn and plunged into Oak Creek. Pam's parents demanded Ethan be brought up on manslaughter charges, claiming that she'd gone off the road because he'd been chasing her. But because he wasn't actually in Pam's car, there wasn't any alcohol involved and no witnesses, he was acquitted." Jane leaned closer. "Pamela was pregnant," she whispered. "And Ethan hasn't been the same since. He's grown hard and unapproachable and is barely civilized to women most of the time. So now do you see why I'm reluctant to tell Paul?"

"No, actually, I don't," Anna said just as softly, trying to follow her friend's reasoning. "What do Alex and Ethan have to do with you and Paul?"

Jane balled her hands into fists on the table. "We were always careful, but we must have slipped up when we went down to Bangor for a couple of days last fall. And now I'm just another woman one of the Knight men knocked up. Paul's going to think I got pregnant on purpose, and everyone else is going to think I'm trying to marry into the richest family around here."

Anna could only stare at her, speechless.

"That's what everyone said about Pamela Sant, that she was just like Alex's first wife, and that was why Ethan was so angry," Jane said. "And that's exactly what Paul will think when I tell him."

"You did *not* get pregnant by yourself."

Jane buried her face in her hands with a sob. "I'm going to end up just like Madeline Fox," she wailed. "Everyone's going to know I'm an easy lay, my kid will be picked on at school, men will come sniffing around, and I'll end up in one loveless marriage after another, just like Madeline did."

"What *are* you talking about?"

Jane looked up, blinking back her tears. "The legendary *Madeline Fox*," she said with a dramatic wave of her hand. "Samuel Fox's daughter. You know, the guy who used to own the mill you bought? His daughter was the town hussy, and every mother— including mine—still uses her as an example of what happens to loose women." Jane started sobbing into her hands again. "My mother is going to kill me."

Good God, her mom's reputation was still the talk of Oak Grove, even though Madeline had left nearly eighteen years ago? Anna stood, skirted the table, and crouched down to wrap her arms around Jane. "You are not going to turn out like Madeline Fox," she said, pulling Jane's hands away from her face. "You're telling Paul you're pregnant, and the two of you will decide what to do—without worrying about family histories and town legends. Understand?" she said, brushing the hair back from Jane's face. "Your *baby* is what's important, not the reputation of a woman who lived here when you were only a baby yourself."

"B-but what about Cynthia?"

"Paul's new girlfriend? To hell with her," Anna

said with a crooked smile. "She's not having his baby, you are. Why did you two break up, anyway?"

Jane looked down. "Things started going bad right after we snuck off to Bangor last fall. By the end of our trip, I . . . " She looked at Anna. "I started talking about our future together. Then a week after we got back, I saw Paul having lunch with Cynthia at the Drooling Moose, and I went ballistic." She closed her eyes and shook her head. "I made a public scene and said some really stupid things. If I were Paul, I'd have run for the hills, too."

"And have you had any contact with him since?"

"Just a few awkward moments when we ran into each other in town."

"And now you have one more awkward moment to look forward to," Anna said as she stood. "When you call him up and invite him out to dinner."

"I can't do that!"

"Someplace private," she continued, "away from Oak Grove. Greenville, maybe. No, that's still too close." She smiled at Jane's shocked expression. "How about here at your sister's house? You can invite him over for a home-cooked dinner. Your mom can watch Megan and Travis for the evening, can't she?"

"He won't come. You have no idea of the scene I made in the Drooling Moose. People are still talking about it."

"He'll come if you pose your invitation properly."

"But what do I say?"

Anna paced away, then turned back to face her.

"How long did you and Paul go out with each other?"

"A little over a year."

"He must have given you gifts in that year."

Jane nodded. "He gave me a sweater for my birthday, and a teddy bear on Valentine's Day last year."

"It's got to be something special. Something sentimental. Did he ever give you jewelry?"

Jane snorted. "Never." She suddenly brightened. "He gave me a figurine that had been his mom's."

"That's perfect," Anna said, pulling her friend to her feet. "Especially since their house burned flat. You can tell Paul you want to give him back the figurine because it was his mother's. He would definitely come for that."

Jane bit her lower lip. "You don't think this sounds like an ambush?"

"You didn't feel a bit ambushed yourself, when you realized you were pregnant? Jane, there's no easy way to tell a man he's about to become a father, especially if you're not married to him. You're just going to have to come out and say it."

"How did you get so smart about this stuff?"

"I watched three of my brothers jump through hoops to get their wives." She patted Jane's shoulder, slipped into her jacket, and headed for the door. "You get on that phone today and invite Paul to dinner tomorrow night, because I want to see the two of you *together* at Pete's benefit dance next Saturday, got that?"

"Today?"

"You're not getting any less pregnant, Jane. *Today*."

"Megan stinks," Travis announced as he walked down the stairs into the kitchen, rubbing his sleepy eyes.

Jane groaned and walked over to pick up the boy, set him in his booster seat at the table, and gave him her tuna fish sandwich. "I'm not ready for motherhood," she said, heading to the stairs.

"I've been told it's easier when they're your own," Anna assured her as she opened the back door. "Promise me you'll call Paul today."

Jane stopped with one foot on the stairs. "I promise."

Anna nodded. "Then I'll see you one week from tomorrow, at Pete's benefit dance. *Together*."

"From your lips to God's ears." Jane rushed upstairs when Megan let out a bellow.

Anna stepped onto the porch, zipped up her jacket, and headed toward the main road as she thought about what Jane had said concerning Ethan. Barely civilized? Hah, when he wasn't being a pain in the neck, he was downright aggravating.

Though not letting her slide down the ravine in her truck had been a very civilized thing to do. But enjoying undressing her while she'd been unconscious, making her sleep on the couch for three nights just because he didn't have running water, and kissing her senseless and then walking away without a word—might those be considered the actions of a man who was angry at women? And maybe at her in particular, because he didn't like that his foreman was female?

Then why insist on having dinner with her every night, following her to town today, and finding fault with any man she showed an interest in? Dammit, Ethan was such a *guy*. She remembered Pamela Sant from grade school as a simpering, fragile mama's girl with pale skin, big brown eyes, and nearly white hair who was always coming up with excuses why she couldn't take outdoor recess. Ethan had dated her? And gotten the little pris pregnant?

Anna walked along the paved road toward Loon Cove Lumber. Pamela was dead, Ethan had fought manslaughter charges, and since then he'd been hard and unapproachable. Had he loved Pamela that much that he still hadn't gotten over her death?

And was it even any of her business? If he was angry at the world, that was his problem—as long as that anger wasn't directed at her.

She should probably stop pushing his buttons then.

Anna caught the sound of a large rig laboring up the long grade behind her and turned and stuck out her thumb. She heard the heavily loaded twenty-two wheeler downshift, and spun back around and started running, knowing the driver couldn't stop in the middle of the hill to pick her up. He passed her with a blast of his air horn, then came to a stop just over the knoll, dust billowing from his tires and drifting on the gentle March breeze.

"Hi, Gaylen," Anna said as she opened the passenger door and jumped up on the step. "Can I hitch a ride to Loon Cove?"

"I hear you totaled your truck," he said, waving her in. His eyes sparkled expectantly. "How much money you got for a new one?"

"About a thousand dollars less than you're hoping to sell me yours for, you old coot. You ought to be ashamed of yourself, Gaylen Dempsey, for trying to take advantage of a poor, helpless woman like me."

Gaylen looked appropriately offended, but the two flags of red appearing on his ruddy cheeks told Anna she'd guessed right. "You're about as helpless as a fisher with its tail caught in a trap, missy," he muttered, running through the gears as he pulled back onto the road. "My pickup ain't much to look at, but it runs smooth as a purring tiger." He glanced at her, then back at the road. "Three thousand dollars, and you tell Davis to quit shorting my loads when he scales them."

"I've seen your pickup, Gaylen. Two thousand, and you tell Clay Porter to stop sneaking pulpwood into your loads," she countered. "We manufacture lumber, not paper."

"I get paid by the board foot hauling for Clay," Gaylen said, his bushy gray eyebrows coming together in a scowl. "And I've told him he's loading me up with marginal logs."

"Then I guess I need to have a talk with your boss," she said. "He's been dirtying his loads a lot lately, and it's got to stop. Two thousand dollars, and you deliver the pickup to Loon Cove by six tonight."

Gaylen sighed in defeat. "I'll have my wife drive it over while I'm unloading, so she can ride back with me." He gave her a quick glance, then began to downshift as they approached the mill. "You know there's an ongoing feud between the Knights and Porter, don't you? Clay had been trying to raise the money for Loon Cove Lumber, but the Knights bought it right out from under him."

"So he started dirtying his loads to us? But he's only hurting himself."

"The bad blood between them goes way back," Gaylen added. "Alex Knight's first wife ran off with Porter, and then there's the fact that Clay is forced to haul his trees over ten miles of Knight road, but they won't let him rebuild it." Gaylen drove through the open gate of Loon Cove Lumber. "It takes me nearly an hour each way to travel those ten miles, which means I can only make one trip a day instead of two. Their feud is cutting into my profits, along with all the other contract drivers."

Anna shook her head. "Two thousand dollars for your pickup, plain and simple," she stated. "I am not asking Ethan Knight to pretty please let Porter upgrade their road so you can bring us two dirty loads instead of one each day."

"Did I ask?"

"You were working your way up to it."

"Jeeze, Anna. You've somehow persuaded thirty hardheaded men to take orders from you. I just know you could talk the Knights into letting Clay fix their road. Though maybe Ethan isn't the one you should ask," he said with a frown, skillfully maneuvering through the busy mill yard toward the man directing him to stop beside the long row of logs. "Grady Knight's your go-to guy. I bet he'd listen to you."

"I'm not a negotiator, Gaylen. I saw logs."

"You just negotiated me out of a thousand bucks," he grumbled, the air brakes hissing as he brought the logging truck to a rocking stop. He started to open his door, then looked back at her. "I suppose if you persuade Clay to clean up his loads, that's something, at least."

"I've left messages on his phone about this, but it seems I'll have to find some other way to get my point across." She gave her chauffeur a warm smile. "Thanks for the ride. We'll settle up when your wife gets here."

"It's a good-running truck, Anna. You know I wouldn't sell you a lemon."

She reached over and patted his arm. "I know you wouldn't, Gaylen. That's why I bought it without a test drive."

"Bought what?" Ethan asked through her side window. "It's nearly four, Segee," he said, stepping down to open her door. "You're late."

"It's my fault she's late," Gaylen said. "I'm having

to baby my rig because those ten miles of your road are taking their toll on it."

Anna rolled her eyes and crowded past Ethan to get out. "I just bought Gaylen's pickup. And I'm salaried, so I don't punch the clock," she told him as she headed toward their scaler, who was already measuring Gaylen's load. "Davis, continue to put the marginal logs in the pulpwood pile when you sort, and we'll start letting these drivers take them to the paper mill on Monday. We might as well sell this junk as let it sit here and rot."

"But we don't actually own it," Davis said in surprise. "We only pay for the timber logs."

"Yet Clay Porter keeps right on sending it to us," she drawled. "So he must want us to have it."

"You'll start an all-out war," Gaylen sputtered in alarm.

Anna looked at Ethan, who merely gave a slight nod, turned, and strode toward the office. She had, however, noticed a distinct sparkle in his deep blue eyes.

Gaylen gave a soft whistle through his teeth. "So the wind blows that way, does it?"

"What way?" Anna asked with a warning look.

"You're obviously on the Knights' side in this feud."

"I'm on your side," she snapped. "If Clay Porter doesn't stop loading you up with junk so you get full scale, then I'm giving you a back load to take to the paper mill so you won't have to run empty partway."

Gaylen suddenly grinned. "That you are, missy." He stepped closer and lowered his voice. "I'm sorry for implying you might have your eye on Ethan. I know you're smarter than that."

"Smarter?"

"You just moved here, so you might not realize that Ethan can be a hard-ass sometimes, especially with women."

Anna chuckled. "Ethan doesn't scare me."

"He should. He's dangerous, Anna. A woman's dead because of him," Gaylen said, leaning closer. "I'm not gossiping or nothing, I'm just trying to warn you so you won't be taken in by his good looks."

"You think Ethan's handsome?" she asked, glancing toward the office to hide her smile. "I hadn't really noticed."

Gaylen harrumphed and nudged her arm. "I'm serious, Anna. Everyone in town knows he's staying at Fox Run through the week, and I'm trying to warn you to keep it only business between you."

She patted his sleeve. "Consider me warned."

He harrumphed again, then ran toward the back of his truck with a shout, complaining that the log Davis was off-loading to the pulp pile was perfectly good timber. Anna left them to battle it out, and headed toward the office to pick up her paycheck—and push one or two of Ethan's buttons.

But it's hard to rile a man who's disappeared. All Anna found in the office was a brand-new twelve-gauge pump shotgun sitting on her desk, a box of number four birdshot, and her paycheck with a note scribbled on the envelope: "I've gone home for the weekend. Lock the gate behind you, don't kill anyone, and try not to miss me too much. Ethan."

Anna picked up the box of shells and snorted. Kill anyone? She'd be lucky to *dent* them with number four birdshot. She might as well be armed with a fistful of rocks.

Chapter Nine

Anna lay snuggled under her thick down comforter, staring at her bedroom ceiling and blaming Ethan for another sleepless night. No matter how hard she tried, she couldn't stop picturing him chasing Pamela Sant down a pitch-black road, then seeing him frantically racing into Oak Creek after the woman carrying his unborn child.

Anna didn't doubt that Ethan had gone in after Pamela and likely almost drowned himself as he'd desperately tried to save her. Hadn't he been just as determined eighteen years ago to save Abigail Fox from the boys who had trapped her in Frost Lake? He'd certainly taken an awful beating—though she knew that two of the boys who'd been taunting her had spent the night in the hospital, and the third boy probably was still running. Dangerous? Oh yeah, Anna knew exactly how dangerous Ethan could be, considering she'd carry to her grave the image of him battling her bullies that long-ago summer.

Would anything have come of her childhood crush on Ethan if she hadn't been dragged off to Quebec? She had quietly adored him from afar, her young heart thinking he hung the moon. Hell, part of her still did. That was why she couldn't stop pushing his buttons every chance she got. She was finally getting to play out her childhood fantasy, only better, because Ethan didn't equate her with the shy, gangly daughter of Oak Grove's legendary tramp.

Abigail Fox had ceased to exist the day André Segee had brought her, kicking and screaming, to his home in Canada, where he'd legally changed her last name and started calling her by her middle name, Anna. It would take more than a few bullies to intimidate her now, as she'd grown strong and self-assured under the watchful eyes of a quietly generous stepmother, four bossy half brothers, and a determined father who insisted the French Canadian blood running through her veins would give her the strength not only to survive, but to thrive.

And she had, to the point where he'd been brought to tears four months ago when she'd told him she was accepting her inheritance from Grampy Fox and moving back to Maine. When she'd explained that she needed to prove to herself that she was more than her Segee name, the blood in his veins had started to boil. And despite his hiding her SUV and managing to freeze all her assets, she had stubbornly boarded a Maine-bound bus with only a few possessions and the two thousand Canadian dollars her stepmom, Claire, had pressed into her hand on her way out the door.

Anna finally sat up in bed with a sigh of defeat. Apparently it didn't matter which direction she crossed the border; she was doomed to be riddled with guilt, be it eighteen years of not seeing her Grampy Fox or four months of missing her daddy's frustrating habit of trying to micromanage her life.

And since she obviously wasn't going to get any sleep thanks to *all* the maddening men in her life, Anna decided she might as well start the generator and go over her laughable budget. She threw back the comforter, picked up her flashlight as she scuffed her slippers, put on her dark flannel bathrobe, and went downstairs. She walked through the living room, shining the light on Bear in his bed next to the woodstove, then at the empty squirrel shelf on her way through the kitchen, and opened the back door.

She hadn't taken two steps toward the generator shed when she heard a noise that sounded like something falling inside the cookhouse across camp. She immediately snapped off her flashlight and stepped back inside, quietly closed and locked the door, and covered her racing heart with both hands. Damn, she hated it when things went bump in the night!

Especially with Ethan conveniently gone.

Which meant that it was a vigilant, *earthly* someone snooping through her buildings. Still, even though her brain knew there were no such things as ghosts or tree-squeaks or side-hill gougers, she sure as hell wished her pounding heart would settle down.

"It's raccoons," she said out loud, so she wouldn't feel so completely alone. "It's an animal or person going through my outbuildings, not a ghost. And I've had enough, dammit, and it ends tonight!" She marched into the living room and picked up the shotgun Ethan had loaned her. "At least I can scare whatever's out there." She kicked off her slippers and crammed her feet into her mud boots.

Making sure the safety was engaged on the shotgun, Anna loaded a shell in the chamber, then filled the magazine with four more shells. She shoved her flashlight in her pocket, tightened the belt on her robe, and headed through the kitchen to go out the back door.

Bear bumped against her leg, trying to squeeze out ahead of her. "No, pup, you can't come with me. I don't need to worry about you," she whispered, gently pushing him back inside as she slipped out the door.

Anna straightened and peered into the darkness encompassing the old mill site, took a fortifying breath, then quietly crept off the porch. She wished the moon was out so she could see better, but the warm front that had arrived this afternoon was creating a thick blanket of fog—which meant her intruder wouldn't be able to see any better than she could.

With her thumb resting on the safety, Anna worked her way around the side of the house and used familiar trees to guide her toward the shoreline so she could approach the cookhouse from the lake. The melting snow didn't crunch under her feet, so she wasn't worried anyone would hear her, but the dense fog fueled her imagination, making her jump at every little shadow she couldn't immediately recognize.

When another loud bang came from the cookhouse, she immediately scurried behind a large boulder and went perfectly still. Oh God, what *was* she doing out here? "Courage is being afraid but acting anyway," she whispered. "I'm just going to scare those raccoons as bad as they're scaring me."

But what if she found a two-legged creature? Exactly what did she intend to do then? March the man at gunpoint back to her house and call the sheriff?

No, she would simply ask him what in hell he was looking for, and once she got an answer she'd give him a piece of her mind, then escort him off her land with a warning that the next time he showed up, she would shoot first and ask questions later. A shotgun blast over his head would tell him she meant business.

Feeling a bit braver being armed with a plan as well as five rounds of birdshot, Anna started following the shoreline—but froze again when she spotted a large dark shadow on the lake. She waited, holding her breath and listening, but the shadow didn't move or make a sound. She silently crept closer, feeling the jagged transition from shore to lake with her feet as she stepped onto the ice.

The large blob remained silent and unmoving as she drew nearer, then slowly took on a form she finally recognized, and Anna started breathing again. A snowmobile. So that's how her intruder had been coming and going without her hearing him; he arrived by lake and hiked in.

Careful not to make any noise, Anna lifted the cowling, grabbed the ignition wire, and unplugged it so the sled wouldn't start when he turned the key. Then she closed the hood and headed to shore, mentally patting herself on the back for disabling his only means of escape.

She grew braver with every step she took, barely flinching when another loud bang, this time followed by a human curse, came from the cookhouse. She could just make out the weak beam of a flashlight moving around inside, but when she heard whispering, Anna rethought her plan. There were two intruders? Maybe she should shoot *first*—to get their attention and immediate respect—and *then* ask questions.

She quietly stuck the tip of her shotgun through one of the broken windows, aimed it toward the roof, and slid off the safety, then braced the butt of the gun against her shoulder and pulled the trigger. The muzzle blast was deafening and the recoil bruising, but she was prepared for both. She was not, however, prepared for the large hard body that slammed into her side.

Anna twisted, elbowed his head, and drove the butt of her gun into her attacker's ribs, then before he could finish gasping for breath, she scrambled to her feet and swung the gun down over his shoulders as he rolled to his knees. He went back down with a pained grunt, and Anna was torn between hitting him again or running like hell for home when she heard heavy footsteps scrambling through the junk-cluttered cookhouse.

Putting all of her weight into it, Anna kicked the guy in front of her as he tried to get up again, then ran around the building to head off the others as they made their escape. They didn't turn toward the lake, but headed at a dead run toward the road that led out of camp. Anna shouldered her shotgun and fired another round over their heads, then took off after them when they yelped in surprise and started running even faster.

She lost them in the fog but stumbled onto the lane leading to the main highway and guessed that was where they were heading—while their battered accomplice beat a hasty retreat to his snowmobile. Boy, was he in for a surprise. But she'd deal with him later, once she made sure these guys were well on their way.

An engine roared to life up the lane, and Anna

ran toward it as she jacked another shell into the chamber. A set of three taillights appeared through the fog up ahead, and she could tell by their pattern that it was a pickup. She shouldered her gun and fired, aiming right between the lower two lights, smiling smugly when she heard the tiny lead missiles pepper the tailgate. By God, they'd think twice about snooping through her buildings again!

For added insurance, and maybe because it felt so damn good, she jacked another shell into the chamber and pulled the trigger one final time—just as she was knocked off her feet by a heavy body slamming into her again.

"Dammit, quit shoo—"

Anna cut him off by shoving her elbow into the side of his head, but he managed to get hold of the shotgun before she was able to drive the butt into his ribs. There was a desperate tug of war over the gun, which Anna valiantly fought but eventually lost. Her attacker tossed the weapon away, spun her onto her back and straddled her hips, and caught her fist before it could connect with his face.

"Quit hitting me!" he growled.

Anna stilled and blinked up at the dark figure towering over her. "Ethan?" she whispered. "Dammit, I thought you were one of them!"

He pinned her hands on the ground by her head, hunching over until his face was only inches from hers. "If you hit me again, I'm going to stuff you down a fishing hole."

"Then stop tackling me."

"I was trying to stop you from shooting that damn gun."

"If you didn't intend me to use it, then why did you leave it on my desk?"

He lifted slightly but didn't let go of her hands. "I thought it would make you feel safer to have it. I didn't think you'd leave the house, much less actually shoot at anyone."

Anna struggled to get free, but he only tightened his grip and shifted his weight over her thighs, his knees squeezing her like a vise. "Why in hell were you shooting at them?"

"I wasn't shooting *at* them, I was aiming over their heads. I just wanted to scare them, so they'd realize there's a crazy woman living here who's willing to use a shotgun."

He looked up the lane, but because she couldn't make out his expression, she didn't know if he was shocked or angered. She was getting madder by the minute. Her adrenaline rush was starting to wane, the wet snow was seeping through her robe, and her bare legs were growing numb with cold.

"I'd say you accomplished that," he said with a chuckle—which meant he wasn't angry. He let go of her hands and rubbed his jaw, but stayed straddling her hips. "Where'd you learn to fight like that, Segee?"

"Four older brothers. You going to let me up anytime soon?"

"Eventually," he said, gently feeling his ribs. "Once I stop hurting." He settled his hips more firmly over hers. "I seem to be comfortable right where I am."

Anna simply snorted. "You're lucky I only had a shotgun tonight. Let's consider us even for that punch you gave me last month."

"I think you cracked one of my ribs."

Anna reached up and patted his cheek. "Poor baby. Would a kiss make you feel better?"

"Jesus, you're reckless," he whispered, pulling her hand from his cheek to pin her back down, then staring at her mouth as if considering her offer.

"You kiss me again, Knight, and you better plan on sticking around to finish it this time."

He snapped his gaze to hers, every muscle in his body tense. "Excuse me?"

She hadn't *really* said that, had she? Why had she just challenged him to take her to bed? Maybe she should stuff *herself* down a fishing hole.

Or . . . maybe she should really shock him, and at the same time finally put her childhood fantasies to rest once and for all. Anna shrugged one shoulder. "But I'll understand if you're not up to a no-commitment, no-regrets affair. Maybe I've been reading what's been going on between us all wrong."

He just stared down at her until Anna began to feel like a bug under a microscope. How the hell long did it take a guy to decide whether or not he wanted sex, anyway? Geesh, you'd think she'd proposed marriage to him. Anna wiggled more robustly to get free—which was why she didn't see it coming when his lips touched hers.

She would have expected him to come at her like a house on fire once he'd made up his mind, but again Ethan caught her off guard with a kiss so tender, she found herself responding without even thinking of laying down ground rules.

He released her hands and she immediately wrapped them around his neck, parted her lips, and went in search of his tongue. Ethan just as immediately retreated, sliding his mouth along her jaw in a succession of teasing kisses. With a shiver of delight and a moan of frustration, Anna gripped his hair and tried directing his mouth back to hers.

But he wouldn't be rushed; he simply continued his deliberate journey, moving his wonderfully skillful mouth down the curve of her throat. Anna arched her spine and threw back her head to give him access, sliding her arms under his and wrapping them around his torso to draw in his warmth.

"Yes," she urged with building desire, digging her fingers into his back as she moved her legs against his imprisoning thighs. She gasped when his teeth gently raked the skin over her collarbone on his downward journey, and pushed at his hips until she was able to finally free her legs and wrap them around him.

He suddenly sat up and looked down, pulling aside the edge of her robe. "What *are* you wearing under there?" he asked, his voice thick.

"My nightie," she said, taking advantage of his distraction by placing her hands on his shoulders and giving him a gentle push. "Can we maybe take this into the house? I'm getting soaked to the bone."

He hesitated, and Anna knew he was wondering if she would change her mind if the mood was broken. "I'm pretty sure I've got some condoms in my bureau," she offered, giving him a more urgent push. "And flannel sheets beat a snowbank hands down."

She might as well be shoving against a pine tree for all the good it did her, considering he was more interested in fingering the delicate lace covering her breasts.

"Have you made love in many snowbanks?" he asked.

Oh great, a curious lover. "Not since seventh grade, when Tommy Dubois kissed me in the school yard while we were waiting for our rides home." She touched his cheek so that he'd look at her. "I won't change my mind, Ethan."

With a deep sigh, he finally braced his hands on the ground and got up, then pulled Anna to her feet. He made a noise that sounded suspiciously like stifled laughter as he gathered the edges of her robe to her throat and lifted her face to his. "Why am I not surprised that you're out here shooting at trespassers in a sexy little nightie the size of a napkin?"

Anna shrugged. "I wasn't aware protecting hearth and home required special clothing."

He covered her mouth with his, and this time it

was exactly what she expected: his lips were commanding, his intentions blatantly obvious, the anticipation he sent coursing through her intoxicating. Anna melted against him and met the thrust of his tongue with bold and equally urgent desire. A shudder ran through her, and she pressed closer to his warmth.

But he broke away again, pulling her head against his chest on a harsh sigh. "If you keep kissing me back like that, we won't see those flannel sheets," he said, his lips touching her hair, making her shudder again. "Damn, you turn me on, Segee."

He kissed her again, briefly but no less intensely, then captured her hand and started leading her toward the house. He stopped to pick up the shotgun, releasing her to empty out the one remaining shell.

He shook his head and made a tsking sound. "Have you ever thought about anger management therapy?" he asked as he laced his fingers through hers and started walking again.

"I don't have an anger problem. Why do you guys think that if a woman stands up for herself, she's either a shrew or really a man trapped in a woman's body?"

He squeezed her hand with a laugh. "Knowing your preference in underwear, I doubt there's one male hormone in that lovely body of yours. So what happened to Tommy Dubois when he kissed you in the snowbank? Did you send him home with a bloody nose?"

"Why would I do that? I was more curious about kissing than he was," she said, stumbling over a rock in the path.

Ethan pulled her up against his side by wrapping his arm around her. He suddenly turned serious, his hand on her hip tightening perceptibly. "We do this, Anna, and people will talk," he softly warned.

"Not if you don't go bragging at work that you nailed your foreman," she countered. "I believe it's called being discreet."

He stopped walking and turned her to face him. "It's not me I'm worried about."

"You're worried *I'm* going to say something?" She rolled her eyes. "Oh, that would make my life easier."

"I know you wouldn't *say* anything, but when a woman's gone to bed with a man, people can . . . well, they can *tell*."

"Oh?" she asked evenly.

"Yeah." He led her toward the house again. "Women act different around a man they've slept with. You get all clingy and possessive and . . . all moody, all of a sudden."

Anna pulled him to an abrupt halt. "I do not *cling*. And if you don't shut up, you're never going to see the rest of this sexy nightie, much less what's under it. I want to sleep with you—period. I don't want to possess you in any way, and I'm not *moody*. We keep it fun, uncomplicated, and discreet. Any problems with that, Knight?"

"No, ma'am."

Anna started walking again, this time leading. "I don't suppose you have any condoms on you?" she asked, stepping onto the back porch.

"You said you have some in your bureau."

She reached in her pocket for her flashlight as she stepped into the dark house. "I must have lost my flashlight when you tackled me. Hold on, I have a kerosene lamp I can light."

"I can start the generator."

"I don't want to leave it running all night." She located the lamp, then slid her hand along the counter until she found the jar of wooden matches.

"So do you have any condoms or not?" he asked.

"I'm pretty sure I do." She struck the match, blinking when the flame flared to life, then lifted the glass on the lamp and touched the match to the wick. "Ah, do they have expiration dates?" she asked, not looking at him.

He didn't immediately answer. "Exactly how old are yours?"

She picked up the lamp and walked into the living room, Ethan following behind her. "I bought them one, maybe two years ago," she said, settling Bear back in his bed before finally looking at Ethan. "Maybe three," she admitted as she slipped out of her boots. "Do they actually go bad?"

"I know we're not supposed to carry them around in our wallets for more than a year," he said, straightening from removing his own boots and taking the lamp from her, then lacing his fingers through hers to lead her up the stairs. "Which means I should have thrown away the one I'm carrying months ago."

So they'd established that neither of them was in the habit of bed-hopping. Anna smiled in anticipation of what could prove to be a very interesting night.

Chapter Ten

Ethan led the way up the stairs to Anna's bedroom, undecided if he was about to become the luckiest man this side of the Canadian border or the sorriest. He hadn't lied when he told Anna she turned him on; he hadn't wanted a woman this badly in years.

He entered the bedroom he'd spent three sexually frustrating nights in, Anna silently following, her pliant hand nestled in his. He'd been expecting her to either come to her senses and tell him she'd changed her mind or start ripping off their clothes downstairs. He wasn't sure what to make of her getting all quiet on him all of a sudden.

He let go of her hand to set the lamp on the antique bureau. "Okay, let's see your goods."

Her eyes widened and she held her robe closed at her throat.

"The condoms," he drawled, nodding toward the bureau.

She turned and pulled open the top drawer, but not quickly enough for Ethan to miss her blush. She rummaged through the drawer for several seconds, shuffling tiny bits of lacy underwear back and forth with increasing urgency. "I know they're here some-where," she muttered, closing the drawer and pulling out the one below, then rummaging through it. "I'm pretty sure the box is blue."

Ethan unbuttoned his shirt and shrugged it off. He was sharing Anna's bed tonight, by God, condoms or no condoms. If she didn't find them, they would just . . . dammit, they'd figure it out when they got there.

"Here they are," she said, turning with a semi-crushed blue box in her hand. She went perfectly still, the box forgotten as her gaze traveled down his naked chest, stopping at his hands unzipping his fly.

"What's the date on them?" he asked.

"Ah . . . " She held the box near the lamp. "It only has a year stamped on it." She glanced over her shoulder just as he dropped his pants, then quickly turned back to the bureau. "It's this year. I don't know if that means they're still good or . . . or not," she said, her voice trailing away when he reached around her waist and unknotted the cloth belt holding her robe closed.

"You aren't getting all shy on me, are you, Segee?"

he asked, his lips brushing her hair as he slid her robe off her shoulders. He gently kissed her skin next to one of the thin straps of her nightie, then began to slowly nibble his way toward her throat. "Because I really admire a woman who isn't afraid to go after what she wants," he added, sliding her curls out of his way to continue up the long slender line of her neck. "And I was under the impression you wanted me," he whispered against her ear.

She leaned back into him, a soft sound of pleasure escaping on a sigh. "I do want you," she admitted.

Ethan wrapped one arm around her just under her breasts, and took the condoms out of her hand and tossed them on the bed behind them. "I'm glad," he said, reaching up to slide first one and then the other thin strap off her shoulders. "Open your eyes, Anna," he softly commanded, watching her in the mirror over the bureau, her flawless skin glowing alabaster in the soft flame of the kerosene lamp, a sensuous contrast to the deep red lace of her nightie.

She opened her eyes and stared, transfixed, as the lace slid down over his arm, exposing two full, beautiful breasts tipped with large almond-rose nipples. He positioned his hand just beneath one plush nipple and trailed his thumb lazily across it, watching it pucker into his touch. He lifted his gaze briefly to see Anna watching his hand in the mirror, then buried his face in her throat to draw in her scent.

"You're so beautiful," he rasped, his throat closing with the need to possess her.

She turned in his embrace, and Ethan felt the delicate silk slip to the floor as she reached up, cupped the sides of his face, pulled his mouth down to hers, and parted his lips with her tongue. Ethan opened his eyes and nearly *swallowed* her tongue when he saw her sleek, naked length in the mirror; her long, wild hair draped over his arm around her, her trim waist and the slight flare of her hips, her heart-shaped backside topping long, athletic legs. Reaching a hand behind her knees, he swept her up in his arms and settled them both on the bed.

"Is that rain I hear on the roof?" she asked, her hands on his shoulders holding him still as she listened.

"Maybe. Or my heart trying to pound out of my chest," he offered with a provocative smile, taking her wrists to hold her arms to her sides, sliding down her body until his mouth was even with her breasts. "You sure are put together nicely, Segee."

She used his grip on her wrists to pull herself into a sitting position, and Ethan had to look up between her breasts to see her face. "If you want to maintain your distance by calling me Segee, that's okay," she said, her expression as fierce as her voice. "But you say it like a lover, not an adversary."

"Yes, ma'am," he contritely agreed, dropping his gaze to her nipples not an inch from his nose. "Anything in particular you want me calling these two little ladies?"

"That does it!" She flailed her legs beneath his

and twisted her wrists in his grip. "I am *so* going to have you begging for mercy!"

Here was the Anna he knew, her outrage only serving to slap her breasts against his face. Ethan burst into laughter and lifted her hands over her head, then used his body to push her back until he covered the length of her, successfully subduing her struggles.

"Now, play nice," he cajoled, covering her mouth with his, not letting her come up for air until she softened beneath him. "I've been begging for your mercy all week," he said, shifting to take one of her enticing nipples in his mouth, turning whatever she'd been about to say into a strangled moan of what he sincerely hoped was delight.

Lord, he had never worked so hard to make love to a woman; one minute she was soft and pliant, the next she was giving him hell. Ethan suckled her nipple, coaxing it to life in his mouth, feeling her quiver beneath him as she wrapped her legs over his thighs and pulled him tightly against her. She was so damned responsive, so uninhibited, so . . . unpredictable.

The moment he let go of her wrists to better attend to her breasts, she grabbed hold of his hair and started trying to direct him again. Ethan didn't care if she pulled out his hair, he refused to be rushed. He greedily took his fill of her left nipple, then kissed his way to her right one, teasing it with his tongue until she was moaning and squirming and pulling his hair a good half inch longer. Oh, he was going to pay for this, he knew; the moment he dropped his guard, she would try to move in for the kill.

Better get his licks in while he could.

Ethan pinned her arms to her sides as he shifted lower and kissed her belly. Her heated skin contracted and she cried out, arching her back and lifting her pelvis into his chest. He continued his downward journey, each little sound she made encouraging, each quiver of her writhing body urging him to explore further.

She was so amazingly responsive.

The old house surrounding them creaked, resettling on a gust of wind that brought driving rain as the storm finally broke with deafening thunder. But Ethan's focus remained on the heated storm building beneath him, moving lower and lower until his mouth reached the juncture of Anna's thighs and he kissed her most intimately.

Her cry of pleasure went straight to his groin, and he continued his gentle assault, feeling her shudder with each flick of his tongue as she tightened her legs around him, her building passion sending him to the very edge of his control.

"Come into me, Ethan," she cried, freeing her hands to tug him upward. "Now!" she demanded, her shout echoed in another house-shaking rumble of thunder.

Ethan rose to his hands and knees, and found the box of condoms near one of the pillows, just about to slide off the bed. He made a lunge for it. "If you don't quit squirming, we won't need the damn condoms," he growled, shaking out one of the packets and ripping it open with his teeth.

Her hands were all over him, working him into such a frenzy it was all he could do to get the condom out of the packet.

"Maybe you should put two on," she said, her impatience obvious as her hand trailed down his stomach toward his groin. "They really are old."

He dropped the condom on her belly to chase after her hand. "I'll be lucky to get *one* on," he hissed, her determined fingers curling around his shaft just as he pulled them away. "Anna, you're not helping."

The little vixen actually smiled up at him. "You're not very adept at this, are you?" she said, her eyes sparkling in the flickering lamplight. "Except for your very competent mouth."

Ethan took the hand he was holding and lowered it to where his competent mouth had been, pressing her fingers intimately against her. "Do you think you could keep yourself occupied for just ten seconds, Segee?" he ground out. "While I try to get my act together long enough to protect us?"

Her scowl quickly turned into a gasp of surprise, then into a moan of pleasure as he slowly worked Anna's fingers against her sensitive bud. Ethan forgot all about the condom, becoming utterly mesmerized by her response.

Holy hell, what had made him think taking Anna to bed would put her out of his head once and for all?

The way she was coming alive, he'd never get enough of her.

"Hurry, Ethan," she entreated, shifting her hips directly beneath his and lifting them up, her hand brushing his scrotum—sending a shudder through him so powerful, he nearly lost it there and then. "I want you inside when I come."

He started to sweat and his hands shook as he tried to slide on the condom, and he actually *shouted* when her delicate fingers suddenly rolled it down around him. She did *not*, however, have to show him what to do with his safely packaged package. Ethan captured her wrists to hold her still long enough to position himself, but she suddenly used his grip to pull him down on top of her.

He'd barely started to ease inside her when she crested, her body arching against him. He'd been trying to be gentle, but she blew his noble intentions to hell with her long, keening cry—which immediately cut off all the blood to his brain and sent it shooting straight to his shaft, buried deep inside her. At the first pulse of her orgasm, he began thrusting into her contracting heat with mindless need.

She not only matched his enthusiasm, she braced his shoulders and used her legs wrapped around his to better his angle, her hoarse, breathless cries of approval competing with the deafening rain drumming the roof. He fought the urge for release, desperate for the powerful sensations coursing through him to last; but when she suddenly crested again, Ethan drove deeply into her and went perfectly still, letting her contractions of pleasure pull him over the edge, pulsing so powerfully that every muscle in his body shook with the force of his release.

It was a long time before the blood started flowing back to his brain. The first thing he noticed was Anna softly caressing his sweat-beaded chest; the second was the satisfied, smug smile that reached all the way to her shining eyes.

He closed his, back to wondering if he was lucky or crazy—because although he was feeling quite smug himself, he doubted Anna was going to let him enjoy the glow very long.

"Say something, Ethan."

"I think my ribs really *are* cracked."

Her fingers dug into his chest a tad too much, and he leaned down and kissed her mouth, gently pulled out of her and rolled free, and folded one arm over his forehead. He stared up at the ceiling in silence, trying to find the words he knew every woman needed to hear . . . after. But what could he possibly say that wouldn't go straight to her beautiful head? *That was mind-blowing, Segee. The absolute best I've ever had. Can we do it again in ten minutes?* The possibilities as well as her responses snapped through his mind with the same fury as the rain on the roof, his loss for words stretching long and awkward between them.

"Your sled won't start because I unplugged the ignition wire," she finally said, her voice barely audible over the drum of the rain.

"Thanks for the heads-up."

"What were you doing over here tonight?"

Okay, small talk worked for him. "I thought your ghost might take advantage of my being gone, and that I could pay the rest of my rent by finding out what's so intriguing about your mill."

"Thank you."

Was she thanking him for checking up on her or for screwing her brains out? Better to stick with the small talk. "Now we know a couple of things we didn't before," he said. "One, there's two ghosts; and two, they're searching for something specific."

He felt her turn her head on her pillow to look at him. "How do you know that?"

"I'd been listening to them for maybe twenty minutes before you showed up. They're hunting for something they think Samuel Fox had hidden someplace in camp."

"They didn't say what?"

"No, but they thought it might be in an old mason jar or plastic bag. They just knew they were looking for a waterproof container. Apparently, they'd already done a thorough search of your house shortly after Samuel died, before you arrived. That's probably why your home hasn't been bothered."

She rose up on her elbow to face him. "Are they looking for money, do you think?" she asked. "Could Samuel have hidden cash someplace in camp? I know older people often prefer mason jars to banks."

Ethan forced his gaze from her lovely breasts to

her face. "It could be money. Or they could be looking for a document. A deed maybe, or a will. Do you know if Samuel had a will?"

She nodded, her forehead wrinkling in thought. "He had a will," she said, lying back on her pillow, affording Ethan a wonderful landscape view of her chest.

He saw her shiver and rub her arms, and he immediately rolled to his side, removed the condom, and held it over the edge of the bed, undecided what to do with the damn thing. He finally dropped it on the floor, reminding himself to take care of it later—wondering if there'd be a small pile there in the morning or just the one.

He got up, pulled back the thick down comforter, and picked Anna up and set her down on the flowery flannel sheet, quickly climbing in beside her and covering them.

She immediately snuggled against him, wrapping an arm around his waist and resting her head on his shoulder with a sigh of contentment. Pleased by her response, Ethan smiled up at the ceiling. "Did you happen to notice how many condoms were in the box?" he asked.

"Five in all," she said, her breath tickling his chest hair as her hand gently massaged his ribs. "Enough for tonight."

Her eyelids heavy and her pulse finally starting to calm, Anna lay snuggled up to Ethan's heat, listening to his heartbeat against the backdrop of the rain and occasional rumble of distant thunder. Making love to the fully grown Ethan Knight was far more exciting than any one of her million dreams of him over the last eighteen years.

Too bad he was going to be hell to deal with at work now. Although Ethan felt that women were the ones who clung, Anna knew from watching her daddy and brothers that men were far more possessive of women they slept with, often to the point of making complete fools of themselves. Her brother Damon still hadn't recovered from his last girlfriend, who'd dropped him like a hot potato when he'd shown up at her hotel in Toronto unannounced and uninvited when she'd been on a buying trip for her work. It hadn't mattered that he'd been carrying an engagement ring with him; they'd known each other only three weeks and had slept together all of five times. Simone had immediately—and quite accurately—foreseen a future of spending an exhausting amount of energy dealing with Damon's ego and his efforts to micromanage her life.

But then, all of Anna's brothers took after her daddy.

Not that she was comparing Ethan to the men in her family. Although he had been rather peremptory during their lovemaking, Anna knew her own take-charge attitude sometimes made men feel as if they'd better wrestle her for control or lose it completely. Ethan wasn't the first lover she'd battled in bed, but he was the first one she hadn't minded conceding to—likely due to her lingering childhood impression that he hung the moon. Then again, it might be because Ethan was the first man she'd met who didn't seem overly threatened by her own healthy ego.

Or maybe he simply was incapable of feeling too deeply since losing Pamela Sant. After all, Anna had offered him a no-commitment, no-regrets affair, so maybe he was just taking advantage of the opportunity to end his own sexual drought.

Not that his skills as a lover had suffered for it!

Anna trailed her fingers down his ribs with a sigh, smiling when he emitted a warning growl and captured her hand before she could explore any lower.

"You can't make up three years in one night," he said, kissing her palm before placing her hand on his shoulder with a pat to stay put. "But if you give me a few minutes, I'm willing to help you try."

"You make me sound like a love-starved hussy."

"Hussy?" he repeated, lifting his head to look down at her. "That word has to be older than my father. Where'd you get that?"

"From *my* father," she said. "He used it in every lecture to me about men, my reputation with them, and the consequences of my . . . ah, forthrightness."

He placed a finger under her chin and lifted her face to look at him. "Did you get your propensity for shooting at people from André Segee? Do I need to watch my back for sleeping with his little girl?"

Anna gave him her sweetest smile. "Probably, if he ever speaks to me again. Actually, it's my brothers you should watch out for. They're just as protective of me as my father."

"You the baby?"

"Yup."

"How many brothers?"

"Four."

"There's five Segee men?" he asked in surprise. "No wonder you moved down here. And what do you mean, if he ever speaks to you again? You didn't leave on good terms?"

"Haven't you wondered why I can't even pay my taxes when I come from a family with enough money to run a small nation?" She lowered her hand to his wonderfully broad chest and started working her fingers through the fine down covering his wonderfully strong muscles. "My father somehow persuaded the president of my bank—which also happens to hold the Segee Logging and Lumber accounts—to freeze my checking and savings." She snorted. "And my beautiful truck is probably parked on some logging road a hundred miles north of nowhere."

He turned on his side to face her, pulled the comforter up over their shoulders, and held her restless hand between them. "Your whole family disowned you?"

"Just Daddy," she said with a resigned sigh. "My stepmom, Claire, writes to me regularly and includes money when she can. And though my brothers are siding with Dad, they're still speaking to me. At least I think they are."

"Then why did you do it? Why throw it all away for some run-down mill that's only going to bankrupt you?"

"Have you ever felt like you're drowning in love?" she asked. "Like your family is so determined to see you happy that they suffocate you with attention? My father chose the schools I attended, gave me a job in one of his mills the day I graduated college, picked out the vehicles I've bought, and dragged home most of the men I dated. Last summer, he suddenly decided it would be a great idea if I married the manager of our mill in Debec and got serious about having babies."

"And instead of just saying no, you ran off to Maine?"

"Quebec is a large province, but the Segee name reaches into all four corners, employing thousands of people in the forests and our mills. It wasn't possible for me to stay there and live my life on my own terms. *Your* family lives and works together. Haven't you ever felt like telling them to bugger off?"

He laughed, his handsomely chiseled face softened by the glow of the kerosene flame. "I've been known to pack a sleeping bag and head into the woods for a few days," he admitted. "My father's a lot like yours, though with us being boys he's into scheming to get what he wants, where your dad seems to prefer a more direct approach. How does André treat your brothers?"

"Strictly hands off." She shrugged one shoulder, but couldn't catch the comforter when it slipped down because he wouldn't let go of her hand. Hey, if the man wanted to ogle her chest, why not? Maybe it would restart his engine, because dammit, she wanted to feel him inside her again.

"Since my brothers are exactly like him," she said to answer his question, "Daddy doesn't feel compelled to tell them what to do, how to do it, or who to do it with. If it wasn't for my stepmom, I'd have headed for the loony bin years ago." She nodded toward her bureau. "You have Claire to thank for my sexy undergarments. She was so tickled to have another female in the house, she took me shopping in Toronto and New York every chance she got."

Ethan lifted his gaze from her chest to her face. "If I ever meet your stepmom, I'll have to thank her personally," he said thickly.

Deciding she'd given him more than enough time to recover, Anna suddenly threw her leg over his hip and pushed at his shoulder, straddling him in one fluid motion. His hands immediately went to her breasts, and she made a tiny sound of pleasure as she leaned into his touch—while reaching down to fondle him intimately.

He yelped in surprise and brought his knees up, trying to buck her off. Anna fought valiantly but lost the battle for who would be on top for their next round, finding herself pinned to the mattress five minutes later, panting with laughter.

"I also had brothers to wrestle with growing up," he said, and she was pleased to see he was just as winded as she was. "Am I going to have to sleep with one eye open?" His gaze traveled down to her chest again, which was rising and falling as she tried to catch her breath.

"If I let you sleep at all," she said. "You might want to open the four remaining packets now, and just line them up on the nightstand." She jutted out her lower lip in a pout. "Unless you're not in as good a shape as you appear."

"I'm starting to feel sorry for your father and brothers," he said, lowering his mouth to hers but stopping just short of making contact. "Come for me like you did before," he whispered, the deep timbre of his renewed desire reaching all the way to the pit of her stomach, "and maybe I'll let you be on top *next* time."

And so went their salacious battle of wills far into the rainy night, though the lamp had long since burned out, dawn had come and gone several hours earlier, and they were down to their last condom before Anna finally got to straddle his hips and make him beg for mercy. Or was that *her* voice crying uncle as she collapsed on top of his heaving chest in a quivering puddle of bliss?

Chapter Eleven

*T*he storm must have started up again, and for some strange reason the thunder sounded as if it were yelling her name. But Anna didn't open her eyes—she couldn't have moved a muscle to save her soul.

Ethan managed to lift his arm enough to prod her hip. "Wake up," he muttered. "You have company, and they've let themselves in."

"Anna!" came the shout from downstairs. "Come on, *ma belle enfant!* I've brought you a surprise."

Anna bolted to a sitting position with a horrified gasp. "Damon!" she yelped, rounding her eyes on Ethan. She shoved him hard enough that he nearly fell off the bed, his eyes snapping open with a growl.

"Get up!" she hissed, rolling toward the hall door. "You need to get out of here!"

"Anna!" Damon yelled again as she heard his foot on the bottom stairs. "Where are you? It's nearly noon!"

"Stay downstairs!" she called out, holding her bedroom door open a crack. "I'm getting dressed! I'll be down in a minute."

"What are you doing in bed in the middle of the day?" he asked, sounding as if he had stopped halfway up the stairs. "Are you sick?"

"I got dirty working outside. I'm changing my clothes," she said through the crack, glancing briefly at Ethan to see him on the other side of the bed, smiling like an idiot as he stuffed something in his pants pocket—when he should be stuffing himself into them! She closed the door, silently locked it, and gave him a warning glare as she strode to her bureau. "Hurry up," she demanded in a whisper, pulling underwear out of the top drawer. "The last thing we need is for Damon to find you up here."

He straightened from putting on his pants. "Exactly how protective is dear brother Damon? Better yet, how big is he?" he asked, scratching his chest as he gave a lazy yawn. "Because I don't think I have enough strength left to defend you, much less myself."

"He's five-ten and a full-blooded French Canadian woodsman, which means he's compact and lethal," she said as she slid her camisole over her head.

She jerked opened another drawer and pulled out a sweater and jeans. "And your halfhearted offer is sweet, but I don't need defending from my brother. Unlike you, Damon would cut off his arm before he'd put so much as a scratch on my body."

While slipping into her sweater, Anna was suddenly spun around, and when she popped her head out, she found herself facing a rather foreboding scowl.

"I didn't *know* you were a woman when I punched you."

"And last night when you tackled me? Did you know then?"

His expression turned sinister. "Which time?" he asked in a growl. "Before we hit the sheets or after?"

She reached up and patted his still naked chest— which she'd gotten well acquainted with last night— and smiled. "Damon will take a shotgun to you, and he won't be aiming in the air when he pulls the trigger."

"You're twenty-nine years old, Segee."

"And the only girl in the family, and the baby." She slid into her pants. "It's your funeral. But if I were you, I'd crawl out the window, hike to my snowmobile, and book it for home."

"I am not climbing out the window," he snapped, walking back around the bed to pick up his shirt.

"Anna!" Damon hollered again from the kitchen. "Where's the birdseed? These chickadees are driving me nuts!"

Anna finished buttoning her pants, turned to the mirror to make sure she was presentably dressed, and gasped in horror. "Oh God, I look like a madwoman." She walked to the door, opened it, and shouted down, "In the canister on the counter! And let the dog out!"

She shut the door and walked back to the bureau, working the snarls out of her hair with her fingers. "Will you get out of here!" she hissed, glaring at Ethan in the mirror.

"My boots are downstairs."

She leaned over her hands on the bureau, closed her eyes, and sighed. "This is exactly why I ran away from home."

Strong fingers came around her shoulders. "Let it go, Anna," he said, his voice gently soothing. "Our sleeping together is nobody's business but ours."

She opened her eyes to see Ethan behind her in the mirror, and immediately blushed with the memory of their standing in this exact position last night—and what he'd done to her and what he'd made her *feel*.

He slid his hands up her shoulders and encircled her neck, lowering his mouth to her ear. "If it will make you feel better, I can let him beat me up."

It didn't seem to matter that they'd just spent the entire night exploring every inch of each other's bodies; his hands on her pulse and his mouth moving against her hair sent a shiver of desire coursing through her.

She leaned back into him. "You're right, I'm a big girl. And I won't let Damon beat you up." She turned and wrapped her arms around his waist. "Considering I already did that last night—before and *after* we hit the sheets," she finished with a grin, grabbing his hand and leading him out the door before he could respond to her outrageous boast.

While Anna rushed down to greet her brother, Ethan hung back at the top of the stairs and sized up the man who was staring at the large pair of boots sitting next to his sister's smaller ones.

Anna had accurately described him as compact and potentially lethal. And since Ethan had been in more than one fight with a French Canadian woodsman, and at this point barely had enough strength to keep breathing, he decided he'd put on his civil face and try not to let the man goad him into doing or saying anything stupid.

Anna skipped the last step and threw herself into her brother's arms. "You've come to see me, Damon!" she cried excitedly. "I'm so glad to see you!"

Damon easily caught Anna and held her in a bear hug against his chest, but his eyes were locked on Ethan. Without so much as a word or facial twitch, Damon Segee quite aptly expressed how he felt about finding a man exiting the bedroom with his baby sister.

Ethan decided to remember that look, to use on Delaney's dates when his niece started dragging home boyfriends.

"We've brought you your truck, *belle enfant*," Damon said, finally setting Anna on her feet.

"We?" she asked in surprise, looking around.

"Jean-Paul followed me down to drive me back. He's out inspecting your property." He captured Anna's wild hair and cupped it to her face as he looked deep in her eyes. "How are you surviving your self-imposed exile, *bébé?*" Damon asked, his gaze inspecting her body. "You've lost weight."

"I've only lost what that blasted desk job had put on me," she countered, trailing one finger down his scowling cheek, then throwing herself back against his chest. "Oh, I've missed you so much! How's Claire? And the others? And . . . and Daddy?"

"Ah, *bébé*, we've been miserable without you around to pester us. *Especially* papa. He puts on a face to everyone, but Claire has caught him up in your room more than once, just sitting on your bed staring at nothing."

Ethan held in a snort. If Damon called Anna *beautiful child* or *baby* one more time, he was going to be sick. She was twenty-nine, for chrissakes, not nine. And what sap of a father couldn't handle his grown daughter moving out?

When she tried to hug him again, Damon took hold of Anna's shoulders and held her still as he made a point of looking up at Ethan. "Are you going to introduce me?"

"Oh, yes!" she said, turning to the stairs. "This is

my boss at Loon Cove Lumber, Ethan Knight. Ethan, this is my brother, Damon."

"Knight?" Damon repeated, one brow raised as Ethan walked down the stairs, sat on the bottom step, and put on his boots. "Of the NorthWoods Timber Knights?"

"Yes," Anna answered before Ethan could. "His family just purchased Loon Cove Lumber last month. And Ethan was kind enough to come over today and help me fix the plumbing in the upstairs bathroom."

Ethan barely caught himself from rolling his eyes as he stood up. Did she think her brother would actually *believe* that? "Damon," he said, holding out his hand. "Segee Logging and Lumber's loss is our gain, it seems. Anna's been single-handedly running Loon Cove for months now."

It took him a while, but Damon finally reached out and shook his hand, and it was Ethan's turn to silently get his point across as he merely held his own against a grip strong enough to strangle a moose.

Apparently Anna knew exactly what was happening between them, because she pulled Damon toward the front door. "I can't wait to see my truck. Tell me where Daddy hid it."

"About twenty miles north of the Debec mill," Damon said, letting her lead him out onto the porch. "It was inside an abandoned trailer parked in one of our gravel pits. But he must have forgotten there aren't any roofs on chip trailers. I never would have found it if I hadn't been flying back in the chopper from our Jacquard cutting." He shook his head with a laugh. "It just barely fit inside, and I have no idea how he drove it in there and then got out of the damn thing. He must have climbed out through the sunroof."

"Which shows exactly how angry he was," another man said as he came around the corner of the house, Bear following on his heels. The man suddenly stopped, his expression darkening when his gaze settled on Anna. "You look like hell, *enfant!*"

Ethan finally did roll his eyes. This man could have been Damon's twin but for being eight or nine years older.

"Jean-Paul!" Anna cried, rushing off the porch to throw herself at him. "I've missed you so much!"

Just like his brother, Jean-Paul hugged Anna tightly, though his attention had zeroed in on Ethan. "Your inheritance is a rotting pile of lumber, *bébé,*" he said against her hair as he continued to pierce Ethan with sharp, intelligent blue eyes. "Sell it and come home."

Inheritance? Ethan had assumed she'd purchased Fox Run from Samuel's daughter. So what in hell was the man talking about? Unless he was angry that Anna had spent her inheritance from her grandparents on the rotting pile of lumber?

Anna leaned back in Jean-Paul's embrace, squished his cheeks together so he'd quit talking, and smiled. "Once I get things up and running, Fox Run is going to put Loon Cove Lumber out of business," she told him. "And Papa's going to lose the specialty lumber market to me, because he's too stubborn to expand the Debec mill as I suggested."

This was interesting news, Ethan reflected. Did she plan to continue sleeping with the owner of Loon Cove Lumber while she plotted his demise?

"Who is your friend?" Jean-Paul asked, setting her down and throwing an arm around her shoulders as they climbed the stairs.

"This is the man *bébé's* going to put out of business," Damon said. "Ethan Knight of NorthWoods Timber. His family recently purchased Loon Cove Lumber."

Jean-Paul seemed to relax, apparently assuming Anna wasn't foolish enough to sleep with her competition. But then, he hadn't seen Ethan coming out of her room just now, both of them looking like they'd spent the night having mind-blowing sex.

"Ethan," Jean-Paul said, holding out his hand. "We know of your family's operation. I believe some of our land borders yours?"

"I believe it does," he agreed, returning the handshake.

Anna suddenly took Ethan's hand and also shook it. "Well, I'm sure you've got better things to do today. Thanks for fixing my plumbing," she said brightly—though her cheeks turned pink when she realized what she'd just said.

"You're welcome," he drawled. "Anytime I can be of service, just ask."

"Yes, well, thanks again," she stammered, sliding her arm through his and dragging him off the porch. "Don't forget to plug in the ignition wires on your sled," she tightly whispered.

"Is that your snowmobile parked on the lake?" Jean-Paul asked as he followed them down the steps. "Because it's sitting in about two feet of water."

Ethan looked toward the lake. "All the rain last night must have buckled the ice near shore."

"We can help you drag it to high ground," Jean-Paul offered, then gave Ethan a sharp look when he realized the sled must have been parked there all night.

"Hey, where's my truck?" Anna asked. "And yours, Jean-Paul?"

"Up on the main highway," Damon told her, since Jean-Paul was too busy glowering at Ethan to answer. "The rain turned your gravel road to a sheet of ice. We walked in."

Anna realized she still had her arm looped through Ethan's, and immediately stepped away and marched back up on the porch. "I'm starving. Have you two eaten?"

Two? Since when did two brothers and one lover equal *two*? Dammit, he was hungry; he'd burned just as many calories as she had last night—probably more!

"We've eaten," Damon said, turning to follow her into the house. "And as your cupboards only contain birdseed, peanuts, and dog food, we should have had

Claire fill your truck with groceries instead of more of your belongings."

"Are you coming inside to call for a ride?" Jean-Paul asked Ethan, his foot on the bottom step.

"I'll call from my cabin."

"Your cabin?"

Ethan motioned across camp. "I'm renting a cabin from your sister, to save the drive around the lake every night."

That bit of news didn't settle very well with the older Canadian. Good, he hoped Jean-Paul gave Anna hell. She should have offered him lunch, dammit!

Ethan headed to his cabin with a negligent wave, wondering if there was enough water left in his tank for a shower. He didn't care that it would be luke-warm; he was going to shower, then fall into his rickety old bed and sleep until Monday morning.

He smiled at the realization Anna would have to stay awake to entertain her brothers, likely for the entire weekend. Served her right for not feeding him.

But before Ethan reached his cabin, he walked to the lake and stood staring at his snowmobile sitting up to the engine in water. He pulled out his cell phone, walked several paces until he got a strong signal, and dialed Alex's cell.

"Hello," Alex said after the fourth ring.

"I'm at Fox Run, and it looks like I'm spending the weekend here," Ethan said without preamble. "Unless you need me for anything."

"No, we're set," Alex assured him. "Paul's gone, too. He left last evening after he got a phone call, and then called me this morning to say he's out of town for the weekend."

"With Cynthia Pringle?" Ethan asked in surprise. "That boy moves way too fast when it comes to women," he said, though he'd only known Anna a week. "One of these days it's going to catch up with him."

"And exactly what are you doing at Fox Run all weekend?" Alex asked. "You're not moving too fast yourself, are you?"

"Two of Anna's brothers are down visiting her. I thought I'd spend some time at Loon Cove and get better acquainted with the books. Did you know there are four Segee brothers? No wonder André Segee was able to build his empire; he sired his own management team."

"I met one of them at a logging expo seven or eight years ago," Alex said. "The oldest, I think. Jean . . . something."

"Jean-Paul," Ethan supplied. "Yeah, I just met him. And for the record, I'm glad it was in broad daylight and not some dark alley. Both brothers look like they wouldn't break a sweat felling a tree with a dull ax. Give Tuck and Delaney a hug for me and tell them I'll take them to supper one night this week. I've been missing them."

Ethan heard a chuckle on the other end of the phone. "I'll tell them. And I'll probably stop in the mill Wednesday or Thursday to see how things are going. So, did you finally see Anna's ghost last night?"

"It was two guys looking for something they think Samuel Fox had hidden around here someplace."

"Who are they? And what are they looking for?"

"I didn't get to ask. They ran like rats abandoning ship when Anna started shooting at them."

"She *shot* at them?"

"Over their heads. She's got a bit of a temper, not to mention a reckless streak."

Alex chuckled again. "Maybe you should watch your own back," he suggested. "You did knock her flat on her ass a month ago. I don't know if it was thoughtful of you to leave her a shotgun or just plain dumb."

"This from the man who gave his lead-footed wife a truck when she can't even control a sewing machine."

"I put a block of wood under the gas peddle to limit her speed."

"And I gave Anna number four birdshot."

"Okay," Alex said with a laugh. "Ah . . . Ethan," he added, suddenly turning serious. "Keep a clear head around her, will you?"

"Why? What's up?"

"Dad."

"What? You think he's scheming again? With Anna and *me*?" Ethan asked incredulously. "He knows better."

"I'd bet our tree harvester that he knew all along Bishop had a female foreman at Loon Cove, and conveniently forgot to mention it to us."

Ethan looked toward the main house. Naw, Grady wouldn't . . . "He *knows* better," he repeated.

"It's just a feeling," Alex said. "I thought I should pass it on to you."

"Okay, thanks for the heads-up. I'll see you later this week."

"Later," Alex said.

Ethan closed his cell phone and continued looking toward Anna's house.

Naw, this wasn't a setup. His dad just forgot to tell him Bishop's foreman was female, and he just happened to find Ethan a rental on Anna's property . . . so his bachelor son would be working with the beautiful woman every day and sleeping less than two hundred yards away from her every night.

He sighed and started walking to his cabin. Dammit, he didn't need anyone interfering in his love life—*especially* his father!

Ethan opened one eye and saw it was half past two in the afternoon. He'd been asleep less than three hours, and the idiot pounding on his door was about to die—just as soon as he got the strength to get up.

"Knight!" came Damon's voice through the solid wood door. "Your snowmobile is sinking. Come, we'll help you get it out."

At the moment, he didn't care if the damn sled

sank to the bottom, but Ethan shoved himself out of bed. "It's kind of you to offer to help me," he said as he opened the door to the two Segee brothers, "but I'll just toss a rope around it and use Anna's truck to drag it ashore."

"Oh, but we insist," Damon said, crowding inside ahead of Jean-Paul. "You'll need to wade out to it, so we'll just make sure you don't accidently slip under the ice and not come back up."

Yeah, like he trusted either of them to watch his back. Ethan sat down with a resigned sigh and put on his boots, aware of the two brothers inspecting his living quarters.

"Anna's plan to restore Fox Run to a working mill is a pipe dream," Jean-Paul said as he turned from looking in the bathroom. "This place is past the point of no return. She'll have to raze all the buildings and start from scratch, and that's not cost-effective."

Ethan stood up and reached for his jacket. "Oh, I don't know," he said. "Anna seems to have a head for this sort of thing. I think that if she's determined to restore Fox Run, she will." He leveled his gaze on the older Segee. "With or without her family's support."

"She needs to sell it and come home," Jean-Paul growled.

"I believe Anna feels she is home," Ethan said, stepping onto the porch and picking up the coil of rope the men had brought with them. He turned to them. "Besides, at twenty-nine, don't you think that's her decision to make?"

Neither man answered; they strode off the porch and walked to the lake, Ethan trailing behind them. Now he understood why Anna was so hardheaded sometimes. She had to be just to stay afloat in her family. She definitely was drowning in familial love.

Damon took the coil of rope from Ethan when they reached the shoreline. "I'll feed you the rope as you wade out to your sled, then you can keep it upright while we pull you in."

Ethan looked at the snowmobile sitting on the sunken ice in two and a half feet of water, about a hundred and fifty feet from shore. Damn, the water looked cold. He looked toward the main house. "Where's Anna?" he asked.

"Taking a nap," Damon said. "She claims she's tired from working a lot of overtime for you lately."

Ethan turned back to the lake, shrugged out of his jacket, and rolled up his sleeves. "She's a bit of a micromanager," was all he said as he carefully made his way down the rocks lining the shore. He turned and held out his hand. "Do you happen to know where she picked up that nasty habit?" he asked as Damon handed him one end of the rope.

That question got him pleasant smiles from both men. "She comes by it honestly," Damon said, uncoiling the rope.

Ethan stepped into the freezing water, sucked in his breath as it seeped through his pants and boots, and carefully started feeling his way toward the sled.

"Maybe that's why *bébé* has such rotten luck with men," Jean-Paul said softly in French, his comment obviously aimed at his brother. "She has no tolerance for bossy boyfriends, and no respect for those who let her boss them."

So Anna had a bit of a problem with bossy boyfriends, did she? Not that that was news. "Why do you call her *baby* and *beautiful child?*" Ethan asked. "She's a bit past that, don't you think?"

He glanced back to see Damon shrug. "It's what we've called her since the day she arrived," Damon told him as he fed out more rope. "Can you tie it around both skis?" he asked when Ethan reached the snowmobile.

Numb from the waist down, Ethan nodded, gritted his chattering teeth, and reached below the surface to slide the end of the rope through the ski handles and tie it off. He centered the knot so the pull would put even pressure on both skis, then walked to the side of the sled and turned the handlebars toward shore. "Okay," he said, planting his feet as best he could on the slippery ice. "I'm ready."

Both men had their own jackets off and their sleeves rolled up, and both took hold of the rope and started pulling. The sled pivoted with a sudden jerk, splashing freezing water onto Ethan's chest. Growling through his teeth, he righted the machine when it started to tilt, and slowly walked beside it as they dragged it to shore. But with less then thirty feet to go, the sled suddenly stopped moving. Ethan looked up to see the men standing with their hands on their hips, smiling at him.

It wasn't a nice smile, either.

"Do you have a sister?" Jean-Paul asked.

"No. Two brothers," Ethan said as pleasantly as he could, considering the numbness in his legs had started shooting needles of pain up his spine. "Why?"

"Because having a sister might help you understand what we wish to . . . impart to you," Jean-Paul said.

"And that would be?"

"Two things, really," Damon clarified. "A promise from us, and a sincerely given warning."

"Shall we start with the warning?" Ethan suggested tightly.

Jean-Paul nodded. "Very well. We feel we should warn you about Anna's . . . ah, trail of broken hearts, shall we say?"

"She has a trail of them?"

Jean-Paul nodded. "She doesn't do it on purpose," he said. "She just breaks men's hearts."

"We think it's because of a childhood crush she had on a boy when she was ten or eleven," Damon explained. "It's like she measures each man she meets to him, and none of them can live up to his memory."

"And so you're warning me to . . . ?"

"To guard your own heart, Knight," Damon offered.

"She doesn't do it on purpose," Jean-Paul repeated.

"Yeah, yeah, I got that," Ethan muttered, the needles of pain now shooting across his shoulders as his muscles violently knotted. "Thanks for the heads-up. And your promise?"

Damon's sinister smile returned as he folded his arms over his chest. "We wish to give you our collective promise that if you break our Anna's heart, we will hunt you down, crush every bone in your body, and feed your guts to the wolves. Then we'll go after your family, and not stop until NorthWoods Timber is nothing more than a memory around here."

O-kay, that was certainly plain enough to understand.

Ethan nodded. "Both points taken, gentlemen."

They also nodded, reached down and picked up the rope again, and finished dragging Ethan and his snowmobile to shore.

"The lane seems to have melted enough to travel, so we're off to bring Anna her truck, then go buy her some groceries," Damon said as he tossed down the rope and unrolled his sleeves. "Can we pick up something for you in town?"

"A very large bottle of bourbon would be nice," Ethan said, shrugging on his jacket and heading to his cabin. "You can just leave it outside my door."

Chapter Twelve

The warm front that arrived on Friday had continued straight through the weekend, melting the snow and turning the plowed areas to mud. Ethan sat basking in the brilliant afternoon sun with his feet propped on his porch rail, swirling an icicle in his glass of bourbon as he contemplated Anna Segee.

He had never known a woman like her—not in his everyday dealings, and definitely not in the bedroom. It didn't seem to matter what she put her mind to; Anna approached life with the vitality of a powder keg waiting to explode. She *had* exploded in his arms night before last, and he was still experiencing lingering shock waves. Anna Segee was the first woman who not only matched him in bed, she had come damn close to making him lose his infamous control.

Which was why he'd better find a way to tone her down before their little affair killed them both.

Ethan took a leisurely sip of his bourbon and watched the two Segee brothers say good-bye to Anna as they stood between Jean-Paul's pickup and her late-model SUV, both vehicles covered to their roofs in mud. The old pickup Anna had bought from Gaylen Dempsey was parked beside Ethan's cabin, since she'd loaned it to him to go to Loon Cove earlier today.

Life was good, he decided as he lifted his glass to the departing Canadians, their tires making an obscene sucking sound as they oozed up the lane leading to the main road. "Good-bye and good riddance, you overprotective bastards," he said through his pleasant smile as Damon Segee nodded in return, his own expression conveying the promise to feed Ethan's guts to the wolves.

"Got any more of whatever you're drinking?" Anna asked as she made her way up the muddy path to his cabin, finally choosing to plod through the rotting snow when she nearly fell. "I hope it's at least ninety proof."

"Hard weekend?" he asked, leaning over to pull up another straight-back chair beside him. He handed her his glass when she sat down with an exhausted sigh and propped her feet up on the rail beside his. "I guess so," he said with a chuckle when she downed the rest of his drink in one gulp.

"I nearly took your shotgun to them," she said,

wiping her mouth with the back of her hand as she held the glass out for him to refill. "They had me up until midnight last night trying to persuade me to follow them back to Quebec today. They even promised they'd make Daddy let me open a specialty lumber division at our Debec mill." She shook her head. "They just don't get it. I don't want anyone *giving* me anything; I want to earn it on my own."

"They're just being brothers," he told her, setting the half-empty bottle of bourbon back on the porch. He picked up what was left of the icicle he'd broken off the eave, waiting until she took another long gulp before he could drop it in the glass. "I imagine they were a bit shocked to see what you'd spent your inheritance on."

She looked at him questioningly.

"Didn't you buy Fox Run with the money you inherited from your vitamin-popping grandparents?"

She merely shrugged. "What did the three of you talk about when you pulled your sled off the ice yesterday?"

"They didn't tell you?"

She snorted. "If it doesn't further their cause, they don't tell me anything."

Ethan took the glass from her. "They mentioned something about a trail of broken hearts you'd left behind in Quebec. Though they did say you didn't do it on purpose," he added with a chuckle.

She dropped her feet and sat up straight, gaping at him.

He took another sip, letting the bourbon slide down his throat more slowly before he said, "And while I was standing knee-deep in freezing water, they also explained what would happen to me and my family if I broke your heart." He raised the glass in salute. "Wasn't that friendly of them?"

"You didn't take them seriously."

"I always take threats seriously, Segee."

She snatched the glass out of his hand and downed the entire contents before holding it out for him to refill.

He shook his head and took the glass from her, setting it on the porch beside the bottle. "You're wasting good bourbon. And tomorrow's Monday, and I've heard the Knights have been known to fire people who show up to work with a hangover."

"I think I can handle a couple of—" She stopped in midsentence, her attention turning to the pickup pulling up beside the cabin. "Isn't that your brother Paul?" she asked. "And Jane. Jane Trott is with him!" she said excitedly if not smugly, standing up and rushing down the steps.

Paul got out of the truck, but Jane didn't. Ethan stood up, accepting the fact he wasn't going to get Anna to himself anytime soon, and watched a grim-faced Paul say something to his tearful passenger before he got out and walked to the porch. Anna had rounded Paul's truck, opened Jane's door, and was quietly talking to her.

"What's up?" Ethan asked Paul.

"Jane and I got married yesterday in Bangor."

Ethan could only stare at his brother in silence.

"She's four months pregnant. And we're just coming from telling her parents," Paul said, disgust in his voice. "They went ballistic, saying this was all they needed on top of Pete's accident." He looked up at Ethan, his expression defensive. "I didn't marry her out of obligation. I love Jane."

Ethan shoved his hands in his pockets. "I believe you. Congratulations, then. Have you been over to tell Dad, Alex and Sarah, and the kids?"

Paul shook his head and finally walked up on the porch, bringing his gaze level with Ethan's. "After what happened at Jane's house, I couldn't talk her into going over to tell them." He shook his head. "I don't know why, but she's afraid of you and Alex. She agreed to come here because we thought you were still at home, but she started bawling again the moment she saw you." He gave Ethan an inquiring look. "We need someplace to stay for a few days until we can find our own place, or until Jane calms down enough that we can move in with Alex and Sarah at the sporting camps."

"Why is she afraid of us?" Ethan asked, surprised. He and Alex had never been anything but nice to Jane.

"Because she's somehow come up with this crazy notion that everyone—and you and Alex in particular—will think she got pregnant so I'd have to marry her." Paul made a helpless gesture with his hands.

"Because of Alex's first wife, and ... and Pamela Sant," he finished softly, his eyes not quite meeting Ethan's.

Ethan looked toward Paul's truck and saw that Anna had coaxed Jane out of her seat and, with her arm around the still-sobbing woman, was leading her up the muddy path to her house.

He looked back at Paul and shrugged. "It's obvious we don't have a good track record when it comes to girlfriends." He reached out and pulled Paul into a bear of a hug. "Congratulations, brother," he growled, roughly patting him on the back. "You and Jane will do well together. She's a good woman."

Paul snorted, though he returned Ethan's hug just as robustly. "Not according to her parents, she's not. Her mom actually had the nerve to compare Jane to Madeline Fox."

"*The* Madeline Fox?" Ethan repeated with pretend shock, heading down off the porch. "Madeline may have slept with every man in town, and gotten several of them to marry her before she had to move on to greener pastures," he said as he walked with Paul to Anna's house, "but the one man who got her pregnant was the only one she couldn't get to the altar." He threw his arm over his brother's shoulder. "There's something ironic in that. Don't worry, we'll make Jane feel welcome."

Paul heaved a heavy sigh of relief. "So we can stay here for a couple of days? Anna shouldn't mind, seeing how she and Jane are friends."

"I've got the only cabin that's livable, and it's so small you need to go outside to change your mind," Ethan said, thinking fast. He stopped and looked at Paul. "I tell you what. You and Jane can have it, and I'll bunk with Anna—as long as you give me your word you won't make our arrangement common knowledge in town."

Paul raised a brow. "You and *Anna?*"

"You got a problem with that?"

"No, no problem," Paul said, clearly amused.

"But let's not mention this to the women just yet," Ethan added, climbing the stairs of the main house. "I'll tell Anna this evening, when I show up with my toothbrush in hand." And the brand-new box of condoms he'd driven all the way to Greenville to buy this morning.

"I suggested you invite Paul to dinner so you could talk things over," Anna said as she led Jane to the house. "I didn't mean for the two of you to run off and get married."

"Paul was adamant," Jane said with a final sniffle. "When I called him Friday to invite him to dinner Saturday evening, he rushed over the minute he hung up the phone." She looked at Anna through red-rimmed eyes while she wiped her nose with a mangled tissue. "He must have heard something in my voice, because he arrived at my sister's house with a panicked look on his face. And I just burst into tears and blurted out that I was pregnant."

Anna led her to the kitchen, eased her down in a chair at the table, and put the kettle on to boil. "What did Paul do then?" she asked, keeping one eye on Jane as she got down Grammy Fox's beautiful old china teapot.

"He . . . he was wonderful," Jane said with a stifled sob. "He pulled me into his arms and told me everything would be okay. Then he helped me pack a few of my clothes, and we waited until my sister got back from Bangor—Jenny comes home weekends to spend time with her kids. Anyway," she said with a steadying sigh, "the moment she walked in the door, Paul hustled me out to his truck, telling Jenny he was taking me on a minivacation until Monday. I had calmed down by then, so I don't think she suspected anything. She was just happy to see me and Paul together again. Pete's doing well, by the way. He's getting out of the hospital Tuesday or Wednesday, and should be able to attend the benefit dance on Saturday, though he'll be in a wheelchair."

"That's great news," Anna said, opening a cupboard and taking down one of the five boxes of maple leaf cookies Claire had sent with Damon and Jean-Paul. She carried the box to the table. "Is this what you wanted, Jane?" she asked softly. "For Paul to marry you?"

"I don't know," Jane said in an equally soft whisper. She lifted her chin. "But I love him. And he says he loves me, and that he's been miserable since we broke up."

"And Cynthia What's-her-name?"

"He said he was just trying to make me jealous, that there wasn't ever anything between him and Cynthia Pringle. They didn't . . . they never . . ." She looked down at the table. "He said he told Cynthia right from the start that he still had feelings for me, and he told me they were just friends and she was helping him make me jealous." She looked back up at Anna. "Cynthia's moving to Boston next week. She got a job as a paralegal at some big law firm down there."

"Honest to God," Anna said, shaking her head, "I swear men are denser than dirt. Look at what the two of you went through over a simple misunderstanding."

"It's all my fault," Jane said, rushing to her new husband's defense. "I made such a scene when I saw him talking to Cynthia that day in the Drooling Moose."

Anna smiled. "Well, maybe a little. Just because Paul was talking to another woman doesn't mean he was going to leave you for her. You all went to school together, didn't you?"

"Cynthia stole my boyfriend when we were in eighth grade," Jane said in her own defense. "She's really pretty."

"No prettier than you are," Anna said, going to the stove when the kettle started whistling. "So okay, you're married. Now what?" she asked as she poured the boiling water over the tea bags in the teapot.

"I have no idea." Jane gave a deep sigh as she

opened the box of maple cookies. "We didn't think past getting married. And our one-night honeymoon," she added with a cheeky grin. "Paul splurged for a beautiful motel room, and took me out to a really nice restaurant for dinner."

"And you said your mom and dad exploded when you told them?"

Jane merely nodded, since her mouth was full of cookie.

"And you haven't told Paul's family yet?"

"Uh-uh," Jane said, swallowing quickly. "I couldn't survive another scene like that right now." Her eyes clouding with worry, she glanced toward the living room. "Do you think Ethan's out there giving him hell?" she asked in a stricken whisper. "Where will we stay tonight?"

"Right here," Anna said, placing the teapot on the table and sitting down to pour the tea. "I can have one of the upstairs bedrooms ready in twenty minutes. Though you might want to put the mattress on the floor, as the old bedsprings squeak," she said with a crooked smile, bobbing her eyebrows.

Jane's face turned from blotchy pink to blistering red.

"It's going to be okay," Anna said soothingly, reaching out and covering Jane's hand. "It doesn't matter what anyone thinks, only what you and Paul feel for each other. If people whisper and speculate, just ignore the gossiping bastards. And get your revenge on them by being blissfully happy." Anna jumped up and gave her friend a fierce, tender hug. "I'm glad for you, Jane. Everything's going to be okay. Your mom and dad will come around once they see how happy you are."

"Rumor has it your cupboards are full of human food, Segee," Ethan said as two sets of heavy footsteps tromped through the front door. "And Paul and I are starved."

He walked into the kitchen and directly up to a wide-eyed, pale-faced Jane, then pulled her into his arms. "Welcome to the family," he said, giving Anna a wink over the startled woman's back. He smiled into Jane's eyes. "I can't decide if my brother really is smart after all, or if it's just dumb luck that he got the prettiest girl in Oak Grove to marry him." He gave Jane a brotherly kiss on her blushing forehead, then looked back in her eyes. "And if he ever gives you any trouble, you come to me, okay? I'll help him see things your way."

Anna's heart did a double thump. She had known there was something she liked about Ethan Knight. The guy could charm the bark off a pine tree if he had a mind to—or the nightie off his female foreman. He'd certainly put Jane at ease, if the shy smile she gave her new brother-in-law was any indication.

"Maple leaf cookies!" Paul said, snatching the open box off the table. "I've been trying for years to get Mary to stock these in her store," he said, stuffing a whole one in his mouth.

Anna took the box from him, closed it up, and set

it in the cupboard. "You'll spoil your supper," she said, turning back around to give him a big hug. "Congratulations."

"Thank you," Paul said, returning her hug before stepping away and gazing around the kitchen. "Wow, it's like a time capsule in here." He walked over to Jane and put his arm around her. "Feeling better, sweetie?" he asked softly. "We can stay here until we decide what to do."

"I—I know," Jane whispered before taking a deep breath. "You can bring in my suitcase and take it upstairs while I help Anna fix dinner. Then could you fill the wood box so we can have a fire in the hearth tonight?"

Anna was pleased that Jane had apparently decided to begin her marriage as she intended to go on, giving her new husband a to-do list to keep him out of their hair.

"Uh-oh, it looks like the honeymoon's over," Ethan said, shoving his brother toward the living room with a laugh. "We've just been told that if we want to eat, we have to earn it."

"Oh my God," Jane squeaked, her hands going to her mortified cheeks. "Ethan thinks I was ordering him around, too."

Anna waved Jane's concern away. "He needs the practice." She opened the fridge. "Let's see what I've got in here that's quick. How about chop suey?" she asked, taking out the hamburger. "We can throw that together in no time."

"Anna? A bunch of chickadees just hopped through that hole in your window."

"Oh, they're my pets," Anna assured her, walking up to the window and holding out her finger. "Samuel Fox must have tamed them." Bold little Charlie ignored her finger and fluttered onto her shoulder instead.

"It's really sad what happened to Samuel," Jane said, holding out her hand to another one of the chickadees. "What with him living out here all alone, and no one finding him at the bottom of that ravine for two days." The chickadee hopped on her hand. "Old Samuel always seemed sad and lonely, whenever I saw him in town," she continued, picking up a shelled peanut and holding it out for the bird. "His wife died before I was even born, and his daughter hardly ever came to see him. I think he had a granddaughter, but she disappeared years ago."

Anna set Charlie back on the shelf and washed her hands. "Yeah, I think of Samuel every time I drive by that spot. I'll open a bottle of wine so we can toast your nuptials."

"I can't," Jane said, setting her own bird down and washing her hands. "I'm pregnant, remember?"

"Then we'll have the wine and you can have milk."

Between the two of them, they had dinner on the table in less than an hour. And the wonderfully obedient men had the wood box filled and a roaring fire going in the hearth by the time the food was ready. Since they were taking orders so well, Anna had them move the table into the living room so they could dine in front of the beautiful fire. Bear thought it was a wonderful idea, since he could lie on his bed and eat whatever his sappy-eyed begging could get him.

By the time everyone's bellies were full, some thirty minutes later, there seemed to be an epidemic of yawns going around. Anna was dead on her feet, and it was all she could do to carry the dishes into the kitchen.

"Paul and Jane are taking a walk before they turn in for the night," Ethan said, carrying in more dishes behind her. "Can we leave these until tomorrow?" he asked as he turned Anna around and pulled her into his arms. "I'm beat."

"You got to sleep all weekend while I had to entertain my brothers."

He cradled her head to his chest. "Quit whining, Segee. What doesn't kill you only makes you stronger."

"Oh, great, a philosophizing lover." She yawned, snuggling into his rock-solid warmth and wishing she could cuddle against him all night. But thanks to her houseguests, she would have to lie in bed all alone, and think of Ethan lying all alone in his own bed just two hundred yards away.

Maybe she could sneak over to his cabin once the newlyweds had gone to sleep.

"You haven't fallen asleep on me, have you?"

Ethan asked, ducking his head to see her face. "Come on, I'm taking you to bed," he said, dropping one hand behind her knees and sweeping her off her feet.

"You are not taking me anywhere," she hissed, squirming in his arms as he strode through the living room and up the stairs. "I have company."

But she might as well have been a gnat caught in a spider's web for all the good it did her. Ethan's smile turned darkly promising as he carried her into the bedroom and dropped her on her bed.

Anna immediately rolled off the opposite side and pointed at the door. "Out, before they come back and find you up here."

He pulled something from his pocket and held it up, and Anna saw that it was a toothbrush. "I packed some of my stuff and brought it over," he said, using the toothbrush to point at a small duffel bag on the floor by her bureau. "I gave Paul and Jane my cabin, and told them I'd bunk with you."

"You what!"

He tossed his toothbrush on the bureau, keeping himself between her and the door. "Newlyweds need their privacy," he said, crossing his arms over his chest. "And if my brother's getting some tonight, I intend to get some, too."

"*Getting* some?" She rounded the end of the bed and stepped up to him. "Nobody is supposed to know about us."

"Paul and Jane won't say anything. I have their word."

Anna picked up his duffel bag and shoved it at his chest. "Out."

"The damage is done, Anna," he said, tossing the bag back on the floor. "They already know about us, and they're probably already doing it in my bed." He bobbed his eyebrows. "So let's you and me do it in your bed. I've grown quite fond of your flowery sheets," he whispered, pulling her against him and holding her head to his chest. "I drove all the way to Greenville this morning to buy more condoms. That should tell you I'm determined to keep our affair quiet."

Anna sighed, half aroused as she drew in his wonderful scent while listening to his strong heart beating against her ear. Oh, what the hell. She should heed her own advice to Jane and not worry what any of the gossiping bastards in town might say if they found out. She could "do it" on the hood of her truck in the middle of town if she wanted to.

"No, you can't," Ethan said with a strangled laugh as he suddenly held her away, his expression incredulous.

Dammit, she was so tired she was thinking out loud. She wrapped her arms around his neck and pulled his mouth down to hers. "How many did you buy?" she asked, her lips just inches from his.

"Considering how many we went through the other night," he whispered, moving his own lips closer, "and deciding we need to slow down before we kill ourselves, I only bought three dozen."

"Oh, good, we can add them to the two boxes my stepmom packed in the stuff she sent me," Anna said, her lips brushing his. "Along with some sexy new underwear," she whispered, finally kissing him—passionately enough for him to know she had no intention of *ever* slowing down where he was concerned.

Chapter Thirteen

You go start the generator and turn on the water heater," Anna muttered into her pillow. "I'm right behind you."

"You are *so* lying," Ethan said from beside her, not moving.

Anna turned her head just enough to open one eye and look at him. "Not that I'm keeping a diary or anything," she said, "but how many times was that last night?"

"Four and a half."

"A half?" she repeated, rolling onto her back. "How can there be a half?"

"You slept through one of the times, so it only counts as half," he said, sliding his legs over the side of the bed and sitting up with a groan.

"You don't consider that cheating?" she asked with a laugh, studying the play of muscles on his back as he stretched his arms over his head.

He turned and grinned at her. "I found a rule book on affairs next to the condoms in the drugstore, which I read cover to cover over the weekend so I'd be up to speed. And rule number seven clearly states that if one of the 'affairees' can't stay awake, it's perfectly legal for the other participant to take full advantage of the situation. But it only counts as a half." He finally stood up, not the least bit concerned with his beautiful nakedness.

Anna sat up, clasping the comforter to her chest as she watched him get dressed. "I want to see this rule book," she said, silently marveling at his lean, graceful strength—not to mention his amazing endurance.

He faced her as he tucked his shirt into his pants, his expression deadpan serious. "Sorry. It's strictly for men. It states in bold letters right on the first page that the Male Society of Self-Preservation says we can't let women read it. You'll have to buy the women's version, which is probably in the feminine aisle. Come on, get up," he said when she fell back against her pillow in laughter. "It's going to look suspicious if we both show up late for work."

"I'm calling in sick."

The comforter started sliding away despite Anna holding on tightly, which resulted in her being pulled back up into a sitting position. "Do I have to carry you downstairs and throw you in a snowbank?"

"I don't like being manhandled."

He bent at the waist as he finished buttoning his shirt, getting his face really close to hers. "Yes, you do," he said. "In fact, you goad me into manhandling you every chance you get." He straightened with a derisive chuckle. "Your brothers don't know squat about you, Segee. They believe you don't care for bossy boyfriends, but that you don't respect boyfriends *you* can boss around."

"They said that? To you?"

"No, they were talking between themselves in French while I was freezing my tail off in two feet of icy water."

Anna wasn't surprised Ethan knew French, considering half the workers around here were Canadian. "I *don't* like bossy men," she said, lifting her chin with a haughty glare.

"Sure you do." Sitting down on the edge of the bed to put on his socks, he shot her a wink over his shoulder. "You feel all feminine and stuff when I overpower you with my manly strength, and make you writhe and quiver beneath me."

"Of all the—" She threw her pillow at him. "You got your psychology degree in a cereal box!"

He ducked and was suddenly on her, pressing her into the mattress and pinning her hands beside her head, using his weight to hold her still. "It said in my book of affairs," he teased, "that if we men don't sweep a girl off her feet and keep her off balance with wild, mind-blowing sex, we might as well pack it in and go home, and consider ourselves lucky to have escaped emasculation."

Anna didn't know whether to smack him or kiss him, so she burst out laughing again. She'd never seen this playful side of Ethan; in fact, she hadn't known he even had a sense of humor, *especially* a warped one. The scary part was, she worried there might be a grain of truth in his teasing her about liking manly men. If she still got to be the boss, of course.

"I want to make up for that half a time."

He shook his head. "It won't work if we're both awake. We'll still be a half off."

Anna snapped her eyes shut and started snoring.

"Come on, lazybones," he said, shoving off the bed and taking the comforter with him. "You have a crew of thirty men just dying to spend their day with you bossing them around."

Anna rolled off the bed and sashayed past him, utterly naked but for her smile, and pulled a fiery red satin bra and matching boxer panties out of her bureau drawer. She turned, dangling them from her fingers. "I'm taking a long lunch today," she drawled in her best Mae West voice. "And driving down to Greenville to get me one of them books on affairs for women. I bet it comes with a set of handcuffs," she called after him when he strode out the door—adjusting the fit of his pants.

Anna threw herself back on the bed with a laugh, gathering up Ethan's pillow and drawing in his scent with a satisfied sigh.

* * *

Ethan sat with his feet propped on his battered old desk at Loon Cove Lumber, watching Anna through the window as she stood outside talking to Keith. "What did you say?" he asked Paul, forcing his mind away from her fiery red underwear and bringing it back to his brother.

"Jane wants to keep working," Paul said, frowning. "And I told her I'd rather she stay at home."

"You don't have a home yet. And if you live at the sporting camps with everyone, Jane will feel like a houseguest. Sarah's too efficient when it comes to cooking and housekeeping, so what's Jane supposed to do all day while you're at work? Trust me, a woman needs to be busy."

"But I don't want her working."

"Have you forgotten what it was like when Alex's first wife came to live with us? Charlotte kept trying to nest, but Mom had already created a comfortable nest." Ethan shook his head. "Two women sharing a house doesn't work unless one of them is gone all day, and even then it's iffy. Nesting is programmed into women from birth."

"Then we'll get our own place," Paul countered. "I have enough saved to put a down payment on a house, and Jane can stay home and . . . and nest," he said with a dismissive wave.

"But what's wrong with her working?" Ethan asked, dropping his feet to the floor and leaning his arms on the desk. "Last I heard, pregnancy wasn't a disability. Working as Dr. Betters's receptionist is interesting and respectable, and Jane will feel like she's contributing to your household. Didn't you say she's worried everyone will think she got pregnant so you'd marry her and she'd get a free ride through life?"

"Well, yeah. But she's taken a leave of absence to watch her sister's kids while Pete's in the hospital. She just has to tell Betters she's not going back."

"But *why?*" Ethan asked with growing impatience. "What's wrong with her working?"

"I am quite capable of supporting my wife."

"Ah," Ethan said with a sigh, settling back in his chair. "So this isn't about Jane, it's about you."

"Me?"

"You Tarzan, her Jane? You bring home the bacon and she cooks it. That way people will see what a good provider you are, and everything will be neat and tidy and picture perfect."

"It worked for Mom and Dad."

"A generation ago." Ethan leaned forward on his desk again. "Things have changed since Mom and Dad got married. If Jane wants to work for Betters, then let her, and to hell with what people think." He shrugged. "After the kid's born, then you can see how she feels about working."

"Everyone who goes to Betters's office is sick," Paul said desperately, knowing he was being unreasonable.

"But that's—" Ethan straightened and looked out the window, noting that Anna and Keith had disappeared. "Do you hear that?"

Paul also looked out the window. "I don't hear anything."

"Exactly. The saws have stopped and everything's gone quiet. Dammit," he growled, heading for the door. "What in hell broke now?"

Ethan stepped outside to a completely deserted yard. There wasn't one man in sight, and every piece of machinery looked like it had been abandoned right in the middle of a job.

"Over there," Paul said, pointing toward the massive rows of timber that had been stockpiled over the winter. "I just saw two men running that way."

The only thing behind all that timber was the Kent River, which defined the mill's eastern property line. Ethan suddenly heard the distinct sound of an excavator start up, listened for several seconds, and started running toward it.

"Something's happening on the river," Paul said, loping beside him. "The ice must be going out."

"Or jamming," Ethan said, picking up his pace.

Spring thaw, coupled with the rain they'd had over the weekend, would have swelled the river and broken the ice into huge chunks—all of them being pushed downriver with amazing force. If the ice was building up against their timber, was somebody using the excavator to hold it back? Or were they simply moving equipment out of harm's way?

Ethan rounded the end of a row and came to an abrupt halt. His entire crew—standing on wooden pallets, on rotting snowbanks, and on top of the timber—was watching the mill's metal-lagged excavator make its way through the rising river water littered with floating slabs of ice.

"What's going on?" Ethan asked the closest man, as he scanned the crowd for Anna. "Why is the excavator going out there?" he continued, noticing that the pulp hook that was usually on the end of its boom had been replaced with a large bucket. "Where in hell is Anna?"

"In there," the man said, pointing at the excavator. He then pointed upriver. "She's going after that dog."

Ethan's knees nearly gave out the moment he realized what Anna was attempting to do. The dog—which looked confused and terribly frightened—was stranded on a slab of ice in the middle of the Kent River as the powerful current pushed at the building jam with slow, grinding momentum. The Kent had overrun its banks, effectively flooding a good three or four acres of the mill yard, and it was virtually impossible to tell where the yard ended and the river began.

Ethan found Keith standing at the water's edge and grabbed him by the shoulder. "Get on the radio and call her back," he ordered. "She's got no business going out there."

"She's okay, Ethan," Keith said calmly, turning to watch Anna. "She knows where the yard ends, and she's watching her markers." He glanced upriver toward the dog, which was now barking at the men on shore. "She's gonna reach out with the bucket and try to snag the slab of ice he's on, and work it close enough for us to grab him." He looked back at Ethan and smiled. "Anna could thread a needle with that machine, she's that good. She'll be okay."

Ethan snatched the walkie-talkie off Keith's belt and keyed the mike. "Get in here," he snapped. "Now."

Nothing but static answered him.

"She's too busy to use the radio," Keith said, nodding toward the excavator.

Ethan watched in helpless silence as Anna pivoted the boom to her right and dropped the bucket's sharp teeth into a large chunk of ice that had rammed into the excavator. She gave the machine full throttle, sending black smoke into the air with a deafening roar as she tried to push the slab away. Its weighted momentum caused the excavator to shudder and come to a grinding halt, the heavy knuckles of the giant boom rattling loudly as the bucket's teeth chittered across the polished ice. Using her hand levers to nudge the slab with the bucket, and her foot pedals to urge the lags forward, Anna slowly worked her way free as she finally swung the ice out of her way.

Ethan wiped beads of sweat off his forehead with an unsteady hand. If Anna survived this, he was going to throttle her. He swung around and started running back toward the office, ignoring Paul's shout asking where he was going. He reached the saw shed, jumped up on the forklift loader, and started it up. He dumped its load of sawlogs on the ground, then sped down between the rows of timber.

Several men scrambled out of his path as Ethan drove straight into the flooding water, using the forks on the loader to plow his way through the ice slabs as he angled upstream of Anna. He wanted to kill her for risking her life for a stupid dog!

He picked up the radio mike in the loader. "You need to turn back. Half the banking could already be washed away. You're traveling blind, risking your life over a damn dog," he growled, completely failing to contain his anger when a large slab of ice slammed into him, pushing his loader sideways with a shuddering jolt.

"*You* go back," came her reply, her voice brisk and impatient. "That machine isn't heavy enough, and you're going to roll over. I'm okay, Ethan. I can feel if I'm on solid ground or not," she said with maddening calm. "And I'm almost close enough to reach the chunk of ice he's on. Go back. Please."

Ethan threw down the mike and gave his loader more throttle, spinning the large rubber tires in the gravel beneath the ice-laden water, churning up frothing mud as the machine fought for purchase. He finally got himself positioned just above Anna and used the forks to push away slabs of ice heading for her, all the time watching her inside the cab, looking small and vulnerable as she crept closer to the edge of the main flow of water.

The lags on her rig were completely submerged,

the water beginning to lap against the engine housing. Ethan had never been so scared in his life. The dog—a pup, really—stood with its tail tucked between its hind legs and continued to bark frantically as the ice it was on slowly came closer. Ethan watched Anna extend the boom to its full reach, then roll the bucket out until the four-inch teeth were several feet from the edge of the slab.

He saw her look back and forth at the trees lining the river's original bank and slowly ease the excavator forward to intercept the approaching dog. Ethan also inched forward, lifting his forks and rolling them downward, then plunging them into a large chunk of ice. He reversed gears and gave it full throttle, dragging the ice back far enough to open a spot for Anna to bring in the dog.

She finally snagged the slab it was on. The excavator roared, billowing smoke from its stack as Anna fought the current's force. The bucket's teeth slipped free several times but she quickly resnagged the slab, moving it inch by painful inch toward shore. The dog had scurried as far back as he could on the ice and was cowered into a tight shivering ball, too frightened to bark anymore.

Somebody banged on the door of his idling loader, and Ethan looked over to see Paul standing on the ladder, looking through the window.

"I'll ride the forks while you take me out to him," Paul shouted. "Then I'll grab him and you can bring us back in."

Ethan opened the window. "No, you could fall off and go under. You're not risking your life." He checked how Anna was doing, just as the pup slid off the back edge of the ice and disappeared beneath the water.

He shot back up like a bobber, splashing frantically, and Anna lifted her bucket off the slab, curled it inward, and swung the boom toward the struggling dog. The bucket dipped below the surface behind him, then suddenly reappeared with the frightened pup inside, water and slush pouring out. Ethan heard a loud roar of cheering erupt behind him.

Keeping the bucket just inches above the water, Anna swung it toward Paul, who was wading through the thigh-deep water toward the terrified dog, and she began creeping the excavator toward shore.

As soon as Paul got near, the pup leapt out of the bucket and splashed into his arms, licking his face as it squirmed and whined and most likely peed on him. The crew's cheering grew louder as Anna sped toward shore, now that she didn't have her frightened cargo. Ethan shut off his loader, jumped to the ground, and strode through six inches of freezing water to the stopped excavator. He jumped up on the lag, tore open the door, grabbed the front of Anna's jacket in his fist, and hauled her out.

She yelped in surprise, then started struggling as he dragged her onto dry land. "Ethan!" she hissed, her fingers digging into the arm holding her. "What in hell's your problem!"

He let her go and swung around to face her. "You're my problem! You had no business going after that dog!"

She blinked up at him, then took a deep breath and tugged down the front of her jacket. "You're angry."

Keith approached them, but one look from Ethan and the man beat a hasty retreat. Ethan turned his glare on his suddenly red-faced foreman. "You do not drive into a flooded river to rescue a damn dog," he said, enunciating each word in an attempt to hold his temper in check.

"The excavator's heavy enough that I knew the current wouldn't affect it," she said, her eyes wide with disbelief. "And I could feel the ground was solid beneath me. I couldn't just leave that dog out there, Ethan. It would have drowned or been crushed to death."

What was it with her! Didn't she realize that the bank could have given way at any moment, and the excavator could have fallen into the river with her trapped inside? His hands itched to grab her and shake her, so Ethan balled them at his sides. "You put our equipment and people at risk. You're fired," he ground out. "Clear out your desk and be off this property in ten minutes."

"*What?*" Her eyes suddenly narrowed. "You can't fire me for this."

"I just did," he shot back. "A mill is no place for anyone with a death wish, Segee. Ten minutes."

He strode through the dumbstruck crew, his demeanor daring them to say anything.

"You can't really mean to fire her," Paul said as he walked beside Ethan, the large, shivering pup still in his arms. "We're talking about Anna here."

"She could have been killed."

"But she wasn't," Paul countered, shifting his passenger. "Everything worked out."

Ethan stopped and glared at his brother. "And just that quickly," he said, snapping his fingers, "it could have turned nasty. Some of those slabs were large enough to tip over that excavator, or the vibration of its engine could have caved in the riverbank. She'd have been trapped inside in twenty feet of freezing water."

"Then dock her two weeks' pay or something, but don't fire her. Christ, you're sleeping with the woman."

And that was exactly the problem. Ethan couldn't get the opposing images out of his head of Anna naked and sweaty and sated, clinging to him and laughing, and then of her lifeless body floating face up in the windshield of the sunken excavator, her beautiful eyes blank with death.

"I doubt that I am anymore," he growled, walking away.

Chapter Fourteen

We'll go on strike," Keith said, carrying a box for Anna as they walked to her truck. "Ethan shouldn't have fired you. We'll get him to change his mind."

Anna opened the back door of her SUV and set her box inside, then turned to take Keith's box. "No, I don't want you doing anything to retaliate. I would have fired anyone who did what I did, now that I think about it. Ethan's well within his rights."

"But Tom Bishop hired you because he knew the mill was heading for disaster, and that if you couldn't get us back on track, nobody could."

"You and the crew have had four months to catch on, Keith, and you'll make Loon Cove a good foreman. And Ethan knows more about millwork than he's been letting on. He's got a good head on his shoulders, and he's fair with the workers."

"That's it? You're just gonna walk away without a fight?"

"I have to." She touched her friend's sleeve. "I'd like to think I'm big enough to admit when I'm wrong. Maybe I'll go hit up Clay Porter for a job before he finds out why I was fired."

Keith immediately shook his head. "Porter's okay to work for, I guess, but you're going to piss off the Knights and ruin any chance of your getting hired back here."

"I've heard they don't particularly care for Porter, but I need to eat," she said, opening her driver's door to get in.

"Give Ethan a couple of days before you talk to anyone," Keith entreated. "I bet he'll ask you to come back to work within the week."

She pointed her key at him. "No funny stuff," she warned. "I mean it. You keep everything running perfectly. I can fight my own battles." She gave him a Cheshire smile. "I control the generator at Fox Run, and if Ethan suddenly loses his electricity, well . . . " She lifted her shoulders. "It's not my fault if the wire to his cabin shorts out."

Keith didn't return her smile. "It's going to be awkward, don't you think, with him living out there with you?"

"Naw," she said as she put her key in the ignition. "His cabin's far enough from mine that he can come and go without my even seeing him." She looked back at Keith. "If you know anybody looking for a good-running pickup, I've got Gaylen Dempsey's old one for sale." She shook her head. "I bought it one day too soon. The first two thousand bucks takes it."

"My son's getting his license next month," Keith said, rubbing his jaw, "and he's got fifteen hundred dollars saved up."

"You're all a bunch of damn Yankee traders down here." She sighed and shook her head. "You're going to make me take a five-hundred-dollar loss, aren't you?"

"Gaylen had already bought a fancy new truck when he sold you his old one," Keith told her with a crooked smile, not the least bit offended to be called a damn Yankee. "And he would have taken a thousand for his old one."

"That old poop. He started at three thousand bucks."

Keith laughed. "I'll bring my son out Saturday to see the truck. I know it runs okay, but I want him to figure that out for himself." He sobered again. "I'm sorry you got fired, Anna. I liked working with you. Hopefully you'll be back next Monday."

"Good-bye, Keith. And I mean it, you keep everything tip-top for Ethan. A profitable mill means jobs." She closed her door and started the engine. She waved to Keith as she pulled out of the yard—and noticed Ethan standing outside the office watching her leave, his face and stance rigid.

Anna pulled onto the main road and turned toward home with a tired sigh of defeat. She knew it had been a stupid stunt, but she couldn't have left that pup to face certain death. And she'd *known* what she was doing; she'd been able to judge the ground beneath her, the strength of the current, and the weight of her machine. She hadn't once felt as if she were endangering herself. But to be honest, she would have fired any of her crew if she'd caught one of *them* going after that dog.

Dammit, she just hated that Ethan was right!

"I can't believe he fired you like that," Jane said as she stood amid the ancient clutter in Anna's attic, her arms crossed and her toe tapping the floor. "Paul told me Ethan didn't even let you explain yourself. He just up and fired you, even though you've been sleeping together. I warned you he was a hard man."

Anna straightened from looking in a box and smiled at her outraged friend. "What has our sleeping together got to do with anything? Ethan did exactly what I would have done."

"He's just getting back at you for firing him two months ago," Jane said, opening an old trunk beside her and kneeling to look inside. "At least you found out what a jerk he is before you went and fell in love with him. And your dumping him is exactly what he deserves," she added as she pawed through the trunk's contents. "Maybe you'll find someone nice at the benefit dance Saturday."

"So you don't think I should sleep with Ethan anymore?"

Jane popped her head out and blinked at Anna. "Are you nuts? Not after he fired you like that."

"What's one thing got to do with the other?"

Jane sat back on her heels and gaped, apparently unable to believe that Anna would even *consider* sleeping with Ethan again.

"He's really not a hard man," Anna told her. "Ethan's quite nice, actually. He even has a sense of humor." She picked up the stack of notebooks she'd found earlier and sat down in their place with a sigh. "I've been thinking about it all day, and I bet I gave him a terrible scare, and that's why he got so angry. It probably brought back memories for him of when Pamela Sant drowned in Oak Creek. And truth be told, if I had seen him out in the middle of that ice jam trying to save that dog, I probably would have gone ballistic."

"But he didn't have to *fire* you. And right in front of your crew." Jane shook her head. "You can't keep sleeping with him. He'll get the idea he can treat you any way he wants. And besides, it will make you look desperate."

Anna choked on a laugh. "Desperate?" she repeated. "Maybe this is a good thing. It's impossible to work with someone you're sleeping with, which today certainly proved. So I've decided to start restoring Fox Run. I'll just find a part-time job in town. I can waitress at the Drooling Moose or something."

Jane looked utterly horrified. "You can't go from bossing men around to serving them dinner. It would be humiliating."

"Humiliation is in the eye of the beholder. And I'm not so proud that I can't take a bit of ribbing, especially if it pays my bills."

Jane's huge brown eyes softened. "Call your father. He can't stay mad at you forever. I know the minute he hears your voice, he'll break down and help you."

Anna shook her head. "Two of my brothers were here this weekend, and they said Daddy still feels that if he holds out long enough, I'll get tired of being poor and come running home. What he doesn't realize is that I get my stubbornness from *him*." She turned and headed down the narrow attic stairs. "No, I'm going to begin restoring Fox Run."

"All by yourself? But how?"

"One board at a time," Anna told her, heading down the living room stairs next, then dropping the notebooks on the couch. "Have you and Paul decided where you're going to live?"

Jane flopped down on the couch and picked up one of the notebooks. "His family offered us a place at the sporting camps with them, and I really like Sarah." She shot Anna a quick smile. "Our due dates are only two weeks apart." She opened one of the books and gave it a cursory glance before looking back up. "But Paul thinks we should get our own home. For the entire drive out to his place this afternoon, he kept rattling on about my needing to *nest*." She shrugged. "I have no idea what he was talking about. I just know he doesn't want me going back to work."

"Why not?" Anna asked, adding a log to the fire in the hearth. "You like working for Dr. Betters."

"I love that job, and I don't care what Paul says, I'm going back to work. And after tomorrow, I won't have to watch Megan and Travis anymore, since Pete's coming home." She shut the notebook and stood up. "Is it okay if we stay in Ethan's cabin until we find our own place?"

"Where's Ethan going to stay?"

"He told Paul he intended to sleep at the mill, because it has running water."

"But the cabin doesn't," Anna reminded her. "Are you certain you want to stay there?"

"Sure," Jane said, walking to the door and slipping into her coat. "It's like camping out, sort of cozy and romantic. So can I tell Paul it's okay with you?"

"If that's what you guys want to do. The rent's already been paid. Whatever happened to the dog? Was anyone able to find its owner?"

"He's at our cabin with Paul," Jane said. "We're going to ask around town if anyone's missing a black Lab pup. Paul thinks he's about seven or eight months old, and we've been calling him Kent since he got baptized in the Kent River." She grinned as she buttoned her coat. "Paul said he's never seen anyone operate machinery like you—that you scooped Kent up as gently as if you were plucking an egg out of the water."

Anna dismissed her praise with a laugh. "I've been running large equipment since I was twelve. I think Dad started teaching me as a way to make up for lost time and to bond with me when I went to live with him. Do you have food at your cabin?"

Jane stepped out onto the porch. "We went shopping on our way home from telling Paul's family about us. My *husband* is cooking tonight. Stew, I think."

Anna raised an eyebrow. "That sounds promising. You've gotten yourself a man who can cook."

"Only stew," Jane said with a laugh, trotting down the steps, then looking back. "You're okay?" she asked. "You won't get all depressed tonight and get drunk or anything, will you?"

"I'm going to make a pot of hot cocoa and read those notebooks. They seem to be journals Samuel Fox kept. And then I'm turning in early, so I can start working on my mill first thing tomorrow morning."

"Okay then, good-bye," Jane said with a wave as she started walking down the muddy path.

Anna watched to make sure she didn't slip in the mud, then called Bear, realizing she hadn't seen him for the last hour.

"He's over at our place," Jane called to her. "He seems to be fascinated with Kent."

"Okay. Just send him home if he becomes a pest," she called back with a wave, turning and going inside. "Well, Charlie," she said when the chickadee fluttered down off the curtain rod and landed on her shoulder. "You want to go to a benefit dance with me this Saturday night as my date?"

Anna woke up at the feel of the comforter moving and the bed dipping beside her. "Ethan," she whispered.

He said nothing, rolling to cover her with his body, his naked weight pressing her into the mattress as he captured her hands reaching for him and stretched them over her head. He kissed her full on the mouth with gentle aggression, as if expecting her to push him away. But even before she could respond, his lips began a familiar journey over her jaw and down her throat, not stopping until they came to her breasts, and he started suckling her nipple through the thin silk of her nightie.

Anna gave a cry of pleasure and tried to wiggle free to touch him, but he merely moved both her hands into one of his and continued his gentle assault. His free hand began its own journey then, sending shivers of anticipation sparking through her as his fingers kneaded her flesh, moving down her ribs and slipping under the elastic of her panties.

He'd learned her body quite well in only two nights, and knew right where to touch her to make her writhe beneath him. His strong, calloused fingers dallied over her hip bone, teasing the soft fleshy indent between it and her pelvis as his mouth moved to suckle her other breast. She cried out again, fighting his hold on her hands, but her struggles only settled him deeper into the juncture of her thighs.

"Ethan," she rasped, desperately needing to touch him.

He abandoned her breasts to kiss her again, turning her next petition to a moan as he slowly moved his hips intimately against her, the thin material of her panties compounding her pleasure. Anna realized her only hope of participating would come when he had to put on the condom, so she simply surrendered to her growing desire. But when he lifted his hips, stripped off her panties, and settled back between her thighs, she realized he had already seen to that chore. He slowly began to enter her while stroking her intimately, then held both her hands beside her head and gently embedded himself deeply inside her.

He set a rhythm that was totally focused and maddeningly tender, staring down at her in silence as he worked his magic, building her passion so subtly that when she crested Anna cried out in surprise.

"That's it, come for me," he coaxed, increasing the force of each thrust but not the speed. "Beautiful Anna."

Her pleasure went on in endless waves as he filled her deeply and rocked her gently, his mouth drinking in her sounds of fulfillment. And before she could even catch her breath he began all over again, making love to her body as he held her suspended in emotional awe. And over the next hour she climaxed again and yet again at his tender urging before he finally found his own release. In silence he pulled her against him, wrapping her in his comforting strength as she fell into an exhausted sleep.

As the sun crept through the window come dawn, Anna awoke to find herself alone in bed. She sighed. Poor Ethan. Unsure of his reception, he'd come in like a thief in the night . . . and come dangerously close to stealing her heart all over again.

Anna sank into the claw-foot tub of steaming lavender-scented water, laid her head back with an appreciative sigh, and listened to the soap bubbles softly pop around her. She didn't know if she was more exhausted from working on her mill all week or from spending a good part of the last five nights making love to Ethan.

No, *he* had been making love to *her*.

Since he'd fired her on Monday, Ethan had shown up each night after Anna had gone to sleep, crawled into bed, and made tender yet passionate love to her. And in all that time, she could count on her fingers the actual words they'd exchanged. Which was why sometime around Wednesday morning, when she'd been tearing apart Fox Run's old saw engine, Anna had decided that instead of confronting Ethan about his nocturnal visits, it might be wiser for her to wait him out.

The only thing Anna could figure was that the silent intensity was rooted in Pamela Sant's death. It must have been very traumatic not only to witness but possibly to have caused the accident, and then to have failed to save Pamela. That's why he'd gotten so crazy when he'd seen her in the middle of an ice jam, risking her life for a dog. He just needed some time to rebury the memories her stunt had dredged up.

But dammit, she wanted her lover back! She wanted to laugh with Ethan again, wrestle him to exhaustion, and push his buttons until he exploded. The man had been living up to every one of her childhood fantasies, which was precisely why she intended to shatter his maddening mood tonight.

Claire, André Segee's wife of twenty-five years, had taught Anna most of what she knew about men—as well as how to use that knowledge to her advantage. Though she had inherited four young sons when she'd married the widowed logging baron, then found herself the mother of a frightened eleven-year-old girl just seven years later, Claire had taken Anna under her wing without question or hesitation. She had taught Anna not only to be proud of her femininity, but how to dress, how to subtly hold her own in a relationship, and especially how to be comfortable in her own skin. Most of this Claire had done by example, as Anna had never known a man as contented as her daddy.

Which made Claire Segee the polar opposite of her real mother; Anna remembered Madeline Fox as a woman who was desperately searching for wholeness in the arms of a man. And she was still searching; last Anna had heard, Madeline was living in Arizona or Florida with her sixth or seventh husband.

Anna didn't hate Madeline, much less blame her for anything; she didn't judge her one way or another. She accepted that some people were doomed to spend their entire lives searching for happiness outside themselves.

That Madeline had been leading her young daughter down the same dead-end path eighteen years ago . . . well, Anna knew she owed her maternal grandfather an immense debt of gratitude for selflessly asking André Segee to come get his daughter before she followed in her mother's footsteps. Though she hadn't understood just how much Gramps had loved her then, she certainly did now, after reading the notebooks that were eighteen years of daily letters Samuel had written to his lost granddaughter.

"I love you, too, Gramps," she whispered. "And I'm going to restore your mill and make you proud. Just as soon as I take care of a little problem with my *Knight* in shining armor."

Anna lifted her sponge and squeezed it over her shoulders and across her chest, drawing in the calming lavender scent as she smiled in anticipation of tonight's benefit dance.

Claire not only had sent down the condoms and new undergarments, but also some of Anna's dressier clothes, her collection of perfumes and lotions, and her jewelry box—into which she'd tucked a note asking Anna not to sell any of her jewels, that André would eventually come to his senses. The envelope containing the note had also held two thousand Canadian dollars, which Anna had added to the four thousand Damon and Jean-Paul had tucked in her hand before they'd left. That was why she hadn't been in much of a hurry to look for a new job. She'd dumped some of the money on her back taxes, saving the rest for a rainy day.

Things had been blessedly quiet at Fox Run all week. The newlyweds had moved into a rented house in Oak Grove on Wednesday, and Anna hadn't had any more ghostly visitations. Apparently getting shot at by a crazy woman was an effective deterrent.

The only nightly visitor she'd had to deal with lately was a recalcitrant lover, and that was about to change. Anna slipped under the water to wet her hair, then surfaced and reached for the shampoo. The poor man was about to get the surprise of his life this evening, when his ex-foreman showed up at the dance wearing makeup, a cute little black dress, and three-inch heels.

Chapter Fifteen

I've changed my mind," Daniel Reed said as Ethan downed the last drop of beer in his bottle. "I'll fight you for her if I have to."

"What are you talking about?" Ethan asked over the sound of the band playing on the far side of the school gymnasium.

"Anna. You Knights can't have a monopoly on all the beautiful women around here," Daniel said, glancing at Ethan before looking across the room again. "I'm going to ask her out."

"Anna only invited you to dinner that day to be nice. She won't actually date you."

Daniel snapped his gaze back to Ethan. "Why not?"

"Because she hates guns," he said, straight-faced. "And you carry one for work."

Daniel stood up. "Then I'll quit my job." He took a long swig of his beer, set the bottle back on the table, and smoothed down the front of his shirt as he looked across the room again. "For her, I'd quit breathing."

Turning to see what had his friend so riled up, Ethan immediately shot to his feet. Apparently he wasn't the only male in the place who felt like he'd just been punched in the gut; to a man, conversations stopped, heads turned, and mouths dropped open.

"*That's* the tomboy you've been working with all winter?" a woman at the next table hissed, which she followed up with a loud smack to her husband's arm. "She's no *tomboy*."

Ethan was torn between running across the gym and stuffing Anna back in her coat and bursting out laughing. The little witch was showing enough leg to make a giraffe envious. Most of the men appeared shocked to realize Anna actually *had* legs. And she'd piled her wild curls on top of her head, exposing her long sexy neck and cute little ears—which were adorned with glittering studs. Jewelry? Legs? A *dress*?

What in hell was she up to?

Daniel took another gulp of his beer, cleared his throat, and smoothed down the front of his shirt again. But he didn't exactly rush over to Anna—probably because he was afraid to trip over his own tongue.

"You're going to have to get in line," Ethan drawled,

watching Frank Coots walk up to Anna. "I hope she brought a dance card. She's going to need one."

"God dammit," Daniel growled, sitting back down and grabbing his beer again, only to realize the bottle was empty.

Ethan pulled two more beers out of the cooler he'd brought, repositioned his chair to watch the show, and sat down. "Don't worry," he said, sliding over one of the beer. "She'll chew up Coots and spit him out in under five minutes."

"What's he doing back here? I thought we got rid of that bastard years ago. Isn't he living in Boston or something?"

"Rumor has it he's offering Kent Mountain to a group of developers if they take him on as a partner."

"Hell," Daniel said, his scowl returning when Frank and Anna started to dance. "Just what we need, another resort."

Ethan only half listened as Daniel disparaged their old high school buddy, and instead watched the dance floor, unable to take his eyes off Anna. As beautiful as she was naked in bed, wrestling him to exhaustion, she was far more stunning and even sexier in that tight little black dress, dark nylons, and heels tall enough to bring her eyes level with those of most men.

Apparently it was payback time for the way he'd been treating her all week. But he wasn't ready to let Anna kick him out of her life. Not yet. Not until he scratched her surface enough to find something about her that would allow him to walk away unscathed.

And there had to be something. He just needed to find her fatal flaw, and then he'd be freed from the spell of her challenging eyes, quick mind, and explosive energy.

"I guess you do clean up nice," Frank Coots said, his smile appreciative as he led Anna onto the dance floor and took her in his arms. "Daddy finally come through?" he asked, his gaze locking on her simple diamond stud earrings.

"They were a sixteenth-birthday gift."

"Have you thought any more about selling Fox Run?"

"Not really. In fact, I've already started restoring it."

Frank's congenial expression immediately cooled, his arm around her back tightening perceptibly. "You're not really serious about reopening that mill?"

"I dismantled the saw this week, and I'm looking for someone who can tool the parts I can't buy." She shrugged. "The saw house will have to be rebuilt, but most of the equipment is in surprisingly good shape."

Frank suddenly guided her toward the edge of the crowd, then led her to an isolated table and sat her down. He then pulled up another chair that put his back to the gymnasium, effectively giving them some privacy.

"How would you like to be part of a deal that would be a lot more lucrative than running a mill?" he asked quietly over the music. "I'm in contact with a group of developers who want to build a multifaceted resort near Oak Grove." He glanced over his shoulder when the music stopped, leaned closer, and lowered his voice. "If we were to offer them my mountain and your shore frontage on Frost Lake, we'd have a package they couldn't resist. They'd make us full partners, and in three or four years you'd be able to buy a lovely necklace to match those earrings," he said with a promising grin, his gaze dropping to her bare throat. "Hell, you'd be able to buy all the diamonds your little heart desires."

"These *are* all the diamonds I desire," she said, touching one of her earrings. "Fox Run's not for sale, Frank."

His eyes hardened. "Did you know your deed is questionable?" he asked, his voice threatening. "And that half of your land used to belong to my father? Five years ago he sold Samuel Fox a thousand-acre plot that runs from the main road down to the lake." He leaned closer, crowding her a bit. "For only twelve thousand dollars," he growled, his complexion turning ruddy. "That's barely ten dollars an acre, for a chunk of land worth over a million."

"My lawyers researched all the titles to Fox Run thoroughly when I acquired it," Anna told him, refusing to lean away. "And I specifically remember seeing that deed from your father to Samuel. All the i's were dotted and the t's were neatly crossed. The sale was legal."

"Not if my father wasn't of sound mind at the time," Frank rebutted. "He's been in a nursing home in Dover for the last three years, wearing a diaper and talking to imaginary people."

"So it's your intention to contest your father's sale of that acreage to Samuel Fox?"

"Unless you decide to come in on the deal. It'll be more cost-effective than for each of us to rack up huge lawyer fees."

What he was threatening just didn't ring true. If it was a simple matter of proving Samuel Fox had taken advantage of his father, Frank would have gone to court long before now. Maybe he was her ghost and had been looking for evidence to back up his claim. "Where have you been this past month, Frank? I haven't seen you around town."

"In Boston," he said impatiently, just as the band started playing again. "I'm returning on Monday." He stood up and held out his hand. "Let's finish our dance while you think about my offer."

Anna stood up without taking his hand. "Thank you, but the gentleman I've been waiting to speak with has just arrived." She leveled her gaze on him. "And I don't need to think about it, Mr. Coots. I have no desire to be part of a resort, and if I have to go to court, then I will."

Anna walked across the gymnasium, taking the time to study the man stuffing a thick envelope in the donation jar. He might be considered handsome in an approachable sort of way. Just a tad taller than her, he had sandy blond hair, gold hazel eyes, and an easy smile.

"Mr. Porter," she said when he turned from speaking to the woman soliciting donations. She held out her hand. "I'm Anna Segee. I was the foreman at Loon Cove Lumber up until this past Monday, and ever since Keith Blaine pointed you out to me in town last month, I've been meaning to visit your cutting and introduce myself."

He seemed startled, but his easy smile quickly returned and he took her hand in his. "Anna Segee," he said slowly, his gaze traveling down her dress before rising to meet hers. "Either I'm the biggest idiot north of Boston, or I've been in a coma for the last five months." His eyes crinkled at the corners. "Did you say 'up until this past Monday'? Does this mean you're currently unemployed?" He slipped his arm through hers and started to escort her to a table, then noticed the sea of faces watching them and turned toward the entrance. "It's a lovely evening," he said. "Would you care to take a walk?"

"Are you trying to ensure I don't get hired back at Loon Cove?" she asked with a laugh, stepping outside ahead of him.

He tucked her arm through his again. "What do you mean?"

"I'm well aware of the feud between you and the Knights. This little stroll could very well ruin my chances of getting my job back."

"You approached me, Miss Segee," he reminded her as they headed down the walkway that led to the parking lot. "And my feud with the Knights is over. They've agreed to let me rebuild their road."

"Please, call me Anna. And I doubt Alex Knight
will ever consider the feud over."

"Ah, so you've heard about my brief insanity, have
you?" he said, bringing them to a halt. "And I'd rather
call you Abby, Miss Fox."

Anna went utterly still.

"My father dated your mother for a short time, not
long after you left for Quebec. You have Madeline's
eyes." His smile was genuine. "Don't worry, your secret's
safe with me. You wouldn't be going by Anna Segee if
you wanted people to know."

"Segee is my legal name. And Anna is what I've
answered to since I was eleven." She inclined her
head slightly, hugging her arms against a sudden chill.
"But I appreciate your not saying anything. I'm not
ashamed of my past; I just prefer to keep it there."

He immediately took off his suit jacket and settled
it over her shoulders, holding on to the lapels. "So tell
me why you intended to come out to my cutting."

Anna slipped her arms through the sleeves and
folded the jacket around her, releasing his hold as she
batted her eyelashes at him. "Why, to share my vast
experience, of course, and help you figure out the dif-
ference between a sawlog and pulpwood," she drawled
in her thickest Canadian accent.

Clay burst out laughing. "And here I thought
you liked those dirty loads, since you started selling
the pulpwood to the paper mills." Then he offered,
"Come work for me. I'll pay you double what the

Knights were, and I'll give you free rein to build a sawmill on my land. And I promise not to fire you for saving a dog."

"So you heard about that."

"Are you kidding? Everyone in the county has heard about your driving an excavator into the Kent River and scooping up that pup without so much as putting a scratch on him. Come help me build a mill and teach me to run it."

"I'm sorry, Clay, but I have my own mill to build."

"You're not really going to try and restore Fox Run, are you? It's too far gone. Start from scratch, but on my land."

"I'm opening a specialty lumber mill," she explained. "And that's not what you need. But I will buy any bird's-eye or tiger maple you come across while cutting, as well as cherry, clear oak, and white birch." She lifted an eyebrow. "Assuming you don't dirty my loads," she added, turning to walk toward the parking lot full of cars and trucks.

From the sound of Clay's sigh as he fell into step beside her, she knew that though he was accepting her refusal for employment, he would continue asking. His companionable silence probably meant he was considering a different approach right now. Anna started walking between the rows of vehicles, studying each pickup she came to.

"Are we looking for something in particular?" Clay asked as he strolled beside her. "Or just admiring the mud?"

"I'm looking for birdshot dents," she explained, veering off to check the tailgate of a truck that was parked nose out.

"Birdshot," Clay repeated when she returned.

"Of the number four variety," she said, continuing on. "It would leave a noticeable dent, don't you think?"

"From how far away?"

She glanced over at him and smiled. "How far to notice the dent, or how far away was I standing when I pulled the trigger?"

He stopped walking. "It's quite possible Ethan had reason to fire you. May I ask why you shot at a pickup?"

"Because its occupants had been rifling through my buildings at night."

"Okay," he said, continuing down the row of vehicles, moving away slightly to look at the trucks parked in the facing row. "Did you call John Tate?" he asked across the short distance.

"Tell the sheriff I actually shot at someone?" She laughed softly. "That would have gone over well, I'm sure. So, why dirty your loads to Loon Cove Lumber if you've ended your old feud with the Knights?"

Clay shrugged, his grin prominent in the lamplight. "Just a bit of tail tugging. The sneaky bastards bought Loon Cove right out from under my nose. I never saw it coming; I was too busy trying to pull together the financing." He stopped searching tailgates and looked at her. "So why did you seek me out tonight, Anna? My dirty loads to Loon Cove no longer matter since you don't work there anymore, and apparently you don't want a job from me."

"Just curious," she said, walking around the end of a row and starting up a new one as he followed. "I've heard a lot about you, both good and . . . interesting, depending on who I was talking to. What do you remember about Pamela Sant's death, and Ethan's trial after?"

Clay caught the sleeve of his jacket and stopped her again. "If I take you back inside and we dance, am I going to reignite my old feud?"

"Probably."

He chuckled. "I don't know if Ethan is lucky or brave."

"Did he love Pamela Sant?"

"My personal opinion? No," he said, shaking his head.

"How come you sound so sure?"

"My family got along quite well with the Knights before Alex's first wife robbed me of all common sense. And the Ethan I knew back then had a bit of a . . . *Knight in shining armor* personality." He smiled again. "You should know; he came charging to your rescue that summer, didn't he?"

"We're talking about Pamela."

"Pamela was in desperate need of a knight herself, and somehow Ethan fell into the role." Clay made a dismissing gesture with his hand. "Whether by choice or by Pamela's design, I don't know."

"Who was he rescuing Pamela from?"

"From herself, if you ask me. She seemed like a woman who couldn't have her hair cut without someone deciding for her how it should be styled. She was fragile, both in body and personality." He shrugged. "Maybe in a protective sort of way, Ethan did love her. Men need to be needed."

"People have said he changed after the accident."

"It certainly hardened him. And left him cynical about women. Nobody but Ethan and Pamela knows what happened that night, and since Pamela can't tell, I doubt Ethan ever will. He didn't utter one word at his manslaughter trial. He just sat in court and stared at nothing." Clay eyed her speculatively. "Most of the women around here consider him dangerous."

"Really? You don't think a little elbow grease could polish his tarnished armor?"

He laughed, then looped her arm through his and started walking back toward the school. "I *think* Ethan's in really big trouble, but that it's going to take a lot more than polishing for him to realize exactly how much. Maybe if a forklift loaded with sawlogs ran over him," he said, "he *might* see the light."

"I'd been leaning toward handcuffs myself," Anna said with a laugh, "but heavy machinery does have its appeal. I guess sometimes a girl's just got to forget subtlety and go for the big bang."

Chapter Sixteen

Is there a reason you're sitting here pounding back beers while Anna is outside with Clay Porter, wearing his jacket?" Paul asked as he pulled up a chair beside Ethan.

"She's probably looking for work," Ethan said. "And this is only my third beer. The empties belong to our disillusioned game warden," he added, nodding toward the dance floor, where Daniel was soothing his battered libido in the arms of a petite and newly divorced woman.

"Disillusioned about what?"

"He took one look at Anna tonight and decided to quit his job and ask her out."

"And?"

"The line got too long for him. Did you see her when you came in? I mean *really* see her?"

"I saw that her hair was up," Paul said, confused. "But she and Clay were walking between vehicles, so all I noticed was Clay's jacket and her hair. Why?"

"Then I suggest you prepare yourself," Ethan said, looking toward the gym entrance. "And try not to let your chin hit the floor. You're a newlywed, remember?"

Paul turned in his seat just as Anna and Clay walked inside. "Holy shit," he said when Anna slipped off Clay's jacket and handed it to him. Paul turned and glared at Ethan. "You let her come here looking like that?"

Ethan lifted one foot to see his ankle. "I'm sorry, I seem to have misplaced the chain I keep attached to her." He looked his brother in the eye. "Oh, I forgot, *you're* the one with the ball and chain. Go dance with your wife." He gave Paul a brotherly shove. "This is your chance to show everyone how much in love the two of you are."

Paul barely took a step before turning back to him. "You've got to get her out of here before she starts a brawl. The wives are going to kill your crew once they see what their husbands' ex-boss *really* looks like. The least you could do is dance with her a few times, so they'll realize Anna's not interested in their men."

"Too late," Ethan said, glancing toward the dance floor. "Dad beat me to it." He pulled another beer from his cooler. "Don't you worry about Anna. She can have her fun this evening, but she'll be leaving with me."

Paul walked away, shaking his head and muttering to himself. Ethan propped his feet on a chair and sipped his beer as he watched one man after another work up the nerve to ask Anna to dance. What was she up to? She wasn't the type to try to make him jealous, and she wasn't a woman who needed to flirt with every man in the room to feed her ego. She didn't even need to bat an eyelash—she simply had to put up her hair, slip into a tight little black dress, and walk through the door wearing three-inch heels.

And she damn well knew it, too.

She certainly appeared at ease, her smile genuine as she glided across the dance floor with partners ranging from fifteen to ninety years old. Anna seemed comfortable in most any setting, be it the middle of a busy mill yard, driving large equipment, chasing after intruders with a shotgun, or in bed. Which made him wonder: Just what *would* rattle Anna's cage?

"I finally looked into that little matter you asked me to," John Tate said as he pulled up a chair and sat down. "And you were right, it is her."

"I thought so," Ethan said. "I just wanted to be sure. You on duty tonight?"

John glanced down at his sheriff's uniform. "If I tell you the truth, you'll realize how desperate I am."

"Women are suckers for men in uniform? Is that your great appeal to the ladies, Tate? Then where's your gun? That would impress them even more than the uniform."

"I'm carrying, but not my service revolver. I don't want to overwhelm them," he drawled, his gaze traveling to the dance floor. "Your girl is causing quite a stir tonight. She's really quite beautiful."

"You'll have to join Daniel in line," Ethan said, "along with every other single male here. What about Anna's intruders? Have you been able to dig up anything?"

John looked back at him. "Frank Coots has been in Boston this past month, though that doesn't mean he didn't hire a couple of guys to snoop around for him. As for the historical society, all the members are old enough to have worked at Fox Run when it was up and running, which means they're too old to be dodging birdshot."

"And Samuel's death?"

"I wasn't on duty the morning they found him, but I went over the entire report and everything pointed to it being an accident. The man was eighty-three, so any number of ailments could have sent him skidding into that ravine. The autopsy said he died of exposure within a couple of hours."

"Don't you think it's an odd coincidence that the exact same thing happened to a young, healthy woman who is more than competent behind the wheel? I've been checking that spot ever since her accident, and I haven't found any signs of an active spring. So where'd the ice come from?"

John shrugged. "I have no idea." He lowered his voice when several people sat down at a nearby table. "A person would have to haul in barrels of water to cover even a short section of that road." He rubbed his jaw in thought. "But it would be a perfect crime. There wasn't any mention of ice on the road in Samuel's report, though it could have melted in the two days it took to find him. That would mean we're talking about murder, and I can't imagine why anyone would want to kill an eighty-three-year-old man."

"A multimillion-dollar resort isn't motive enough?"

"And Anna's accident?"

"Same reason," Ethan said. "She's no more willing to sell Fox Run than Samuel was."

John shook his head again, as if he couldn't believe both accidents had been deliberate. "It's a stretch." He cocked his head. "I still say you should tell her what you think is going on. I'm not comfortable keeping her in the dark. She should be watching her back."

"*I'm* watching her back," Ethan told him. "And I can't just come out and say I believe her grandfather was murdered without having something to back up my claim. That would devastate her."

"She still hasn't told you who she really is?"

Ethan shook his head. "If you were her, would you want everyone in town to know your mother is *the* Madeline Fox?"

"I'm not talking about everyone, I'm talking about *you*." He leaned closer. "It doesn't bother you that the woman you're sleeping with isn't exactly being truthful?"

Ethan shrugged. "She'll get around to telling me, just as soon as she realizes it doesn't matter."

John leaned back in his chair, folded his arms over his chest, and studied Ethan. "You've fallen in love with her."

"No."

"And you're angry about it, and that's why you're sitting here going through a case of beer while your woman is dancing with every eligible man in town."

"Those are Daniel's dead soldiers, not mine," he growled. "And I learned my lesson five years ago. I—"

"Come dance with me, Uncle Ethan," Delaney said, running up to them. "And you next," she told John, her sparkling eyes reflecting the bright blue in her dress. She grabbed Ethan's hand and tugged him to his feet. "You have to save me from Billy Danes," she said in a whisper. "He ambushed me when we walked through the door, but I told him I had promised my first dance to you."

"You want me to take Billy Danes outside and beat him up?" Ethan asked in his serious voice, leading her onto the dance floor. "That is my job as your uncle, you know."

Delaney gave him a devastatingly feminine smile that told Ethan young Billy Danes would be the least of his and Alex's worries in a few years. "If I thought a punch would discourage him, I'd have done it myself before now," she said, gracefully moving to his lead. "You had an awful lot of empty beer bottles on the table," she continued, giving him a look that Ethan had seen on his own mother more than once. "Are you upset that you don't have a date tonight?"

"They're not all mine," he said with patient restraint, deciding he'd better make a trip to the recycle bin the moment he handed Delaney off to John. "And you've got no business punching boys. That's my job."

"Cathy Farmer's all divorced now," she offered, sticking to her obvious agenda. "And you like kids, so it shouldn't bother you that she's got three."

"Cathy Farmer comes up to my belly button," he said with a choked laugh. "Uh-uh," he added when she opened her mouth to continue. "I don't need you matchmaking for me, baby girl."

"You're not getting any younger, you know," she said, ignoring his warning. "Hey, what about her?" she asked, suddenly spinning them so that Anna came into his view. "Isn't that the lady from your mill? God, she's beautiful," Delaney whispered.

"Don't swear."

She looked up with a frown. "I heard you fired her for saving a puppy. How could you, Uncle Ethan? She's single, she seemed really nice when we toured the mill, and she's the prettiest woman here besides Mom." Her face scrunched up again. "But she probably won't dance with you because you fired her."

Nevertheless, that didn't stop Delaney from guiding them toward where Anna and John Tate were dancing. "Try anyway," she whispered. "I'll cut in on Sheriff Tate, and you grab her and apologize before she can walk away."

But just as his niece was about to implement her matchmaking plan, a woman behind Ethan said in a booming voice, "Abigail Fox! Just look at how you've grown up, child!"

To a person, everyone on the dance floor stopped, the band screeched to a stuttering halt, and silence rippled through the gymnasium on a wave of urgent hushes.

"I couldn't believe it when your mother called to see if I had any rooms available," Penny Bryant continued, stepping up to an obviously shocked Anna. "I nearly fell out of my chair when she told me she was coming to visit *you!*" Penny tsk-tsked loudly and shook her head. "Imagine my surprise when Madeline told me you've been living here *five months* now. And you never once came to see your dear old babysitter," she scolded, pulling Anna into a smothering hug.

And that was when Ethan discovered exactly what would rattle Anna Segee's cage. She stood stiff in the woman's embrace, her face completely drained of color, stunned. Ethan found himself looking into the same terrorized eyes of the eleven-year-old girl's the day he'd found her cornered in Frost Lake.

"Abby!" Penny Bryant yelped, her voice admonishing Anna for not reacting properly to her *dear* old babysitter—just as the first rumbles of speculation started rolling through the crowd.

Ethan strode over and pulled Anna free, folding her protectively against him. "She's been going by Anna Segee for the last eighteen years, Mrs. Bryant," he said, his voice heavily laced with warning. "And it seems you've given her a bit of a surprise."

"Well!" Penny said in a huff, her face ruddy with reproach. "She should have come to see me. I had to find out she was here from *Madeline*."

"I'm afraid that's my fault," he said, acutely aware of the rising murmurs spreading through their audience. "I've been monopolizing Anna's time, seeing how we're engaged to be married," he added somewhat more loudly as he briefly smiled down at Anna's blank, unseeing eyes. He looked back at Penny Bryant. "We're planning a May wedding."

"Oh, Abby—I mean *Anna*!" Penny gushed, reaching for her.

Ethan turned to put Anna out of the busybody's reach. "And if you will excuse us, I think I'll take my fiancée home." He started to turn for the door, still holding Anna tightly against him, but stopped and looked back at the owner of the only bed-and-breakfast in town. "When did you say her mother was arriving?"

"Oh. Madeline's flying into Portland on Wednesday," Penny said, puffing up with importance, "but she won't get here until Friday. She and her husband are renting a car and driving up the coast first."

Ethan felt Anna shut down completely, as if a heavy slab of granite had slammed inside her, sealing her off from the world. He reached behind her knees and lifted her into his arms, then nodded to Oak Grove's town crier. "Thank you," he said, striding past the gaping crowd, making eye contact only with Alex.

Alex said something to his wife, rushed to open the door for him, and followed him out. They walked to Ethan's truck in silence, where Alex opened the passenger door and Ethan set Anna inside before shutting the door and turning to his brother.

"Do you know what you're doing?" Alex asked tightly.

Ethan ran an unsteady hand through his hair. "I have no idea," he admitted, glancing over to see Anna sitting stone still, blankly staring out the windshield. He stepped toward the back of the truck. "But I couldn't just stand there and do nothing. Look at her," he growled. "She's nearly comatose."

"Then yes, get her out of there. But why in hell announce that you're engaged?"

"For insurance."

"Against?"

"Against what happened to her before," he snapped. "To make sure it doesn't happen again."

Alex shook his head. "She's not eleven anymore, Ethan. Anna appears more than capable of holding her own against men. She'd been doing a damn fine job of it all evening."

"As *Anna Segee*." He headed around the back side of the truck. "Every goddamn whore hound this side of the border would be sniffing around her within the week if I hadn't said we're engaged." He stopped beside his door. "I may need you to come in and work at the mill. Can you cover it? I have until Friday to snap her out of this so she can face her mother as Anna Segee." He made a helpless gesture. "If I can't, then we're both screwed."

Alex grabbed Ethan's arm when he reached for the door handle. "Why do you care?"

"Because I do." He opened the door and got in the truck before looking at Alex. "Because . . . because I do," he said thickly, and closed the door.

He drove out of the parking lot, acutely aware of the silent, motionless woman beside him as he turned onto the main road and headed toward Fox Run. Dammit to hell! He was so angry, he wanted to roar.

No, not so much angry as *scared*. She was far too quiet. What was going on in her head right now? Anything? Nothing? Anna was so completely shut down, so *not there*, that Ethan suspected it didn't have anything to do with learning her mother was arriving on Friday, but rather that the entire town knew who she was. But could something as simple as Penny calling her *Abigail Fox* turn her back into a terrorized little girl in the blink of an eye?

And terror it had been. From the time he'd found her torn dress on the path leading down to the lake, to when he'd come upon her standing shoulder deep in the cold water, begging the boys to leave her alone, Ethan had instinctively known what was happening. He'd gone after the bastards in a rage, and by the time the dust had settled, she'd taken advantage of the distraction he'd caused and disappeared. He'd never seen her again; his last memory of her was her huge, shattered eyes and pale, bruised face as she'd tearfully pleaded with her attackers to leave her alone.

Ethan sensed her silently looking over at him, and realized that on some level she was cognizant. And though he felt like a bastard himself for asking, he knew he wouldn't have a better chance of getting an honest answer out of her. Besides, he needed to know exactly what he was dealing with if he hoped to help her—as well as finally put to rest something that had haunted him for eighteen years.

He took a calming breath and said as gently as possible, "I was never sure, exactly. Were those boys threatening you for sport, or did they rape you?"

"One tried, but couldn't," was her barely audible reply.

He took a shuddering breath, his hands tightly gripping the steering wheel as his rage resurfaced. How in hell could anyone be as free-spirited in bed as Anna was, after such a devastating experience? "Which one?" he gently probed.

"I don't know."

After turning off the main road and onto her lane, he stopped the truck, shut off the engine, and stared through the windshield.

"Craig Logan died in a logging accident about nine years ago," he told her. "Peter Wright moved to Texas right after high school, and Ron Briggs lives down in Greenville now." He looked over at her. "Briggs has been in and out of jail for the last fifteen years and works odd jobs when he's not too drunk."

She hugged her arms, staring at the dash in front of her. "You weren't surprised when she called me Abigail," she whispered, her voice devoid of emotion.

"I've known for some time," he softly admitted, opening his door and getting out of the truck. He walked to the gate, realized he didn't have the key, and stood there in the beam of the headlights—damn near close to shutting down himself. He dropped his head instead, and took another shuddering breath.

The lights on his truck went out, and he heard the passenger door open and close just before he heard Anna's footsteps on the gravel. "We'll have to walk. I don't know where my purse is," she said flatly, rounding the gate and starting down the lane.

Ethan ducked under the metal bar and fell into step beside her and they headed down the mile to her mill in silence. But a short time later she suddenly stopped and grabbed his arm for balance to take off her shoe. He'd forgotten she was wearing three-inch heels. Before she could undo the strap, he lifted her into his arms and started walking again.

"It's too far to carry me."

"Hush. You'll cut your feet if I don't." He smiled at her. "Besides, this way I get to enjoy how nice you smell."

Anna took his edict to heart and stayed mute in his arms the rest of the way—while Ethan silently wondered if she had heard him tell everyone that they were getting married next month.

Chapter Seventeen

By the time he climbed her porch steps, Ethan's arms had gone completely numb. He didn't know if Anna had fallen asleep or simply withdrawn inside herself, because she hadn't so much as twitched in the last half hour.

Deciding that if he set her down he'd never be able to pick her up again, he fumbled the door open and carried Anna upstairs. He set her on her feet in her bedroom, holding her until he was sure she could stand, alarmed that she remained so uncharacteristically malleable.

He lit the kerosene lamp on the bureau, then unzipped the back of her dress. "How about if I draw you a bath and make you a cup of hot cocoa?"

She clasped her hands to the front of her dress

so it wouldn't slip off. "I—I can undress myself," she whispered, looking straight ahead. "Thank you for bringing me home. Could you feed Bear before you leave?"

Leave? He wasn't stepping one goddamned foot off this property, knowing she'd be halfway to Quebec by sunrise.

"I'll go run your bath and put on the kettle." He hesitated at the door, but she still didn't move. "Just throw on your bathrobe and I'll come get you in a little while."

When she still didn't respond, he headed down the stairs, so angry that he wanted to pound something—preferably Penny Bryant. That self-serving bitch couldn't have waited until she'd gotten Anna alone. Oh no, she'd had to make her announcement to the entire town.

"We don't need armies to invade a country," he muttered to himself, putting the kettle on to boil. "We could just send in one single busybody to start a vicious rumor and the whole damn place would implode from the chain reaction."

Ethan went out and started the generator to kick on the well pump and lights, then went into the bathroom, put the plug in the tub, and started running the water. He spotted the assortment of bottles on the shelf, reached for the purple one labeled BUBBLE BATH, and took off the cover and sniffed it. Lavender; that's what Anna smelled like. He poured a quarter of the bottle in the tub, watching the water froth into bubbles as the air filled with the scent of flowers. Ethan gave a tired sigh, in need of a hot soak himself.

Leaving the tub to fill, he strode back into the living room and out onto the porch, and whistled to Bear. The dog came lumbering up the steps and inside, and Ethan propped the door closed with a heavy chair, then sat down and took off his boots. He stood with a groan, rolling the kinks out of his shoulders, and looked up the stairs as he listened for sounds of movement. All he heard was the hum of the generator and an occasional creak of the old house settling into the thawing ground.

He fed Bear, set out some seed for Anna's critters, shut off the boiling kettle, then went in and shut off the water in the tub—which now had bubbles cascading over its rim. "What do you think, old boy?" he asked Bear, who had forgone his dinner to come sniff the bubbles instead. "Any suggestions on how we can get her through this?"

Bear nudged Ethan's hand and gave a soulful whine.

Ethan rubbed the dog's ears. "I'm tempted to just pack us all up and take her deep into the woods." He returned to the living room, Bear padding behind him. "But that would only postpone her crisis, not resolve it. And she's already spent eighteen years keeping what happened bottled up inside her."

He stirred the dying embers in the fireplace, added some kindling, then sat down on the stone hearth and turned to Bear. "So if it takes a month of Sundays, she's going to deal with it now. And I'll be right beside her the entire time, no matter how hard she tries to push me away."

Bear's cataract-clouded eyes looked up at him, his whole body shaking with his wagging tail as he wheezed out a soft woof.

"I agree," Ethan said with a final pat before he stood up and headed for the stairs. "The Segee clan did such a good job smothering her in love that they raised an entirely different person from the one who left here eighteen years ago. Now we have to find a way to make Abby Fox and Anna Segee into one *whole* confident woman again." The old Lab wagged his tail, and Ethan quietly headed up to Anna's bedroom.

He found her lying on her bed facedown, wearing thick flannel pajamas that had feet, softly snoring. This was good, he decided as he settled a blanket over her, though he was amazed she could fall asleep. He didn't dare close his own eyes, for fear his imagination would fill in the rest of what sort of hell she'd gone through that day when those bastards had torn off her dress and tried to rape her.

He rubbed a hand over his face in an attempt to wipe away the frightening image. Good God, Anna had been *Delaney's* age. He turned and walked downstairs into the bathroom, and just stared at the tub of bubbles. Well, dammit to hell. He stripped off his clothes, climbed in, and sank into the steaming lavender-scented water. He still couldn't shut down his mind the way Anna had, but his muscles finally started to loosen.

Afterward, Ethan dried and dressed, then sat down in front of the fire. He spotted the stack of old, dusty blue journals on the coffee table and thumbed through them until he realized what they were. He looked for the book dated eighteen years ago, opened it to the first page, and started reading.

Anna woke up sticky with sweat and stuffy from the strong smell of flowers, the source of both apparently being the large male body enveloping her like a Swedish sauna. But if Ethan was sleeping with her, why had she put on her flannel pajamas? And why in heck did he reek of lavender?

Then she suddenly remembered last night, how Penny Bryant had shattered her carefully constructed wall of protection in front of the entire town, like a rogue wave crashing down with the force of the entire Atlantic behind it.

All Anna remembered was feeling utterly naked and completely helpless—emotions so foreign to her that she'd simply shut down. She had no recollection of what happened after, only a vague sense of being carried off by a dark, familiar figure whose anger had been a palpable thing.

Ethan. But had he been angry at Penny Bryant or at her? It must have been a shock to learn the woman he was sleeping with was the same person he'd rescued eighteen years ago. No, not the same. Abigail

Fox no longer existed; she was Anna Segee now, and she was afraid of no one—especially a town full of gossiping busybodies.

Then why couldn't she shake this feeling of dread? And would she be able to put that frightened little girl back in the bottle and cork it as tightly as she had before? Now she understood why her father had fought her returning to Maine. He'd instinctively known that she might be risking her very existence. And as for Ethan . . . By coming back she had also risked her fairy-tale childhood memory of him in exchange for the reality of the man he had actually become.

And hadn't she seen a glimpse of the real Ethan last night, and hadn't he been as frighteningly dangerous as everyone kept telling her? But despite knowing who she really was, he'd brought her home and stayed with her. Out of a sense of obligation, or worse, out of *pity*?

Ethan had felt compelled to protect her—just as he had eighteen years ago, and just as he had tried to do for Pamela Sant. The man really did have a knight-in-shining-armor complex; he still couldn't turn his back on a woman in distress.

How . . . noble of him.

Feeling so stifled she could no longer breathe, Anna carefully raised Ethan's arm from around her waist and slipped out of bed. She tiptoed to the bureau, gathered up some clothes, and quietly walked downstairs. She stopped upon entering the bathroom

THE STRANGER IN HER BED 263

and frowned at the tub full of cold, murky water. Ethan had taken a lavender *bubble* bath?

She pulled up the sleeve of her pajamas, reached into the water with a shiver, and pulled the drain plug just as Bear came padding in and butted his head against her leg. "Hey, pup." She wiped her wet hand on her pajamas, then gave his ears a gentle rub. "Are you hungry?" she asked, going into the kitchen to fill his dish, only to find it overflowing with food. She crouched down and held his head to look him straight in the eye. "You can't stop eating, Bear. I know I'm a poor replacement for Gramps, but I love you. Please don't start wasting away from a broken heart."

Bear answered with a soft whine and licked her chin. Anna buried her face in his neck with a sigh. "I know. I know," she whispered. She scrambled to her feet. "Let's take a walk down to the lake and see how close the ice is to going out," she suggested, trying to sound excited as she returned to the bathroom and quickly dressed.

She exited through the back door, pleased to see that Bear's mood immediately perked up once they were outside—just as hers did when she took a deep breath of the fresh spring air laced with pine and spruce. Okay, she thought, as she headed down the path to the lake. This was only a minor setback. So what if everyone knew who she was? She'd killed off Abigail Fox once, she could do it again.

But alone? Eighteen years ago she'd had the entire

Segee clan showering her with so much love, she'd been too busy trying to keep up with them to worry about what had happened, where she'd come from, or even where she was going.

"But I can't keep using them as a crutch," she told Bear, rubbing his head as they stood staring out at the ice, which had melted away from the shoreline a good hundred yards. "I can run back to the safe little world they created for me, or I can face my past here and now and be the granddaughter Gramps had hoped I'd become when he gave me up." She walked out onto the old dock, sat with her feet dangling over the end, and wrapped one arm around Bear's neck. "So what do you think? Will you help me? I can't move you to a new home at your age, and I would never abandon you."

Bear licked her cheek, his tail thumping the dock.

"Then it's settled. Together we'll turn Fox Run into the best specialty lumber mill on *both* sides of the border."

"Anna! *Anna!*"

Bear stood at the familiar voice and barked loudly.

Ethan was running down the path from the house, his shirt half buttoned and his boots unlaced, his panicked gaze searching the shoreline. When he spotted her sitting on the dock, he came to a sliding halt and seemed to instantly relax—though he did eye her suspiciously.

"Ah, would you like me to cook you some breakfast?" he asked, finishing buttoning his shirt. "I think there's still some bacon left."

Anna stood up and walked toward him. "Thank you for bringing me home last night," she said. "And I'll cook you breakfast before you leave." She started walking toward the house. "And I'll refund the rest of your lease just as soon as the bank opens tomorrow," she added as he fell into step beside her. "How long have you known?"

"Quite a while. When were you going to tell me?"

She stopped and faced him. "Never."

"Why?"

Anna waved a dismissive hand. "What would have been the point, since Abby Fox no longer exists? Besides, it doesn't matter who I was, or even who I'll be ten years from now. The past and future don't define a person, only the present."

Ethan started walking again. "So let me get this straight—you never intended to tell me because you don't see our past affecting our future? Have I got it right?"

"No, I don't see our past affecting our *present*," she clarified, stopping with her foot on the bottom step of the porch. "I never think about the future, since it's an exercise in futility most of the time. Stuff happens, and life changes direction in the blink of an eye."

He rubbed his forehead. "It's too early for philosophical talk, Segee. You're giving me a headache."

"Then go home, Ethan. You've done your good deed."

He got that suspicious look again. "You're high-tailing it to Quebec the moment I leave, aren't you?"

"No. I'm going back to work on my mill."

"And your mother coming on Friday? You're telling me you're going to be right here, waiting to greet her with open arms?"

Anna walked up the steps onto the porch, but stopped at the open doorway. "What happened to my door?"

"I didn't have the key last night."

"Oh." She looked up at him. "I haven't spoken to Madeline in over eight years. I don't even know which number husband she's on now."

"How come she and Samuel never stayed in contact with you?"

"That was my father's idea. He only agreed to come get me if Gramps and Madeline promised to cut me out of their lives."

"That's a little extreme, don't you think?"

"Daddy's an extreme sort of guy. Segee Logging and Lumber wouldn't be what it is today if he was anything else." She shrugged. "Apparently after Gramps explained what had happened to me, Dad came down the very next day and somehow got them to agree to his conditions. I never spoke to Gramps ever again, and Madeline has only called me twice—on my sixteenth and twenty-first birthdays."

"And you never once tried to contact Samuel?"

She finally walked in the house, but stopped in

the middle of the living room and turned to him. "It would have devastated my father if I had. And I was *eleven* when I left. For years, I thought Gramps had sent me away because what had happened at the lake was my fault. And by the time I realized differently, I . . . I was . . . too much time had passed," she finished, turning away.

"Giving you up must have been hard on Samuel."

Anna eyed the stack of journals sitting on the coffee table. "Yes, he loved me very much."

"I'd like permission to read his journals," Ethan said, walking over and picking up the one he'd left on the couch. He opened it and leafed through the pages. "I started reading them last night, but quickly realized they're very personal."

"I don't want them leaving here," she said, taking the notebook from him and putting it with the others. "And if you know they're letters to me from Samuel, why would you want to read them?"

"Because I think they might give us some insight into what your intruders are looking for."

She shook her head. "I'll keep that in mind as I read, but I don't want them leaving here," she repeated.

He walked into the kitchen. "You're a little slow catching on this morning, Segee. I'm not leaving."

"Yes, you are," she said, scowling when he opened the fridge and started pulling out bacon and eggs and setting them on the counter. "I'm fine now. I just got caught off guard last night. And I sure as heck don't need a babysitter who thinks I would throw myself in the lake."

He straightened to glare at her over the fridge door. "I wasn't worried you'd jumped in the lake. I thought you might run off to Quebec."

"I'm not running away."

"That's good," he said, his head buried in the fridge again. "Because we have less than a month to plan our wedding."

"Wedding?" she choked out.

"Yep," he said calmly, closing the fridge and carrying the butter over to the stove. "Last night I told everyone we're planning a May wedding."

"For God's sake, why would you say something like that!"

He turned with his fists on his hips, his expression defensive. "Because it was all I could think of at the time."

"Why did you have to think of anything?"

"You didn't see their faces, Anna. And you have no idea how everyone around here still feels about Madeline. The woman slept with half the men in this town before she took off to greener pastures."

"What has that got to do with me or our 'wedding?'" She took a deep breath and shook her head. "I'm never getting married," she said with forced calmness. "So you'll just have to tell everyone it was a misunderstanding on your part."

"Never?" he repeated incredulously.

"Yes, never."

His eyes narrowed. "So if you happen to fall in love with someone, you intend to have a fifty-year *affair* with him?"

Realizing she was getting defensive, Anna took another calming breath. "This conversation is crazy. I realize your knight-in-shining-armor complex made you blurt out that we're getting married," she said, "but saying you're going to marry me will only prove to everyone that I'm following in Madeline's footsteps and that you're about to become my first pigeon." She laughed a bit hysterically. "No, I take that back. Madeline was on husband number three by the time she was twenty-nine. Now that they know who I am, everyone will assume I left a trail of husbands in Quebec and came down here to look for more victims."

He folded his arms over his chest and leaned back against the counter. "So you'll make sure no one can say you're just like your mother by never getting married," he softly surmised, only to suddenly frown. "What do you mean, my 'knight-in-shining-armor complex'?"

Anna blinked at him. "You really don't see it? Ethan, you keep rushing in to rescue women."

"Women? Plural? Who in hell have you been talking to? I did my 'rescue' thing eighteen years ago, and admittedly again last night, but you're the only woman I seem to have a problem with." He puffed up his chest. "You actually see me as a knight in shining armor?"

"*Rusted* armor," she clarified, feeling a blush climb into her cheeks. "And what about Pamela Sant?"

In less time than it took her to blink, Ethan went from amused to menacing. "What about her?"

"I know you loved her," she whispered, wanting to kick herself for bring up Pamela's name. "And that she was pregnant when she died."

"And did you also happen to hear that I killed her?"

"I heard she missed a turn and crashed into Oak Creek, and that you tried to save her but couldn't," she said, not quite able to meet his eyes.

"Look at me, Anna."

It took some effort, but she lifted her gaze to his.

"Pamela was pregnant, but with Parker Sikes's child, not mine," he told her. "I'd stopped seeing Pam a couple of months earlier." He pushed away from the counter and walked up to her. "And yes, we did argue that night, when she asked to meet me someplace where people wouldn't see us. So we met in an old gravel pit up by our hauling artery."

"Why did she want to talk to you, if she'd broken it off?"

"To ask me what to do. Parker was in Boston at the time, interviewing for a job, and Pam was afraid if she told him she was pregnant, he'd want her to move to Boston with him."

"And she didn't want to go?"

"*Bangor* was too big a city for Pamela. She was scared to death of moving to Boston. But she was even more scared of staying here and having a baby without a husband."

"Why does everyone think Pamela was pregnant with *your* baby?" Anna asked.

"Because I never said differently," he said, dropping the bacon into the frypan.

"Why not?"

"To what end? Pam was dead, so it really didn't matter. And Parker was shaken up enough by her death. They'd been high school sweethearts, and I think he never stopped loving her."

"But you could have gone to jail for manslaughter."

His back to her, he broke eggs into a bowl. "If the trial hadn't gone my way, I'd have spoken up."

Anna felt like kicking him. "*Now* do you see what I mean? You've got this compelling need to protect everyone. Including some guy who got your ex-girlfriend pregnant."

He turned around to face her, folding his arms over his chest and leaning back against the counter. "And since when is it a crime to care?" he asked softly.

"When your own life gets screwed in the process," she snapped. "When you're only twelve years old and you get beaten to a bloody pulp, when you stand trial for manslaughter for something that wasn't your fault, and when you tell half the town that you're getting *married* next month!" She walked over to the stove and turned off the burner under the bacon. "Go home, Ethan. I want to be alone."

He turned the burner back on, then returned to fixing the eggs. "You're just going to have to pretend I'm not here," he said. "Because I'm not leaving."

"I am not running off to Quebec," she said through gritted teeth.

He shrugged. "Still, I think I'll stick around just in case you change your mind."

"Why?"

He turned and faced her again. "Maybe because I'd like to see what it feels like for someone to rescue *me*."

Anna looked blank. "What?"

"I'll admit I didn't exactly think it through last night, but I was trying to head off a problem for you. But now it seems that *I'm* the one with the problem. My reputation in this town isn't exactly sterling, and if we don't get married next month, I might as well head to Quebec with you."

Anna rolled her eyes. "Of all the— Ethan, you just have to do a bit of damage control and it will all blow over in a couple of months. You can't really expect us to get married just to save your reputation."

He shrugged again. "It's a viable solution."

Anna spun on her heel and headed into the living room, deciding she'd had enough. She ran upstairs to her bedroom and rummaged in the bottom of her closet for her work clothes. The man was certifiably insane. Did he actually think she'd marry him just to save his reputation?

I'd like to see what it feels like for someone to rescue me.

Anna plopped down on the floor. Was that really how Ethan felt, or was it just a line to get her to cooperate? But what did he need her cooperation *for*?

To continue their affair?

Or . . . was this payback for not telling him who she was?

Chapter Eighteen

Ethan spent the rest of Sunday morning on the couch, reading Samuel's journals while Anna and Bear were out at the saw house, likely up to their ears in grease. He should have felt guilty for not helping, but he was too intrigued by Samuel's journals. Besides, Anna obviously needed to vent her frustration on something, and better a rusted old engine than his rusted suit of armor.

He couldn't decide if she was angry at him for refusing to walk out of her life, or at herself for not handling last night's public disclosure as well as she would have liked. Then there was the little matter of their upcoming wedding—which was why he'd hidden the shotgun under the couch.

He smiled as he turned the delicate journal page

that was more ink than paper. Imagine deciding never to get married. For someone who didn't care to dwell on the future, Anna had obviously thought long and hard on that particular aspect of it. Which meant he had three weeks to change her mind—because for some reason he refused to dwell on himself, the idea of their getting married was starting to appeal to him.

Ethan frowned and turned back the page to read the last paragraph again. He dropped his feet to the floor and sat up straight, vaguely noticing when the back door slammed and Anna came into the kitchen. He stood up, still scanning the page as he walked out to her. "Did you know that Samuel sold a good chunk of Fox Run to Joshua Coots to raise cash to restore the mill?"

He looked up when Anna didn't immediately answer and found her guzzling a tall glass of water. And yup, she had smudges of grease on her cheek and chin. Ethan glanced down at Bear and saw even the dog had grease on one ear.

"No, you've got it wrong," she finally said, setting down her glass and walking over to look at the journal in his hand. "Joshua Coots sold *Gramps* the thousand acres that runs from the main road to the lake five years ago." She looked up with a frown. "Frank told me about it last night, and he wasn't happy that his dad sold it for only twelve thousand dollars."

Ethan closed the journal, keeping the page marked with his finger, and showed her the year written on the cover. "Samuel sold Joshua that piece of land two years after you'd left for Quebec," he explained, opening the journal back up and pointing at one paragraph in particular. "He writes that he hated to give up any of the land, but that he was determined Fox Run would be a working mill again when you inherited it."

Anna read the paragraph, then reached over his arm and turned back the page to read it again.

"And here," he said, pointing at the bottom of the next page. "Samuel goes on to tell you that he and Joshua drew up a legal document stating that he could buy back the land for the same price plus twenty percent."

"So that means Gramps sold that acreage to Joshua for ten thousand dollars sixteen years ago, then bought it back five years ago for twelve thousand?"

Ethan turned and headed into the living room, going to the coffee table and rummaging through the stack of journals until he found the one dated five years ago. "It would seem so, if that's what Frank told you last night," he said. He opened the book to the first page, quickly scanned it, and started turning pages. "It wasn't uncommon in that era to barter land back and forth as collateral. My father bought the sporting camps they're living in now, along with the six hundred acres they're sitting on, with the stipulation that the original owners could pick out ten acres from our land closer to town to build their new home. And that was only four years ago."

Anna had picked up the older journal Ethan had been reading and started leafing through the pages that followed the disclosure of the first sale. "Then if Gramps got ten thousand dollars to start restoring Fox Run, where is it? He obviously never spent it on the mill."

"We're probably going to have to read all the journals to find that out," Ethan said, still turning pages. He sat on the couch, pulling her down beside him. "You read forward from sixteen years ago, and I'll start reading backward from when he bought back the land from Joshua five years ago."

"That'll take us forever."

"Just scan the pages." He leaned the journal against his chest and looked over at her. "What else did dear old Frank have to say last night?"

"Only that his father has lost his mind, and that he's going to try and get a judge to void the sale on the grounds that Gramps took advantage of Joshua by paying so little for land worth nearly a million dollars." She grinned derisively. "Or I could become his partner and we could combine his mountain and my mill and offer the package to the developers."

Ethan tapped the book she was holding. "That means Frank Coots could very well be your ghost. Or he might have hired two men to do his dirty work. They must be looking for the document that states the conditions of the original sale. Frank could very well argue that his father was already showing signs of dementia five years ago, but if you show up with the original sales agreement, it would prove Joshua Coots was merely honoring a promise he made sixteen years ago."

"But wouldn't that document have been with all the papers my lawyers got when Gramps died? Land sales have to be recorded."

Ethan shook his head. "Only the deed needs to be recorded. And you know how old people are; most of the time deals are sealed with only a handshake. This was likely a private agreement between Samuel and Joshua, but your grandfather was smart enough to actually put it in writing."

"And Frank knows about the agreement, and he and his goons are trying to find that document so I won't have any proof it was a legitimate sale?"

"Frank must know about it; his father also would have had a copy. But we're all assuming Samuel didn't tear up his copy of the agreement after he bought back the land." Ethan lifted the journal in his hands. "Let's hope he told you about it in his letters."

With a sigh, Anna propped her feet up on the coffee table and looked down at her book. "He wrote about every other detail of his daily life, so it's probably in here somewhere."

Ethan reached out and pushed the book down to her lap so that she'd look at him. "Anna," he said softly. "I have a suspicion that Samuel's accident wasn't really an accident."

She went utterly still, her face paling and her

bright green eyes going wide. "What makes you say that?" she whispered.

"And I don't think yours was an accident, either." He turned to face her, his hand still covering hers. "I haven't found a spring anywhere near that section of road, and it's been completely free of ice since you spun out there."

"But how . . . "

"That piece of road is quite steep and curving, and if someone were to dump enough water on it so that it froze to black ice, you wouldn't be able to negotiate the turn."

"But they said it was an accident with Gramps. That's what the sheriff's office told Daddy when he called to find out what happened."

He squeezed her hand. "I don't have any proof otherwise—just a gut feeling. Don't you think both incidents are a little too coincidental?"

"But that would mean Gramps was murdered."

"And that someone attempted to murder you. Or at least get you out of the way long enough to find what he's looking for."

She leaned back into her couch cushion. "You really think someone tried to kill me?" She suddenly narrowed her eyes at him. "You've obviously given this a lot of thought. How long have you suspected the accidents were deliberate?"

"Since yours."

"And you never said anything to me. Why?" She dropped her feet to the floor and leaned toward him, getting right in his face. "Honest to God, if you say you were trying to protect me, I'll smack you clear into tomorrow."

Ethan settled back and started reading. He could feel her glare boring into him for a full minute before he heard her sigh, put her feet back up on the coffee table, and start reading as well.

He'd dodged a dent in his armor that time, though he'd probably be wise to sleep with one eye open tonight—since he didn't want to miss even one moment of Anna driving him crazy.

"What do you mean, you're not going to work? You can't expect Keith to run Loon Cove all by himself," Anna said.

Ethan tucked his shirt in his pants and buckled his belt as he eyed Anna's pajamas—which she'd slept in again last night—with loathing. He might have bullied his way into bed, but her flannel armor made it clear that he wouldn't be making love to her.

Lord, she was wonderfully stubborn.

"Alex is working the mill today," he told her, sitting down on the bed to put on his socks. "So I can stay here and help you finish tearing apart your saw engine. Or start demolishing the building around it, if you'd prefer." He stood up and faced her. "Or we could take the day off and run down to Bangor and shop for wedding rings."

Anna's eyes widened and her jaw dropped. She spun around and stomped into the hall and down the stairs, the soft flannel feet of her pajamas completely ruining her display of outrage.

It was obvious she knew he was hanging around to make sure she didn't suddenly head for Quebec, and she didn't care for the notion that he didn't trust her word not to run. But the fact was, he didn't trust himself not to chase after her, and he definitely didn't relish the idea of facing all four Segee brothers on their home turf.

He stepped into the hallway. "I hope our kids have my disposition," he called down after her.

"Bite me!" she shouted from the kitchen.

Giving her a moment to cool down, Ethan made the bed and straightened up a bit—which included leaning out the window to pick up the dirty clothes that Anna had thrown onto the porch roof when she'd realized they were making the bedroom reek of grease. He tossed them into the hallway to remind him to put them with the rest of the laundry, then stuffed a baby-pink bra in the drawer and straightened the lotions scattered all over the bureau. He picked up the diamond stud earrings she'd been wearing Saturday night and shook his head at her carelessness.

He softly whistled when he lifted the cover of her jewelry box and discovered that Miss Anna Segee owned a small fortune in jewelry. He stared at the colorful array of gems set in a couple of rings, three or four necklaces, and several pairs of earrings. He picked up one ring that particularly caught his eye and examined what he suspected was a genuine ruby surrounded by small, glittering diamonds. He hadn't thought about Anna coming from money; she was . . . well, she was just *Anna*, his bossy ex-foreman, aggravating landlord, and mind-blowing lover.

What if her decision to never get married had as much to do with gold-digging boyfriends as it did with Madeline's parade of husbands? And what if she thought *he* wanted to marry her for her money and not for the way she made him crazy-happy?

Aw, hell. Why couldn't she just be the owner of a broken-down old mill that was going to take a year of Sundays to restore instead of heiress to a logging empire with the assets of a small nation?

Maybe he could offer to draw up a prenuptial agreement between them, so she'd realize he didn't want any part of her inheritance. Or he could have a private man-to-man talk with her daddy. *After* the wedding, so he'd get to enjoy his honeymoon before the Segee brothers showed up en masse and tried to feed his guts to the wolves.

Ethan closed the jewelry box and scowled at himself in the mirror over the bureau. He didn't care if Anna had more money than God; he was marrying her in three weeks if he had to single-handedly take on André Segee and his four sons.

Ethan suddenly sat down on the bed, stunned. He loved her, dammit. Sometime in the last couple of weeks, he had fallen in love with Anna. And not the grow-old-together sort of love, but the walk-through-the-fires-of-hell kind of love that turns a guy's mind to mush and twists his insides into knots until he doesn't know if he's coming or going.

Ethan rested his arms on his knees and hung his head. Well, hell. He hadn't even seen this coming. He'd always assumed that when the right woman came along, he'd instinctively know she was the one. But he hadn't expected her to come walking out of his past. Who would have thought, eighteen years ago, that the shy, quiet little girl he'd caught more than once eyeing him from afar would be the future Mrs. Knight?

Ethan lifted his head with a snort. *Maybe* she'd be Mrs. Knight, if he didn't do anything dumb in the next three weeks—like act too protective, get too bossy, or become so frustrated with her that he threw her in the lake.

But he did intend to burn those flannel pajamas.

With the resolve of a brave and noble knight with slightly tarnished armor, who was facing the greatest test of his courage, Ethan stood up and walked downstairs. He found Anna sitting on the couch, sipping tea and reading one of Samuel's journals, still in those damn pajamas.

"Are we tearing apart the saw engine or not?" he asked on his way to the kitchen.

"I have no idea what *you're* doing," she said. "But I'm finding that sales agreement today."

"What makes you think you can find it in one day if your ghosts have been looking for it for the last six months? They had this entire place to themselves right after Samuel died, and they never found it," he called to her as he poured lukewarm water over his tea bag. He really needed to get a coffeemaker; Anna's tea just didn't have the morning kick he needed.

"They didn't have Gramps's journals," she called back. "And I'm not leaving this couch until I find out what he did with that document."

Ethan poked his head into the living room. "I've thought about that, and I think we're looking in the wrong direction. Instead of reading backward from the sale five years ago, we should read forward from it. It's *after* the sale that Samuel would have either filed away or torn up the agreement."

"But he didn't have to actually *have* it to buy the land." Her forehead wrinkled in a frown. "Joshua and Gramps knew about their agreement, so producing the piece of paper was unnecessary." She shook her head. "I think Gramps hid it right after he sold the land to Joshua sixteen years ago, and I also think he told me where." She canted her head. "If Gramps had died before he bought back the land, do you think the agreement would have passed down to me?"

Ethan shrugged. "That depends on whether Samuel stated that condition." He took a sip of tea as he thought. "Having learned a lot about your grandfather from reading those journals, I'd say yeah, he would have made sure you could buy back the land."

"Then we have to find that document before Frank takes me to court."

"Which means we have to think like an eighty-three-year-old man," Ethan mused.

"Or a sixty-seven-year-old man if he hid it sixteen years ago."

Ethan walked into the living room and sat down on the hearth facing her. "And we know your grandfather's generation didn't trust banks after the depression, so what *did* they trust?"

"Old mason jars buried out back."

"Hell, that leaves two thousand acres for us to dig up."

She lifted the journal on her lap. "Gramps wouldn't have hidden it very far away. It's got to be someplace here in camp. A root cellar or springhouse, maybe?" She shook her head with a laugh. "Or it's as easy as digging under the porch."

Ethan eyed Bear snoozing in his bed. "I bet he knows," he said, using his mug to point at the dog. "And them, too," he added, pointing at the chickadees roosting on the curtain rod. "They would have seen Samuel coming and going to his stash over the years, which means that it's got to be someplace easily accessible for an old man. Samuel wouldn't have risked his valuables anyplace that could burn down, so that rules out buildings, including under the porch, since the ground would get hot enough to ignite any papers buried there."

Anna stood up. "I'll get dressed and we can start walking the property, looking for ground that's been disturbed."

Ethan shook his head. "He wouldn't have buried it in the ground, either. The frost would have prevented him from getting to it in the winter."

She ran up the stairs. "Then we'll look for a spring-house or root cellar or something," she said, her voice trailing off as she entered her bedroom. She suddenly stuck her head back out her door. "Making the bed does not give you brownie points, Knight," she called down to him.

"I am not a suck-up," he shot back, carrying her empty mug into the kitchen to rinse it out.

He noticed his vitamins sitting on the counter and smiled. So she wanted him to live to be a hundred, did she? He popped the pills in his mouth and turned when she came running into the kitchen, completely dressed. "That was fast," he commented, just before washing down the horse pill with his cold tea.

"We'll hunt until sunset and read the journals in the evening, if we don't find it today," she said, slipping on her jacket.

Ethan nodded agreement, not wanting to point out that she had enlisted his help without bothering to ask. Apparently as long as he was useful, he could stick around. "You go get started," he said. "I want to call Alex and make sure he's doing okay at the mill. I'll join you in a few minutes."

The second she was out the door, Ethan headed upstairs, picked up the pajamas that she'd thrown on the bed, and crammed them as far back under the bureau as he could. Satisfied he'd taken care of that little problem, he pulled out his cell phone and walked back downstairs, stepped out onto the front porch, and dialed Alex's number.

"This place is a madhouse," Alex said without preamble when he answered his phone. "And this yard is so goddamned tight, you've got to step outside the gate to change your mind. How's Anna doing?"

"She's fine," Ethan said with a chuckle. "And welcome to my world."

"If she's fine, then come to work before I padlock the gate and give everyone a paid holiday."

"She's not *that* fine. I'm still afraid that if I let her out of my sight, she'll head for Quebec."

There was a heartbeat of silence, then Alex said softly, "Maybe that's for the best, Ethan. It's going to be hell for her to live in this town now."

"I'm marrying her in three weeks."

There was a long silence. "Are you sure you know what you're doing?"

"I'm sure," he told Alex. "I love her."

"And does she love you?"

Ethan hesitated. "She must. She keeps feeding me vitamins."

Alex snorted. "She's probably laced them with rat poison."

Ethan grinned. He hadn't thought about that. "She's still here," he offered. "And I'm still here with her."

"Ethan, you can't force it just because you want it."

"I just need some time alone with her. She'll come around."

"Then why don't you spend your time together *here*, running Loon Cove Lumber?" Alex growled. Ethan heard an air horn blast in the background.

"I fired her, remember? If I hire her back, it will look bad to my crew. Besides, I need *quality* time alone with her. Did you find her purse and coat at the school?"

"Sarah did," Alex told him. "And we drove Anna's truck to Loon Cove and parked it just inside the gate."

"Thanks. By the way, do you remember where Grampy Knight used to hide his valuables? I know he had a secret stash outside someplace, but I can't remember where."

"Grampy's stash?" Alex repeated, obviously confused.

"Yeah. I remember being just a little kid and him telling me that a wise man kept his valuables tucked in a safe place out of the house. Anna and I are looking for a document Samuel Fox would have wanted to keep safe. Where was Grampy's stash?"

Alex's chuckle came over the phone. "I think he kept a gallon jug buried out by an old rock down the path to the lake. But Samuel's stash could be anyplace. I remember Grampy telling me it was sort of an ongoing contest between men as to who could come up with the most inventive hidey-hole. He told me about one man who hid his entire savings someplace on his property, then couldn't find it for nearly three years because he hadn't even told his wife where it was. Another guy thought he was being smarter than everyone else by hiding his stash under a false bottom in their rain barrel. But the squirrels chewed through the wood because he'd used an old peanut butter tin, and they ate his money. Samuel could have hidden his stuff anyplace on Fox Run."

"Damn," Ethan muttered.

"Honest to God," Alex snapped, obviously running. "I never realized what big babies these truckers are. That load needs to go over there!" he shouted. "I have to go," he said in a rush. "If you want your mill to still be standing, you and Anna better be here tomorrow morning."

The connection cut off, and Ethan headed down the steps to catch up with Anna.

"Everything okay at Loon Cove?" she asked as he drew near.

"Running as smooth as a baby's butt," he told her, taking her hand to guide her in another direction. "He wouldn't have hid it in the machine shed, or any other building that could burn down. Is there a spring-house around here?"

"No, just an old hand-dug well that's dried up, over there," she said, pointing a few hundred feet behind the house. "And I seem to recall that Gramps had a root cellar. I remember not wanting to go down inside it, and I cried whenever he did, because I was afraid the spiders would eat him."

"Where is it?"

She looked around, turning in a slow circle. "I can't remember. I must have blocked out its location because it scared me."

"How about if we take a ride someplace and get away from everything?" he suggested. "We could go down to Portland and spend the night, or head to the coast and rent a cabin on the water. It's not tourist season yet."

"I want to look for that document."

"Sometimes the harder you push at something, the more it resists. Some time away might help us see things in a different light."

"I can't leave Bear."

"We'll find someplace that allows animals. Come on, it'll be fun. We'll bring Bear and the journals, and we'll read until our eyeballs fall out."

"It won't work, you know," she said, smiling up at him. "You're not going to seduce me into marrying you."

Ethan gave her his best innocent look and covered his heart with his hand. "On my honor, Segee, I would never use sex to get what I want."

She snorted, then gave him an assessing look. "We'll only be gone one night?"

"We'll be back tomorrow by sunset," he promised. "Unless you're having such a good time that you want to stay another night. It'll be your call."

She looked around the mill camp, then back at him. "And we'll bring the journals?"

He nodded.

"Can we take my truck? It's got satellite radio and navigation."

He grabbed her hand before she could change her mind and headed toward the house. "If you want. Sarah found your purse and coat at the dance, and Alex drove your truck to Loon Cove last night. We'll swap vehicles on our way."

She pulled her hand free and ran ahead of him, clearly warming up to the idea. "You pack Bear some food and gather up the journals. I'll pack us some clothes," she said, running up the front steps and into the house.

Ethan followed at a more leisurely pace, shoving his hands in his pockets and whistling a happy tune. This was definitely a promising turn of events.

"I can't find my pajamas!" she called down as he entered the house. "I know I left them right here when I got dressed," she said, stepping into the hall to look down the stairs at him.

He shrugged. "I wasn't wearing them. Just pack one of your nighties."

"No matter," she said, disappearing back into the bedroom. "I've got another pair in my bureau."

Well, damn.

Chapter Nineteen

$\mathcal{T}$hey arrived at $\mathcal{L}$oon $\mathcal{C}$ove Lumber just as the last of several fire trucks went speeding into the mill. Ethan pulled up outside the gate and parked well out of the way, and Anna was out of the truck before he even shut the engine off. She ran toward the man who appeared to be the fire chief, shouting orders as he stood upwind of the black smoke billowing out the windows of the saw building.

"You need to start watering down the sawdust pile so we can bucket it away from the building," she told him as she looked for Keith amid the swarming chaos of men. "If we try to move it dry, the dust will combust."

"Who the hell are you?" he asked, taking hold of her arm and trying to turn her away.

Anna stood firm. "I'm the foreman here, and I've fought several mill fires in Quebec. How many have you dealt with?"

He let go. "None," he admitted, and looked toward the saw shed. "The point of origin seems to be the saw itself, according to what your crew told me."

"I'll use our excavator to punch a whole in the roof to vent it," she said, still looking for Keith as she spoke. She finally saw him talking with Ethan and Alex as they headed toward her, their faces lit by the flames shooting out the central windows of the long and narrow saw shed. She looked back at the chief. "You need to set up your largest hoses at each end of the building and keep pushing the fire toward the center. Once I get it vented, it'll go up instead of spreading out and will eventually suffocate itself."

He grabbed her arm when she turned away. "We'll vent the roof," he said, again trying to push her toward the office.

She shrugged free. "It's not safe to place men on the roof, but I can punch a hole in it with the excavator."

"My crew will—"

A sudden explosion sent flames and fumes out through the windows and both ends of the building. "Get those hoses going!" she yelled, running toward Keith and Alex and Ethan.

"Keith, switch the loader forks to the bucket, and as soon as they get that sawdust pile watered down, start pushing it away from the building. But keep an eye on what's happening around you. If the fire gets too close, get out of there. Ethan," she shouted over the noise, "there's a hydrant that runs to the river beside the machine shed and three diesel-powered water pumps inside. Get the men to start watering down the buildings and all the rows of timber. They know where the other hydrants are. Alex, you put a couple of men in pulp loaders and start moving the timber you were going to saw today."

Keith leapt into action, but Alex and Ethan stared at her as if she were speaking a foreign language.

"I've fought fires at our own mills, and I can tell you that if we don't get going, every inch of this property will go up in flames. Let's go!" she yelled, giving Ethan a nudge.

He held his ground. "What are you going to do?" he shouted.

"Vent that roof!" she told him, running to the excavator.

He caught up with her within three strides and swung her around to face him. "You go start the water pumps. I'll vent the roof."

Anna thought about arguing, but it would only slow things down. "Okay," she said. "Just get in close enough to drop the boom through the roof to make a hole, then get the hell back out of there fast."

"Yes, ma'am." He ran for the excavator.

Anna watched him climb into the big machine, then ran to join several of the crew who already had the pumps hooked up to the first of three hydrants. "Okay, guys," she shouted. "We've practiced this enough that you can do it in your sleep. Hose down everything and watch your backs. There's a mess of equipment working here. Mills can be rebuilt; bodies can't."

"You got it, boss lady," they said to a man, grinning broadly as they scrambled into action.

Anna ran nonstop for the next five hours, going from team to team to see how they were holding up, while keeping an eye on Ethan to make sure he didn't slip into his knight's armor and rush to the rescue of someone. Once the fire chief realized that her plan to contain the fire to the saw building was actually working, he started consulting her on each step of their hard-fought battle.

"You're going to have to leave a truck and crew here for the night," she told the chief, sitting down on a stack of wet lumber for the first time in hours. She wiped her face with the tail of her shirt. "And we'll leave several of our own crew to help you. Mill fires are more stubborn than most, and you'll discover hot spots you thought were completely dead. We'll keep our equipment standing by to tear apart the timber and sawdust piles, in case they're still smoldering inside." She tiredly shook her head. "I've seen spots flare up five and six days after we thought we'd gotten all the embers extinguished."

"You're beat, Segee," Ethan said, plopping down on the stack of lumber beside her. He wrapped an arm around her shoulders and pulled her to lean against him. "God, you stink. Go home. I'll stay and help the crew."

A large group of dirty, exhausted men started to gather around them, and Anna tried to move away from Ethan. But he just hauled her back against his side, grinning down at her from his blackened face and giving her a wink that said he knew his proprietary display made her uncomfortable.

"There's a ton of food set out in the office," Sarah Knight said as she approached with her two children.

"And there's cake," Tucker added, staring wide-eyed at all the dirty men.

Anna stood up, effectively shedding Ethan. "I'm starved," she said, heading for the office.

Delaney fell into step beside her. "You sure looked pretty Saturday night," she told Anna. "Are you really going to marry Uncle Ethan?"

"I'm really not," Anna said, softening her words with a lopsided smile at the girl. "Ethan just said that to protect me."

"From what?"

"Old rumors and town gossip."

"Uncle Ethan's lonely."

"Really?" Anna said, stopping outside the office door. "What makes you say that?"

"He hardly ever goes out on dates, and he's so serious all the time. He needs to find a girlfriend who makes him laugh. Someone like you."

"I think I make him crazy," Anna said, herself

laughing. "And you may have loneliness mixed up with plain old grumpiness."

"But that's just it. Since he's been living at Fox Run, he seems happier. He laughs more, too, when he comes home to visit." Delaney got a twinkle in her eye as she smiled up at Anna. "I think he really likes you, but just doesn't know how to say so." She scrunched up her face. "But he never took his eyes off you all Saturday night."

"That's because he'd never seen me in a dress before," Anna said, opening the door and going inside.

"But couldn't you just *think* about marrying him?" Delaney asked, leading her over to the table laden with food. She leaned in close to whisper, so the women setting out food wouldn't hear. "At least go on some dates with him. I know you could fall in love with Uncle Ethan if you tried."

Anna also leaned down to whisper. "Can you keep a secret?"

Delaney nodded.

"Ethan and I were headed out on a date today when we saw the fire. Would you go out to your uncle's truck and get Bear for me?" she asked as she straightened. "He's been stuck in there for hours. You could bring him in and give him some water."

"Sure," Delaney said, her face brightening with the news that Anna was dating her uncle.

"You, young woman, are enough to make an old man cry, dancing with me one day and saving my mill the next," Grady Knight said as he came up and pulled her into a bear of a hug. "Thank you, Anna," he said, stepping back. "We know how to fight forest fires, but not mill fires."

"They can be stubborn."

"Do you have any idea how it could have started?" he asked, just as Paul and Alex and Ethan came over, looking exhausted and covered head to toe in soot.

Anna shook her head. "Everything in this mill was completely up to code, and that saw shed has a foam extinguishing system. A fire shouldn't have lasted more than two minutes once that system kicked in, and it certainly shouldn't have spread that quickly. Tom Bishop had all the equipment inspected just before you took over."

"Could it have been deliberately set?" Clay Porter asked, walking over and handing Anna a plate of food. He was also covered in soot from his hair to his boots, his shirt torn and his pants wet up to the knees.

"You think someone started the fire on purpose?" Anna asked.

Clay looked over at Ethan, and ignoring his scowl, said, "I was headed to Jackman early this morning to look at a used tree harvester when I noticed a pickup parked off the road beside your northern fence line." He glanced over at Anna and smiled. "And since I've gotten in the habit of checking for birdshot dents, I stopped to look at the truck's tailgate. It had a bunch of tiny pings in it."

"Did you get the plate number?" Ethan asked.

Clay reached in his shirt pocket and produced what looked like a page torn out of a classified ad magazine. "I wrote it down. It was a dark blue Ford pickup, maybe six or seven years old. Straight cab, missing the right outside mirror, and it had a cracked rear window."

"I'll give this to Tate," Ethan said, taking the paper with a nod of thanks. "Did you see anyone hanging around or hear anything unusual this morning?"

"I thought I heard a light tapping from someplace inside the mill, but it lasted only a few seconds and was sort of muffled, so I can't be sure." He handed Anna the cup of punch he'd been holding, and she washed down the sandwich she'd all but inhaled.

Clay looked back at Ethan. "I'm wondering if someone tampered with your extinguisher and set the fire to go off when you started up the saw this morning. The state fire marshal should be able to figure out what happened." He nodded at Anna. "Nice seeing you again, Anna. And my offer still stands," he added with a wink before giving his attention back to the men. "Grady, gentlemen," he said, also nodding to them. "I hate like hell to think we have an arsonist around. Hope that plate number helps," he finished, turning and leaving.

"What offer?" Ethan growled.

Anna swallowed the last of her second sandwich. "Twice what you were paying me to help him build a lumber mill from the ground up." She picked up the cupcake Clay had thoughtfully added to her plate.

"And his promise not to fire me for saving a dog. I'm heading home, soaking in a tub of steaming water, and going to bed." She looked Ethan square in the eye. "Your crew gets a whole week's wages for today," she added, then popped the cupcake in her mouth and left.

"Ronald Briggs? You're sure?" Ethan said.

John Tate tossed his radio mike on the seat of his cruiser. "That's who they said the pickup is registered to. So tell me why you look like you've just seen a ghost."

"Ron Briggs was one of the boys who attacked Anna down at the lake eighteen years ago."

"From which all three of them walked away without so much as a slap on the wrist. I've always wondered why Samuel or Madeline never pressed charges against those boys. But that wouldn't have anything to do with what happened here today," John pointed out. "Briggs will do anything for a price. If he did set the fire, it's because somebody paid him."

"But Clay said Briggs's tailgate was peppered with birdshot, which means he was one of the men Anna shot at that night."

"That only implies that we're probably right: that Frank Coots may have hired a couple of locals to do his dirty work."

"Then why torch *my* mill?"

John rubbed his jaw. "To redirect your attention,

maybe? You've been spending a lot of time at Fox Run lately. It's hard to search a place if someone's always hanging around."

Ethan snorted. "They didn't need to burn down my mill. They could have had Fox Run all to themselves for the next two days. Anna and I were just heading down to the coast."

John laid a hand on Ethan's shoulder. "You only lost the saw building."

"And both saws."

"So you and Anna were heading off together, huh?" John shook his head. "Even covered in soot, she looked a hell of a lot better today than when you carried her off that dance floor Saturday night."

"I'm still a long way from getting her to marry me."

John lifted a brow in surprise. "You mean that wasn't just a ruse? You're really planning on marrying her?"

"I'm going to try." Ethan suddenly stiffened. "My God, if the fire was a distraction, Briggs could be at Fox Run right now. And Anna went home half an hour ago!"

"So whose truck was it?" Alex asked as he strode up, along with Grady and Paul.

"Ron Briggs's," Ethan said, grabbing Alex's arm and turning him toward the parking lot. "And we think he may have torched our mill to cause a distraction so he could search Fox Run. And Anna's there all alone," he explained to his brothers and father as they ran to his truck. "We need to get out there now!"

"I'll lead the way," John shouted to them as he climbed in his cruiser. "Stay behind me."

Alex and Paul climbed in Ethan's truck, and Ethan turned to his dad. "Somebody's got to stay here with the crew," he said.

Grady nodded. "I'll stay. You boys just be careful."

"We will," Ethan promised, climbing in and starting the engine. He pulled onto the main road right behind John, who immediately turned on his siren and flashing lights as they sped toward Fox Run.

"Dammit!" Ethan growled, hitting the steering wheel. "She's been there alone for over half an hour!"

"She's a smart girl," Alex offered. "She'll find someplace to hide if Briggs is snooping around."

Ethan shot his brother a quick glare, then looked back at the road. "You're talking about the woman who went after them with a shotgun. Damn, I hid it under the couch!"

"Why?" Paul asked in surprise.

"So she'd quit shooting at people!"

"You need to calm down, Ethan," Alex said. "We don't even know if Briggs is there."

"Why else would he have torched Loon Cove, if not to pull Anna and me away from Fox Run?"

"There's always your surprise announcement Saturday night," Alex offered. "Maybe he's still holding a grudge for the beating you gave him eighteen years ago, and hearing you're marrying Anna might have set him off when he learned who she really is."

"Then that makes her even more of a target. Dammit, go faster, Tate!" he shouted at the windshield.

"He's going as fast as the road will allow," Paul said calmly. "What exactly is Briggs looking for?"

"An agreement drawn up between Samuel Fox and Joshua Coots sixteen years ago, for a land barter deal."

"What has that got to do with Briggs?"

"We think Frank Coots may have hired Briggs and some other guy to hunt for the agreement. If it doesn't exist, then Coots can take Anna to court and try to get the sale voided on the grounds his father was incompetent." He glance briefly at his brothers, then back at the road. "I also think Samuel's accident was deliberate."

He felt Alex stiffen beside him. "You think the old man was murdered?"

"John's beginning to think so, too, because of Anna's accident in the exact same spot."

"How?"

"Somebody must have iced the road," he said, just as he hit the brakes and turned down Anna's road behind John, the cruiser's flashing lights strobing through the trees like blue and white chain lightning.

"When we get there, John's in charge," Alex warned.

John skidded to a stop behind Anna's truck, and Ethan drove straight up the footpath that led to the back porch.

Alex grabbed his arm when Ethan tried to get out. "The dog looks calm enough, considering we just showed up like an invading army," Alex said, nodding toward the porch. "Briggs must not be around."

"That dog is deaf and blind," Ethan growled, shrugging free and getting out. He was up on the porch in three strides. "Anna! Anna!"

"What?" she asked, suddenly appearing in the door window, her eyes wide with surprise.

Ethan came to an abrupt halt the moment he saw her. He bent over to brace his hands on his knees and took his first full breath in twenty minutes.

He heard the door open. "What's going on?" she asked. "Did the fire flare up again? Did somebody get hurt?"

"We thought your intruders were back," Alex said, walking up beside Ethan. "Ah, you might want to put on some clothes. You're about to have a house full of men."

Still too weak with relief to move, Ethan lifted only his head to see Anna standing in the open doorway, a large towel wrapped around her that she was clutching to her chest, her wet hair dripping over her bare shoulders.

"Were you rushing to my rescue again?" she asked, sighing dreamily. "How gallant of you, Ethan." She turned her provocative smile on Alex. "He's so determined to save me."

Ethan finally straightened and walked up to the

doorway, stopping in front of her. "It's Ron Briggs, Anna. We think he torched Loon Cove and is also your intruder."

Her smile disappeared and she paled, taking a step back. John Tate came walking into the kitchen from the living room, and stopped dead in his tracks when he saw Anna. His face reddened; he spun around and quickly walked back into the living room.

"Ron Briggs?" she whispered. "Y-you're sure?"

"The plate number Clay gave us is registered to Briggs," Ethan told her, taking hold of her shoulders and turning her toward the bathroom. "Where are your clothes?"

"Upstairs," she whispered.

"I'll get them while you dry off."

He softly closed the bathroom door and turned to his brothers. "Put on the kettle and make some hot cocoa," he said, walking past them into the living room. "We should probably take a look around outside," he told John.

"Yeah. I'll start working my way through the buildings."

"We'll come with you," Alex said as he and Paul also stepped into the living room. "Ethan, you stay with Anna."

"Why don't you or Paul stay with her?" he asked, preferring to be the one to find Briggs.

Alex smiled derisively. "Because we already have

our own women to deal with," he said, following John to the door.

The moment the three men stepped outside, Ethan strode upstairs two steps at a time, pulled some clothes out of the bureau, and ran back downstairs.

He knocked softly on the bathroom door. "I have some clothes for you," he said, slowly opening the door.

He found her sitting on the hamper, her face as pale as the towel wrapped around her.

"Why did Ron Briggs burn your mill?" she asked.

Ethan was relieved to see that she hadn't retreated back into her eleven-year-old world. "Maybe as a diversion to get you and me away from Fox Run, so he could continue searching." He snorted. "And maybe as payback for my beating him up eighteen years ago."

"And you all came speeding over because you thought I might have come home to find Ron here." She reached out and touched his arm, giving him a tentative smile. "Thank you. I wouldn't want to confront Ron Briggs alone."

Ethan lifted one brow. "So I do come in handy on occasion?"

She stood up and took her clothes. "Of course. Your armor's much more durable than mine," she said with a cheeky grin, giving him a nudge to leave the bathroom. "And you can cook, too. How about fixing us some bacon and eggs."

Ethan looked back at her. "The others are out searching the buildings."

"Then you should probably scramble a couple dozen eggs," she suggested, closing the door.

Ethan glared at the door. When had "cook" been added to his knightly duties?

Chapter Twenty

Anna lay on top of her bed, fully clothed right down to her boots, and smiled into the darkness as she cuddled into Ethan's warm embrace. It had been a hard-fought battle, and she had four very unhappy men on her hands, but she was here, by God.

This was her property, she'd argued, as well as her future at stake, and she wasn't about to let them tuck her safely away while they spent the night guarding Fox Run. She had finally threatened to sneak back on her own if they sent her away, and then promised to do whatever they told her to do, if they'd just let her stay.

Ethan knew her quite well from their few weeks together, and had been the first to capitulate—once

John had explained that he couldn't lock her up in jail without cause. So the dooryard was empty of vehicles but for the old truck she'd bought from Gaylen, the entire mill was dark and silent but for the scurrying of night critters, and John and Alex and Paul were hunkered down in various hiding spots throughout camp, everyone waiting for Ron Briggs and his partner in crime to show up.

Anna never realized just how much planning, maneuvering, and downright patience went into a stakeout. In order to make it look like they'd all returned to Loon Cove, they'd left Fox Run in their respective vehicles, parked them at the lumber mill, and then returned in Anna's SUV, which they'd hidden on an old tote road over a mile down the lake. From there they had hiked back through the woods following the shoreline and each gone to their assigned hidey-holes to settle in and wait. Paul was up near the main road with a radio, watching the lane leading down to Fox Run; Alex was tucked in the shadows at the mill's old dump site on the edge of camp; and John was down on the shoreline near the cookhouse. She and Ethan and Bear were holed up in her house, which had grown chilly, because to make the camp look truly abandoned, they hadn't even left a fire going in the stove.

"Why wouldn't John call other deputies to come help?" Anna asked in a whisper.

"Because we don't even know if Briggs is planning to show up. We're only working on the theory that he's behind the fire today and is also your intruder. Nor do we have proof that Frank Coots is involved."

"But it all makes sense."

"Still, John can't justify pulling deputies from other parts of the county on a hunch. He did call Daniel Reed, but Daniel's right in the middle of his own case tonight."

Anna sighed. "This really isn't your or your family's fight, you know," she whispered into the darkness. "I could have called my own brothers. They would have been down here in four hours, tops."

Ethan's arm around her tightened. "We can handle this," he said in a low growl. He rested his chin in the crook of her neck, causing a shiver to run through her. "And it *is* our fight. We take care of our own."

"But I'm not 'your own.'"

"You will be in three weeks," he said, his lips against her skin sending another shiver coursing down her spine.

"I feel guilty that the others are outside, sitting on the cold hard ground while we're on a soft bed," she said.

His arm tightened again when he chuckled. "Are you kidding? They—"

The radio sitting on the nightstand suddenly made three short beeps, followed by a pause, then one slightly longer beep. Ethan immediately sat up, pulling Anna into a sitting position beside him.

"Three?" she whispered, her hand covering her suddenly racing heart. "Who's the third guy?"

She felt more than saw him shrug. "Frank Coots is in town. Maybe he decided to join Briggs and his buddy."

The radio beeped again, three long times.

"That was Paul saying he got John's message," Ethan said, reaching for the radio.

"John is the one long beep, right?"

Ethan stood up, pulling her with him. "Yep," he confirmed. "So that means the bastards came in from the lake. I suppose the ice has melted back enough for a boat or canoe to maneuver." Ethan waited until Alex responded with two long beeps, then keyed the mike four times to let everyone know that he and Anna had gotten the message.

"Where's the pepper spray John gave you?" he asked as he quietly led the way downstairs.

"In my pocket," she said, patting her front pants pocket.

"Take it out and keep it in your hand," he instructed. He stopped at the bottom of the stairs and held her facing him. "What would I have to promise to get you to stay out of this?"

"For you to stay out of it with me."

His hands on her shoulders tightened. "What if you freeze up again, Anna?" he whispered thickly. "Like Saturday night."

"I won't, I promise. I was surprised Saturday night, but I'm prepared this time." She patted his chest.

"And I'm just as eager as you are to see Ronald Briggs get his due. I need to be part of this for *me*, Ethan. I need to finally face my past if I ever hope to have a worthwhile future."

Covering her hand on his chest, he leaned down and kissed her. "Okay then, sweetheart," he whispered.

He led her to the back door and picked up the shotgun he had leaning against the counter. "I'm going to tuck you against that huge boulder up back, and I'll be right beside the path that runs from the house to the saw shed. The others are working their way toward us already. You should have an overall view from your position, so it's your job to watch all our backs, okay?"

"Wait," she said as he started to open the door. "Bear's trying to get out," she explained, leaning down to push the dog away.

Ethan pulled her upright. "If Briggs and his buddies are responsible for Samuel's death, don't you think Bear deserves to be part of this, too?"

"But they'll see him and get suspicious."

"They won't see him. He's blacker than the night, and he just might be helpful."

She tugged even harder when he went to open the door again. "He's an old dog, Ethan," she hissed. "He could get hurt."

Ethan turned to face her, cupping her cheek in his palm. "Then he gets to go down fighting, Anna. Give him the chance to decide that for himself."

She thought about what he was saying, and about all the loving things Samuel had written about Bear in his letters to her. "Okay," she said, leaning into his hand. "We're *all* in this together."

"That's my girl," Ethan said, finally opening the door and peering outside.

He let Bear go out first, then slowly crept off the porch with Anna's hand held firmly in his. They walked in silence up the sloping backyard, and since their eyes didn't need to adjust to the dark, Anna soon spotted the boulder that was to be her lookout. She suddenly understood why Ethan had asked her to dress in muted gray clothes instead of black. With half a moon dimly filtering through the canopy of trees, she would blend into the rock when she crouched against it.

"You can see most of the camp from here," he said, his mouth only inches from her ear. He helped her settle into place, then bent close as he handed her the radio. "If it looks like any one of us is getting in trouble, radio the others, okay?"

"I will," she said, gripping the radio in one hand and her pepper spray in the other.

Ethan gave her a quick kiss on the forehead, squeezed her shoulder, then disappeared into the night as silently as a ghost. Anna leaned back against her rock, her eyes wide and unblinking as she strained to separate the shadows from the solid objects. But then she remembered why camouflage worked so well: prey animals were alert to movement, not shapes. So she sort of let her eyes go slightly out of focus and started watching only for movement.

She had no idea where Bear had gone. Ethan had promised to stay near the house—so he'd be close to her, she suspected. Paul would be working his way down from the main road, but it would take him a while to travel the mile in the dark. And John and Alex must be quietly stalking the three men through camp.

Ron had been searching for nearly five months, so what was possibly left for them to search tonight? And why didn't Frank Coots just go to court? If his goons hadn't found the sales agreement by now, wouldn't he figure it no longer existed? Talk about tenacious.

And murderous. Was Frank really responsible for Gramps's death? All over some land and—

There. Just off to her left, halfway between the house and the lake. Something was moving . . . no, several somethings were moving! Anna clutched the radio and pepper spray to her chest. It could be the bad guys, or it could be Alex or John.

Then she heard whispers of conversation coming from the moving shadows, which told her it must be Ronald Briggs and his cohorts. She didn't move a muscle as they came closer, barely breathing as she strained to hear what they were saying.

Dammit, where was Ethan?

"You're sure no one's around?" one of the shadows asked.

"The woman was home for a while, and several men, including the sheriff, were here briefly. But I followed them when they left all at once, and they're at Loon Cove Lumber, including the woman. They'll be there for days, cleaning up that mess," the second man said.

"Then let's just get this over with and get out of here," a third—and familiar—voice said.

"Relax, Frank. Rushing these jobs leads to mistakes. We just set the fires and paddle away as if we have all the time in the world. The whole place will be fully engulfed before anyone even knows it's burning. And with the fire department already exhausted, it'll be nothing but smoldering ashes by morning."

Anna sucked in her breath on a shudder. They were going to burn down Fox Run? Apparently Frank had decided that if he couldn't find the agreement, he would make damn sure *nobody* found it. She scanned the camp, looking for any signs that Ethan or the others were close by, also listening to this conversation.

The talking shadows rounded the side of her house and stopped not a hundred yards from Anna, where the filtered moonlight exposed the three men. One guy was definitely Frank Coots, another of the men was dressed more urban and spoke with a distinct Boston accent, and the third guy was dressed as a local, though Anna didn't recognize him from town. Was that Ron Briggs? He looked . . . well, he didn't look at all scary to her.

"Frank, you start several fires all around the house," the Boston accent said. "Gary, you head to the saw shed and cookhouse and torch them. I'll hit the other outbuildings," he said, walking onto her porch and opening the door to her generator shed. "Bingo," he said, reaching in and pulling out what looked like one of her cans of diesel fuel.

Those dirty rotten bastards; they were going to use her own fuel to burn down her mill! And the Boston guy had called the local man Gary, not Ron. So where in hell was Ron Briggs? Had he been replaced because of his incompetence?

Two men suddenly stepped out of the shadows from different directions. "I think we've heard enough, gentlemen," John Tate said, his gun and flashlight pointed at the obviously surprised arsonists. "You're under arrest."

The local guy, Gary, bolted for the woods, only to suddenly fall flat on his face with a strangled yelp. Anna watched Ethan grab the guy by the collar and drag him back to his feet. "What's your hurry, Gary?" Ethan drawled. "The party's just beginning."

"Now, John," Frank Coots said, holding his hands high in the air, his eyes the size of silver dollars. "This isn't what it looks like."

"Then what exactly is it, Frank?" John asked, walking over and snapping a handcuff on Frank's raised right wrist. "It's a little late to be calling on neighbors, don't you think?"

"We only came here to look for something I lost when I visited Anna last month. I'm pretty sure I dropped my pocketknife someplace in this area."

"I don't remember you being near the back of the house," Anna said, finally stepping away from her rock to join them. "You came and went by my front door," she added, noticing that Alex also had a gun pointed at the men, in particular at the Boston guy, who still hadn't spoken a word.

"Tell them we're partners, Anna," Frank pleaded.

"Did you kill my grandfather, Frank?"

"Samuel?" he said on an indrawn breath, his gaze darting over his shoulder at John, who was just fastening the cuffs behind his back. Frank violently shook his head. "I had nothing to do with that, Tate," he said in a desperate whine. "That was completely Ron and Gary's doing."

"We were only trying to get the old man out of the way," Gary rushed to say, Ethan still holding him by the collar. "We weren't trying to kill him."

"And Anna?" Ethan growled, giving his prisoner a violent shake. "If you didn't want to kill anyone, why set up her accident the same way?"

"It was Ron's idea again," Gary confessed, cringing from Ethan's anger. "He said she'd just get banged up, because there was plenty of snow this time to cushion the crash."

"Where is Briggs?" Ethan asked, giving Gary another shake when he didn't immediately answer.

"He split. He's probably halfway to Mexico by now, since he found out a sheriff's car had visited his house."

John stepped over and quickly handcuffed the Boston guy, who seemed way too calm and cooperative to Anna.

John asked, "Who's your new partner, Frank?"

"Shut up, Coots," the man said in a warning growl. "Keep quiet and I'll have us out on bail by noon."

"Your city lawyers won't be much help to you up here," John said, grabbing his arm and turning him around. "Our judges aren't real fond of folks burning down our mills."

John tossed a set of handcuffs to Ethan, then reached for the radio mike attached to his shoulder. "We're all secure here," he said into the mike. "Three to transport. Move in."

"Roger that, Tate," dispatch returned. "ETA, ten minutes."

Anna breathed a sigh of relief that more officers were on the way, despite the fact that everything seemed to have gone quite smoothly. If she could only shake the feeling that something still wasn't quite right.

"Paul," Alex said into his own little radio, "where the hell are you? It doesn't take that long to get down here."

He released the button and waited, but Paul didn't answer.

"Paul!" Alex snapped more forcefully. "Answer me."

"Shit," Ethan growled, shoving Gary toward the other two prisoners. He walked over and took Anna's radio from her and held it up to his mouth. "Dammit, if you're lost, admit it," he said. "Where the hell are you?"

The radio remained silent.

"He might have fallen and is hurt, and dropped the radio out of reach," Anna offered, laying her hand on Ethan's tensed arm. "Or maybe he just fell and his radio is broken. We'll go find him."

"Sit down right here on the steps," John said, pushing his three prisoners toward the porch stairs. "Anna, you still got that pepper spray?"

"Right here," she said, walking over to John.

"Are you comfortable watching them while we go look for Paul?" he asked.

She nodded. "I'll watch them."

"They're secured, and I've patted them down for weapons. A couple of deputies will be here soon, but if any one of these guys so much as twitches," he said, addressing the three men more than her, "you just point that pepper spray at his face and pull the trigger. Got that?"

"I got it," Anna said, holding the spray so they'd see it.

Ethan put his arm around her shoulders, giving her a gentle squeeze. "You'll be okay," he assured her, handing her back her radio. "And we'll be within earshot. Just give us a holler if they give you any trouble."

"Maybe you should leave me a gun," she said.

John immediately yelped "No!" and Ethan just laughed.

"Let's go," Alex said, already heading into the woods toward the main road. "We'll split up. John, take the lane. Ethan, you search in between us."

"You'll be okay?" Ethan said again, this time as a question.

"I'll be just fine," she promised, giving him a nudge to get him moving. "In fact," she said a bit louder for her prisoners' benefit, "I hope one of them *does* try something." She turned back toward them, aiming the pepper spray directly at their faces. "As soon as they're out of earshot, I might spray you all anyway, for intending to burn down my home," she said in a tight whisper.

"Anna," Frank entreated, leaning away from her threat. "None of this was my idea."

"You knew about that old sales agreement, didn't you? Is that what you were looking for, Frank? So I couldn't prove Samuel hadn't taken advantage of your father?" She kicked him in the shin, holding the pepper spray up when he yelped. "You killed my grandfather, you bastard! Over money."

"I didn't have anything to do with that," Frank said. "That was Ron and Gary's idea. I never asked them to touch the old man."

Gary side-kicked Frank in his other shin, and Frank yelped again, wiggling closer to the Boston guy to get away. But the Boston guy shoved him back with his shoulder just as something solid slammed into Anna's side, knocking her down to the ground and landing on top of her with a jarring thud.

"Well, look who I got here," her attacker said, lunging for her hand just as Anna pulled the trigger on the canister of spray.

The air immediately filled with atomized pepper, and both of them started coughing. The pepper burned Anna's nose and pricked her eyes with burning tears. She pressed the radio's talk button at the same time she shoved her elbow into her assailant's ribs and lashed out with her feet—all as she twisted to roll away from him.

"There's a fourth guy!" she yelled just before convulsing in a fit of coughing, the acrid spray making her mouth burn nearly as badly as her eyes were.

Even though the fourth man was coughing just as violently, he lunged for her again just as somebody else landed on top of both of them. The Boston guy, Anna realized, and she closed her eyes tight and pulled the trigger on the canister again, twisting to roll away. Handcuffed, he wasn't able to avoid the spray and shouted when it caught him square in the face. Anna rolled free and stood. Blinking through her burning tears, she pushed the talk button again. "I need hel—"

Her plea was cut off when she was tackled again.

But just as she was about to punch the guy in the face with the radio, a deep, hair-raising, lethal-sounding growl came from the shadows mere feet away and the man went perfectly still.

Anna dropped her head and the man reared up just as Bear lunged, the primordial sound the old dog made sending a chill down her spine. Her assailant cried out when Bear bit down onto some part of his anatomy, the animal's momentum carrying them both away from her. Anna blindly scrambled to her feet, stumbled into the guy from Boston, who was frozen in surprise at Bear's attack, and gave him another shot of pepper spray to make sure he stayed down. Then she blindly ran after Bear, the vicious sounds of battle guiding her.

Ethan suddenly appeared at her side. "Stay back," he shouted, pushing her away to go after Bear himself.

Anna stumbled after them, but arms of steel wrapped around her. "Stay back," John said.

Then the air filled with the sound of sirens and strobing lights. Blinking her stinging eyes, Anna was barely able to see Bear and the man locked in battle, Ethan approaching them at a run.

Suddenly, Bear and the guy vanished.

John let Anna go and ran up to Ethan, shone his flashlight through the trees, then finally pointed it down at the ground. Anna could just make out the gaping hole in the earth.

She ran up to Ethan and clutched his arm to look down in the hole. "Bear!" she cried when she spotted the old Lab's body half under the man in a foot of water at the bottom of the old well, both of them unmoving.

"Don't get too close," Ethan said, holding her against his side like a vise. "We don't know how stable the ground is."

"He's dead, isn't he?" she whispered into his shirt, her stinging eyes flushing with tears.

"His neck's broken," Ethan said into her hair, obviously knowing who she was referring to. He used both arms to hug her to him. "It was instant, Anna," he whispered. "He couldn't do anything to help Samuel, but he was still able to save someone he loved. He died a hero."

"H-he was so vicious," she said. "He went after that man like a . . . like a powerful young dog."

"I saw, sweetheart," Ethan said, hugging her tightly. "He definitely got his revenge on Briggs."

Anna sucked in a shuddering breath and buried her face in Ethan's chest. Her attacker was Ron Briggs?

The sound of multiple sirens echoed through the forest, growing louder as vehicles sped down her lane. The blue and white strobes of two sheriff's cruisers finally broke through the trees, their headlights shining up the hill when they stopped below. Alex suddenly stepped out of the dense woods with his arm around an unsteady Paul, who was holding what looked like a torn piece of flannel shirt to his bleeding forehead.

"Paul!" Anna said, running toward him. "What happened?"

"Briggs was hiding just outside of camp," he said, wincing when she lifted the cloth away to see his wound. "He blindsided me when I walked past him. I'm okay," he said, apparently more embarrassed than hurt.

"You got a ladder around here, Anna?" John asked. "We need to get Briggs out."

"It's hanging on the back of the house," she said, wiping her eyes on her shirttail.

Ethan appeared beside her again and started guiding her down the slope. "Let's get your face washed off," he said. "That's the problem with pepper spray. It affects its user almost as much as the intended victim."

"Where the hell is Gary Simpson?" John growled from ahead of them. "Dammit, he ran off!"

"He won't get far in handcuffs," Alex said, leading Paul down to the house. He handed off his brother to Ethan. "I'll go get the idiot," Alex said with a tired sigh.

Ethan led Anna and Paul into the house, then left his brother in the kitchen to take Anna into the bathroom. "Flush your eyes with cold water," he told her. "Where's your first-aid kit?"

"In the cupboard over the birdseed," she told him,

already running the water. "Can you start the generator and give us some light?"

"Sure." He headed out the back door. "Tate! Just bring up Briggs," he hollered. "I'll bring up the dog myself."

Anna hung her head over the sink. Poor, valiant, big-hearted Bear. He'd rushed to her rescue with the same noble courage as Ethan. How blessed she was to be loved so much.

Just as the power kicked on, she lifted her head and blinked through her tears at the mirror. Did Ethan truly *love* her? And could Delaney be right, that her uncle simply wasn't able to put his feelings into words?

Dammit, did *she* have the same problem? Anna snorted and hung her head again, splashing water onto her face. What a fine pair they made—neither one of them willing to admit their feelings to each other. She loved Ethan more than life itself—hell, she'd always loved him; yet she hadn't even been able to admit it to *herself*, much less to him, because she'd been afraid her childhood fantasy would die a horrible death if he rejected her love.

And Claire had known. That's why she'd sent down the condoms, jewelry, and dress clothes. Her stepmom had known it wasn't only her inheritance Anna had been coming here to claim, but also the man she'd loved since she was eleven.

And her daddy had known, too—that's why he'd

fought so hard for her not to leave, knowing that his only daughter could very well end up living the rest of her life in Maine.

Anna sighed, and reached for a towel to dry her face. Three weeks wasn't much time to plan a wedding.

Chapter Twenty-one

The first rays of sunshine were just breaking over the lake as Anna and Ethan stared down into the dark well. Anna was holding a quilt she'd found in a trunk in the attic, and Ethan was holding Bear's ratty old bed and a powerful spotlight.

"Spread your blanket on the ground," he said softly. "And I'll carry him up and lay him on it. Have you decided where you want to bury him?"

Anna swiped at her eyes and took a deep breath. "Up with Grammy and Gramps." She shook out the blanket on the ground, then set Bear's bed it on top. "In the small family cemetery up the lane."

Ethan handed her the spotlight. "Shine this down for me, so I can see what I'm doing." He turned and stepped onto the ladder. "Don't cry," he said, his own voice thick with emotion. "We know he died happy, doing what he needed to do."

Anna wiped away another persistent tear and shuddered out a heavy sigh, aiming the light into the well as Ethan climbed down. "I know," she said. "Just get him out of there, please."

But carrying a seventy-pound dog out of a fifteen-foot-deep well that was only four feet wide was no easy task. Ethan finally put Bear over his shoulders, then started climbing back up the ladder. Suddenly he stopped halfway up.

"Shine the light over here," he said, nodding toward the rocks lining the well on his right. "There, angle it a bit lower, would you?"

Anna stepped around the well and shone the light on the dark, moss-covered rocks. "What are you looking at?" she asked, bending to see.

Ethan laughed. "I believe I'm looking at Samuel's stash! There's a good-sized cavity hollowed out in the side of the well that's been neatly lined with rocks. And there's a big tin can sitting in it, about three or four gallons. That cunning old fox. "

Anna moved yet again, first looking across the well past Ethan, then going back and peering straight down. "It's virtually invisible from up here," she said.

"He positioned the rocks so it would be hidden from anyone looking down."

Ethan shifted Bear on his shoulders and continued climbing, stepped onto firm ground, and carefully lowered the old Lab onto his bed. Anna took the edges of the quilt and started rubbing him dry.

"We'll get the tin after we take care of him," Ethan said, folding the blanket over Bear's limp body. "Bring the shovel," he told her, picking up Bear and walking down to Gaylen's pickup truck.

Anna grabbed the shovel on their way past the house and put it in the truck bed beside Bear. They climbed in and drove a quarter of a mile up the lane until they came to the tiny cemetery tucked in the woods on a knoll. She got out, grabbed the shovel, and walked through the broken gate to Samuel and Mary Fox's headstone.

She stared down at the granite marker. "I'm going to have to get the monument people to come out this summer and carve in the date of Gramps's death."

"Have them add Bear's name as well," Ethan said, gently setting the dog on the ground. He straightened and wrapped his arm around her shoulders. "How come you missed Samuel's funeral?"

"None of us even knew he'd died until Tom Bishop drove up to Quebec and told us. Nobody contacted us when it happened."

"Not even Madeline?"

Anna shrugged. "According to Tom Bishop, she was a little shocked to find out Gramps had left everything to me."

"She's a piece of work, isn't she?" Ethan said drily.

"I feel sorry for her more than anything."

Ethan's arm tightened around her as he leaned

over and kissed her hair. "Still, we're not inviting her to our wedding."

"We have to. She's my mother."

Anna looked down to hide her smile when she felt Ethan go suddenly rigid. "Right here," she said, pointing beside her grandparents' grave. "Let's put Bear to rest beside them."

The man still didn't move.

Anna slipped out from under his arm, picked up the shovel, and started digging. It took Ethan a good two minutes before he silently nudged her away and took over the chore. While he worked quietly, Anna began picking up broken branches and other debris that had fallen on the cemetery over the winter, then went over and tried to straighten the rickety old gate.

"This cemetery needs attention," she said, looking around at the leaning older gravestones and broken fence. Only Grammy Fox's grave was tidy from the years Gramps had tended it, and from when Anna had visited when she'd arrived last fall. "I think I'll plant some tulip bulbs and daffodils to come up next year. I seem to remember Grammy loved tulips. Daddy and Claire will be arriving later this evening."

Ethan stopped digging and looked at her.

"I called them while you were in the shower. I'm surprised you didn't hear Daddy's bellow clear into the bathroom."

"Are your brothers coming with him?"

She nodded.

Ethan started digging again.

"I won't let them feed your guts to the wolves."

He said nothing, just continued digging, until he finally drove the shovel into the pile of dirt, then turned and picked up Bear. He dropped to his knees and carefully lowered the dog into the hole he'd made, then lifted the shovel again.

Anna flinched when the first shovel of dirt dropped in the grave, and she said a quiet prayer that Bear and Gramps were united again, happy as two old ducks in a frog pond.

Ethan finally patted down the shallow mound, wiped his brow as he leaned on the shovel, and stared at the grave. "We should get a dog," he said. "A Lab like Bear."

Anna slipped her hand into his.

He squeezed her fingers. "Are you ready to go see what Samuel hid in his stash?"

"I want to be the one to go down and get it," she said, leading him by the hand through the gate. "So I can see the cavity."

They climbed back in the truck in silence, drove home, and Ethan held the spotlight while Anna started down the ladder into the well. She stopped three rungs down and looked up at him. "Ah . . . it's too early in the season for spiders to be out, isn't it?"

He nodded. "I didn't see any earlier."

She continued down, forcing herself not to look too closely at the rocks lining the well, but when she saw the cavity she forgot all about watching for creepy critters. "Wow," she said, staring into the niche. "It's a work of art. The rocks look like each one was expertly cut to fit."

"It's the perfect hiding spot," Ethan said, lying on his belly to better shine the light toward the cavity.

"Gramps must have made this when the well dried up and he had to have a new one drilled."

"Can you hand the tin up to me without losing your balance?"

"I have perfect balance," she scoffed, only to groan when she tried to pick up the tin. "Good Lord, it's heavy."

Ethan chuckled and set the light on the ground beside him in order to reach down to her. "Maybe it's full of gold."

Anna worked the tin out of the cavity, leaned her hips into the ladder, then hefted the tin over her head. Its weight suddenly disappeared and the spotlight beam reappeared, filling the well with light again.

"Take this to see how deep the cavity is and make sure there's nothing else inside."

Anna took the light and aimed it into the hole. "It's only big enough for that tin, and it's empty. "

Ethan took the spotlight she held up to him, then held the top of the ladder. "Okay, come on up."

She was up the ladder and into the sunshine in the blink of an eye. Ethan picked up the tin and they walked to the house and went inside, where he set it on the kitchen table.

"Any guesses why it's so heavy?" he asked as they eyed the dented, rusty old tin.

"Maybe more journals?"

Ethan snorted. "Or the rare parts to fix that old saw."

Anna rubbed her sweating palms on her pants, then reached out and tried to pry off the lid—but it wouldn't budge. Ethan got a butter knife from the drawer, and methodically worked it around the edge of the lid, slowly lifting it off one side and then the other, until it popped free and went skidding across the table.

They both leaned forward to peer inside.

Anna groaned. "They *are* engine parts."

"And more!" Ethan reached in and pulled out a thick sheaf of papers, tore open the plastic they were wrapped in, and began leafing through them. "These look like Samuel's important papers: his marriage license, birth and death certificates, deeds. Here's *your* birth certificate," he said, holding it up. "Abigail Anna Fox," he read before handing it to her. "And here's the original sales agreement with Joshua Coots," he said, also separating it from the pile.

Anna set down her birth certificate and started pulling out the engine parts. She found another box in the bottom of the tin, this one made of a sturdier metal. The lid came off easily, and she sucked in her breath.

"Grammy's wedding ring," she whispered, pulling it out. She slipped it onto her finger and then stirred through the other stuff in the box. "What are these?" she asked, holding up a little plastic bag of tiny white stones.

"Baby teeth," Ethan said with a laugh, taking them from her. He turned the bag in his hand. "*Your* baby teeth," he clarified, showing her the name written in ink on the back.

Anna reached in the smaller box again and pulled out a locket, which she opened to find her baby picture inside, next to a picture of a very young Madeline Fox. "I vaguely remember this," she said, holding it up for Ethan to see. "It was Grammy's. She died when I was five, and I don't remember ever seeing it after that."

"There's a small notebook in here." Ethan pulled it out and opened it to the first page. "This seems to be the first journal Samuel started. It appears he's explaining why he called your father." He closed the delicate old book and handed it to her. "It's going to be hard reading, Anna," he warned.

She went to reach for the book, but instead covered her mouth when she let out a huge yawn.

Ethan chuckled and set the book down. "All this stuff will be right here when we wake up," he said, taking her hand and leading her toward the stairs. "The last twenty-four hours have been hell. I'm locking the doors and we're taking a long nap."

When Ethan appeared in the bedroom two minutes later, his own yawn quickly turned to a look of obvious disgust. "When are you going to stop wearing those damn pajamas?"

"Just as soon as you admit that you love me."

That certainly wiped the scowl off his face. His eyes widened and his jaw dropped, and Anna wasn't sure, but the poor man appeared to stop breathing. She buttoned the top button on her pajamas, pulled back the comforter, and crawled into bed, facing the wall so he wouldn't see her smile.

And when she woke up later that afternoon, she was still wearing her smile—and her pajamas.

Anna padded downstairs, her nose following the smell of frying bacon, and walked into a crowded kitchen.

"Daddy!" she yelped.

He stood and swept her into a hug so fierce that she squeaked. "Ah, *bébé*." He leaned back and looked her straight in the eye, his own gleaming with unshed tears. "You look like hell."

Anna kissed his cheek and hugged him tightly. "Daddy," she whispered.

He finally set her on her feet and turned with his arm around her. "Calm your mama," he said, nudging her toward Claire. "You've sent her in a tailspin, asking her to plan your wedding in only three weeks, in *America* no less."

Anna stepped into Claire's outstretched arms. "Thank you for everything," she whispered, hugging her tightly.

Someone cleared their throat, and Anna turned to see Ethan standing by the stove, a spatula in his hand and a towel tucked in his belt as an apron. "Ah . . . Daddy, Claire, this is Ethan Knight," Anna said, her face prickling with heat.

"We've met," Claire said with a warm smile to Ethan, taking Anna's hand and grabbing a notebook off the table as she led her into the living room. "Come, we'll start on the guest list and leave the men to cook supper."

Anna looked helplessly over her shoulder at Ethan.

"When are your sons arriving?" she heard him ask her father as he turned back to the stove.

"In the morning," André said as he began rolling up his sleeves. "Jean-Paul and Damon are especially anxious to see you again, they told me."

"He's beautiful," Claire whispered once they were out of earshot. She settled Anna on the couch and sat down beside her. "So tall and strong and handsome. Now I understand your fascination with him."

"He didn't look like that eighteen years ago." Anna leaned over to peer into the kitchen.

Claire pulled her back upright, only to suddenly notice what she was wearing. "Pajamas?" she said, arching one perfectly plucked eyebrow.

Anna sighed and leaned back against the couch. "It's a long story," she said. "I have three weeks to get him to admit he loves me."

The other eyebrow also arched. "You told me on the phone that the wedding was *his* idea."

"It was. And he definitely wants us to get married. I just don't think he's quite ready to admit *why*. We're like oil and vinegar most of the time," she said, breaking into a huge grin. "But when you shake us up real good, the combination is heavenly." She shrugged, taking the notepad from Claire. "You taught me subtlety, so I'm trying it."

"Until you finally lose your patience and smack him with a frying pan?"

"I've been leaning more toward handcuffs," Anna said with another sigh. "Eighteen years is a long time to be patient."

Claire gave a laugh and hugged Anna to her. "Don't you worry, *bébé*, he'll come around. Just the fact that he's still here, despite knowing the boys are arriving tomorrow, means he must love you very, very much."

Claire still called Anna's brothers *boys*, though they were grown men rugged enough to worry a small army. "They better not try anything," she warned, "or I'll take a shotgun to all four of them."

"My, my, such fierceness. You love him very much, no?"

Anna gave Claire a desperate look. "Yes. And I need him to say the words before I walk down that aisle. It doesn't matter that I know he loves me; I need to hear it from him."

"You will," Claire said with brisk assurance, taking back the notebook and pulling the pen out of the wire binding. "If the pajamas don't work, I'll give you my wedding present early. That should do the trick. Now, give me the names of his family, and who you want to be in your wedding party."

"I want Ethan's niece, Delaney, to be my maid of honor," Anna said, leaning forward as Claire began to write. "She's eleven, and she's adorable."

They spent the rest of the afternoon roughing out a wedding plan, stopping only to eat. After dinner, Ethan took André on a tour of Fox Run and Claire and Anna went back to work, filling most of the pages in Claire's little notebook. And by ten o'clock that evening, Ethan retired to his old cabin across camp, André and Claire took Anna's bedroom, and Anna curled up on the couch with Charlie the chickadee perched on the lamp shade over her head. Despite how aggravating her brothers could be, Anna couldn't wait to be back in the bosom of her entire family.

Chapter Twenty-two

Two and a half weeks later—a mere three days before her wedding, to be exact—Anna was impressed by how well things were going, especially with her brothers and Ethan. The fact that Loon Cove Lumber had been torched because of her may have had something to do with her family's stellar behavior, but Anna liked to think the Knight and Segee men had more than just *her* in common as the seven brothers joined forces to get Loon Cove's two saws up and running again.

Grady and her daddy had instantly hit it off, and were spending their days hitting every trout brook between Oak Grove and the Canadian border. They hadn't, however, been bringing home any fish—which meant either the trout weren't biting yet or the two aging loggers spent more time talking about the old days than paying attention to their fishing lines.

The Knight and Segee women had certainly come together with a bang, and the wedding plans were moving along at warp speed. Delaney was excited to be Anna's maid of honor, though Anna suspected the young girl wanted to wear nylons and two-inch heels nearly as much as she wanted her uncle Ethan to get married.

As for her mother, Anna had actually been looking forward to finally seeing her again after all these years, and had gone with Ethan to Penny Bryant's the day Madeline was supposed to arrive. There they had been presented with the news that Madeline—and husband number *eight*—had suddenly decided a cruise to Brazil was more appealing than visiting Maine during mud season. Anna had been disappointed but not all that surprised, considering Madeline hadn't even made it to Gramps's funeral—thereby adding yet another chapter to her legend.

By day, Fox Run was overflowing with Segees, but at night two of Anna's brothers, along with their wives and children, stayed at Penny Bryant's bed-and-breakfast. Jean-Paul and his wife, Michelin, along with their four children, had commandeered all the remaining bedrooms upstairs. Damon had insisted on bunking with Ethan in his cabin, and Anna was stretched out on the couch with Charlie—who'd grown quite plump along with his buddies, since everyone had gotten in the habit of carrying birdseed in their pockets.

So everything was good—except Ethan still hadn't said the words she so desperately needed to hear.

Was the man really that stubborn? Or that scared?

Or maybe Ethan *wanted* to tell her that he loved her but hadn't been able to get a word in edgewise since her family's invasion.

Anna bolted into a sitting position, causing Charlie to flutter away in surprise. That was it! She just needed to get Ethan alone long enough for him to say that he loved her so much, he couldn't imagine his life without her. And dammit, she wanted him to *ask* her to marry him.

Anna rummaged around under the couch for the gaily wrapped little box Claire had given her that morning. Clutching it to her chest, she ran over and grabbed her raincoat hanging by the front door, ran into the bathroom and tore off her flannel pajamas, and slipped into the beautiful wedding present. She covered it up with the raincoat, went into the kitchen and put on her sneakers, then snuck out the back door.

Now she just had to figure out how to get Ethan out of his cabin without waking his self-appointed watchdog.

Anna tiptoed off the porch and headed toward Ethan's cabin, coming to an abrupt halt when a movement caught her eye over by the small fleet of trucks parked up near the saw shed.

Holy smokes, her ghost was back!

She slowly inched backward along the side of the house, never once taking her eyes off the shadow as it silently moved around her SUV. She suddenly felt the shovel leaning against the house and, gripping it in both hands, ducked down and ran toward the saw shed, going from one large tree to another to cover her progress. By God, if Ronald Briggs was out on bail and looking for revenge, she'd make the bastard wish he'd broken *both* legs when he'd fallen down that well.

Darting behind a large tree, Anna momentarily lost sight of her intruder. Using her trick of focusing only on movement, she slowly let her gaze scan the area around the parked vehicles. And there—just in front of her SUV—something dark moved in the shadows.

Crouching low again, she crept up to the parked trucks, then slowly made her way between her SUV and Jean-Paul's pickup. The shadow fluttered, and she raised the shovel and lunged, swinging it in a low arc to cut him off at the knees.

Just as the shovel connected with the boneless apparition, Anna realized it was a jacket hanging from a branch. A band of steel suddenly came down over her arms, pinning them to her sides and lifting her off her feet just as a large hand covered her mouth, trapping her scream.

"You bloodthirsty little witch," Ethan whispered in her ear.

"Ethmmp!" she muttered, squirming to get free.

He tossed her over his shoulder, effectively knocking the air from her lungs.

"You scared the hell out of me!" she hissed once she got her breath back. She grabbed his belt and gave a hard tug. "You set me up with that jacket hanging on a branch. What are you doing out here?"

There was a soft click of a truck door opening and a light suddenly came on. Ethan bent over and set her down in the rear of her truck. "I might ask you the same question."

She blinked against the brightness of the interior light, then pulled the bottom edges of her raincoat together and straightened her belt. "I was on my way to your cabin to get you. When I saw someone moving around over here, I thought Ronald Briggs had gotten out on bail and come back."

Ethan folded his arms over his very broad, very masculine chest. "Why am I not surprised that instead of alerting a camp full of men, you grabbed a shovel and went after him all by yourself? And what were you coming to get me for?"

"I—I wanted to talk to you," she whispered, looking down so she'd quit noticing how big and strong and beautiful he was.

"About . . . ?"

Anna suddenly forgot *what* she'd wanted to talk

about when she foolishly glanced up again and found him looking ready to pounce, his eyes dark with . . . Lord, she hoped it was lust. He really was big and strong and . . . and . . . beautiful. It had been nearly three weeks since she'd felt his naked skin rubbing against *her* naked skin, or felt him deep . . . or . . .

"Dammit, I love you!" he growled. "Take off your clothes."

She gaped at him, utterly speechless.

"Anna, if I don't get you naked beneath me in the next sixty seconds, I swear we're both going for a swim in the lake."

"I love you, too." She kicked off her sneakers and crawled into the back of her truck, only to find it full of blankets and pillows. "I see you've given this some thought."

He crawled in behind her and started taking off his boots.

"Aren't you going to close the door to shut off the light?"

"Just as soon as you show me what's under that raincoat," he said, unbuckling his belt.

"Did you bring any condoms?"

His hands stilled on his fly. "Did you?"

Anna sighed. "I didn't think that far ahead."

He reached out and began undoing the belt of her raincoat. "We don't need them. We've got three nights to see if we can keep the Knight family tradition going."

"What tradition?"

He gave her a lopsided smile. "Of us Knight men marrying pregnant women," he said, his fingers next going to work on her coat buttons.

Anna crushed the lapels of her raincoat at her throat. "A *baby?*" she whispered. "You want us to have a baby?"

"With beautiful green eyes and hair down to her waist."

Anna covered his hand when it went to the next button. "What if she wants to own a mill when she grows up?"

"Then we'll give her Fox Run," he said, working his fingers under hers until the button released. "It *might* be in full operation by then. Ten seconds left, Segee, before you're going in the lake."

Anna slowly pulled the edges of her raincoat apart, finally revealing what she was wearing. "Claire told me to tell you that this is her wedding present to you," she said, letting the coat fall to the blankets.

It took him a few moments, but he finally lifted his deeply appreciative eyes to hers. "I really like Claire," he said thickly. "And I love *you*, Anna. Will you marry me?"

She plopped her chin in her hand and looked up at the ceiling to think about that.

"You're down to four seconds," he growled, reaching back and closing the door, plunging them into darkness.

Anna lunged before he could guess her intention

and had him pinned flat on his back with two seconds to spare. "Say it again," she demanded, wishing the light was still on so she could see his face.

"Umm ... say what again? I seem to have lost my train of thought. Maybe if you *say* it again, I'll remember."

Anna shook her head, realized he couldn't see her, and wiggled her hips to settle more firmly against him, knowing he got *that* gesture when he shuddered beneath her. "Guess what I found in the drugstore, next to the women's book on affairs?"

"Toys?" he asked way too eagerly, his own hips lifting.

"No, a book on marriage," she purred, lowering her mouth real close to his. "And it said we women need to make sure you men say it first. It said you're supposed to say it three times a day, four times on Sundays."

"Oh," he said, sighing in disappointment. "It didn't even *mention* toys?"

"Nope. But it did come with a nice set of handcuffs."

He went still beneath her. "For you or for me?"

Anna brushed her lips against his. "Say it again, Ethan," she whispered. "So we can start making our baby."

"I love you, Abigail Anna Segee."

"And?"

"And I would be honored if you'd marry me in three days," he added, lifting his head and kissing her.

But just as he got his hands free to capture her shoulders and deepen the kiss, Anna lifted her head. "What *is* that noise I keep hearing?" she asked, trying to see through the darkness. "It sounds like chewing." She scrambled off him. "And it's coming from *inside* the truck," she said, ignoring Ethan's long-suffering groan as she crawled off him to peer over the front seat.

"He was supposed to be a surprise for after," he said, getting on his knees beside her and reaching into the front seat. "Hey, quit chewing on your bow. Now you got it all wet and tangled. Come on, you little varmint," he said, lifting something over the headrest and plopping it in her lap.

The squirming shadow started licking her hands. "A puppy!"

Ethan snapped on one of the soft map lights in the ceiling console, and Anna burst out laughing when the puppy leapt up, his little pink tongue aimed at her face. "Ethan, he's adorable. Where did you get him? And when?" she asked, fighting to control the squirming, licking black bundle.

Apparently deciding he wasn't getting anywhere with her, the puppy suddenly lunged toward Ethan. Ethan caught him with a laugh and quickly subdued him, holding him against his chest, where he immediately began to chew on one of his shirt buttons. "It took a bit of digging, but I found out that old Bear had fathered a litter or two in his day," Ethan told her. "This little guy is Bear's great, great grandson."

"That's perfect!" she said, reaching out to pat the young black Lab. "What did you name him?"

"I'm leaving that to you. Oww!" he said, pulling his fingers away. "I've just been calling him Puddle, because that's what I've been cleaning up in my cabin all afternoon." Ethan's eyes suddenly turned pained as he lifted the pup off his lap. "Damn. Why do babies and puppies think I make a good bathroom?" he growled, looking down at the dark spot on his pants.

Anna took the pup with a laugh, and cuddled him to her. "Take off your shirt," she said.

"It's my pants that got wet."

"Them next. But first put your shirt in the crate for him to sleep on," she suggested. "Your scent will be comforting, and he should settle right down."

Ethan took off his shirt and stuffed it in the dog crate sitting on the front seat, then put the puppy in next.

"Now the pants," she said huskily, reaching up to switch off the overhead light.

Ethan stopped her. "Let's leave it on."

Anna changed direction and reached for him instead, wrapping her arms around his neck to pull him down on top of her. "I love you, Ethan Knight. Forever and ever."

"So you'll marry me on Saturday?"

Anna nodded. "But the anniversary we'll celebrate is today, and for the next sixty years we spend that night in our truck, just like tonight." When he grinned, she frowned up at him. "What's so funny about that?"

He shook his head, his eyes bright with amusement. "I'm just trying to picture us at ninety, making love in the back of a truck. I guess we better keep taking our vitamins." Then his mouth captured hers in a kiss loaded with the promise of what was to come.

Letter from Lake Watch

Dear Reader,

I most often wake up writing. Usually between three and four a.m., the characters in whatever story I'm working on begin stirring in my subconscious, urging me out of my earthbound dreams and into their ethereal world. It doesn't seem to matter that I could use another hour of sleep; these earthbound people are in such a hurry to get on with their lives that they don't much care about mine. They've been quite patient, they point out, to have put their problems on hold while I recharged my mental batteries. And since I had the nerve to imagine them into existence to begin with, I am their only means of achieving happily ever after.

I have awakened to whispered conversations, the sound of something falling in a far corner of my bedroom, and occasional eye-opening shouts that only

I seem to hear. I've tried ignoring these determined figments of my imagination by using my sons' trick of simply pretending I'm still asleep. I've tried directing my thoughts to other things, such as grocery and to-do lists. Sometimes, I must admit, I even shout back. But inspiration is a relentless taskmaster, and eventually I am compelled to get up, get dressed, get over to my studio, and get writing.

This is not an easy thing for me to do in the dead of winter, when the outside thermometer reads ten below, there's a foot of new snow on the ground, and I just happen to be scared of the dark. I think that's why God blessed me with an indulgent husband who, without complaint, will get up, get dressed, walk me to my studio, and open every closet door in the place looking for the proverbial bogeyman. (Though Robbie claims he checks the newspapers regularly, and has yet to see any reports of anyone being accosted by a bogeyman, I still can't make that short trek alone when it's dark out, much less bring myself to open those closet doors.)

Time is an earthly concept, I've decided, designed to give us humans a false sense of control. I came to this conclusion one particularly early winter morning when Robbie and I stepped outside and found ourselves in a fantasy world. Four inches of new snow covered everything in a pristine mantle of white that glittered in the starlight like crystal gems. The world was uncharacteristically silent, and so were we as we gazed around at the splendor laid before us. My eye caught the flash of something overhead, and I looked up to see thick ribbons of green light pulsing across the sky in endless waves of brilliant energy.

The aurora borealis occurs when electrons from the sun's solar winds are drawn into the earth's magnetic field, where they collide with oxygen and nitrogen in the ionosphere. The result is a light show that is unrivaled in its ability to instill sheer awe. And on this particular morning, the sky appeared to be a living, breathing thing.

Time was suspended as the universe gave us a small glimpse of its vast mystical powers, and my incessant need to rise hours before the sun suddenly became clear to me. There are no clocks or calendars out there, I realized, which is why inspiration never seems to arrive with any semblance of order or logic, let alone any concern about sleep, meals, familial obligations, contract deadlines, or a new grandson needing his gram's attention.

Inspiration, like the universe, just *is*.

Many people have asked me where I get my ideas for the stories I write, and I have yet to come up with a satisfactory answer. But not for lack of trying, for I, too, would like to know not only *how*, but *why* these characters step out of the ether and take up residence in my mind, refusing to leave until I tell their stories so that they may enter *your* minds through my books. They want to be known, to inspire us, tug on our emotions, and endear themselves in our hearts. They want . . . they want simply to *be*.

Once I've told their stories, they very quietly get on with their lives and leave me to get on with my own. My peaceful little corner of the world—and my sleep pattern—returns to normal. That is, until another group of characters come marching in like Mardi Gras revelers, shouting and knocking things off my bureau.

Not that I'm complaining. I love these people. Just like you and me, they have wants, needs, secret desires, and dreams of their own. They bravely face their trials and tribulations, and hopefully conquer their fears and triumph in their endeavors. They laugh and cry and feel very much what we flesh-and-blood mortals feel as we try to find our own way in this mystifying world. Yes, the characters in my stories are as real as the northern lights that blessed Robbie and me with the wonderful gift of connective awareness on that utterly magical morning.

So what awakens *you*, and compels you to get up, get dressed, and get going?

Until later, from LakeWatch . . . happy reading!

Janet

Lose yourself in the passion...
Lose yourself in the past...
Lose yourself in a Pocket Book!

The School for Heiresses ❧ Sabrina Jeffries

Experience unforgettable lessons in love for
daring young ladies in this anthology featuring
sizzling stories by Sabrina Jeffries, Liz Carlyle, Julia
London, and Renee Bernard.

Emma and the Outlaw ❧ Linda Lael Miller

Loving a man with a mysterious past can force you
to risk your heart...and your future.

His Boots Under Her Bed ❧ Ana Leigh

Will he be hers forever...or just for one night?

Relive the romance of days gone by with Pocket Books!

Only a Duke Will Do Sabrina Jeffries
The School for Heiresses Series
A duke was the only man who could ever capture her heart—
and the only man who could ever break it.

Fairy Tale Jillian Hunter
To regain control of his castle, a Highlander must fight
the battle of his life…and surrender his heart.

A Woman Scorned Liz Carlyle
Forget fury—hell hath no passion like a woman scorned.

Lily and the Major Linda Lael Miller
In the major's arms she discovered how tender—
and how bold—true love could be.